Darke Blood

Written by

Lee Hall

Text copyright @ March 2017

Lee Hall

All Rights Reserved by

Lee Hall

Published by SatinPublishing

ISBN-13: 978-1546785644
ISBN-10: 1546785647

Author Biography

Lee Hall has been writing creatively since the age of twelve and it has been his dream for the world to read his work. He spends his days working in science engineering and nights with laptop in hand penning various stories of the future or past.

Outside of writing Lee's interests including acting, theatre, immersive television, cinema, and of course, the occasional blog post.

Publisher Links:

SatinPaperbacks:

http://www.satinpaperbacks.com

http://www.satinpublishing.co.uk

https://twitter.com/SatinPaperbacks

https://www.facebook.com/Satinpaperbacks.com

Email: nicky.fitzmaurice@satinpaperbacks.com

AUTHOR LINKS:

www.leehallwriter.com

http://darkecrusadertruth.webs.com/

Twitter: @lhallwriter

Facebook:
https://www.facebook.com/lhallwriter/

Acknowledgement:

To everyone who shared an Open Evening selfie, you helped sell my book and shaped this one. Thank you.

Dedication:

I dedicate this book to my parents and my brother. You have always supported me and without that, none of this would be possible.

Table of Contents:

Prologue

It could be said that you've never known true darkness. I'm talking about the blackest of black where you can't even see your own hand two inches in front of your face; that's the true darkness. There is only one place where the night truly rules all, and that is the Darke Forest.

And abruptly the story begins, out there amongst the trees where the shadows are your only ally or bitter enemy, and that will all depend if you're running or being chased.

"Run. Just drop everything and run," the panicked woman said, breathlessly. Cold damp air slithered over her bare legs and arms. Even in summer at the midnight hour you could find yourself in the fall or bitterness of winter.

"But what about Dad?" a much younger voice asked.

"He'll find us, " she turned back, "come on." Not that it was any use because only the blackness faced her. With both hands stretched out they felt for anything in her path.

"Mum, are you okay?" the kid said from behind, as the woman gasped.

"Yeah, it's just a tree. Where are you?"

"Right here," the kid reached out and met her panicked hands.

"We have to keep moving." The woman led forward in a jog, their hands interlocked.

"Shit, it's dark."

"Watch your language."

The kid was right. Looking up, down, left or right made no difference. The thick trees blocked any skyline or moonlight from shining down; they had no reference point. Being awoken in the middle of the night had given their eyes only a small appreciation of how dark it really was: this was the Darke Forest. The name kind of described it in one.

From nearby came heavy footsteps.

"Quick get down," the woman said lowering herself, as she wrapped her arms around the kid.

"Don't say a word," she added, in a jittery whisper.

Neither of them knew what it was. With clumsy feet, it announced its presence along the soft forest ground; then came a thud.

"Damn it," a voice said, sounding like an older teen.

"Donnie?" the woman called out.

"Yeah, it's me," he said. A small beacon of light shone over his shorts and flashed down to his sneakers.

"Damn torch. Come on work."

Donnie smacked the small torch with the heel of his hand, and again it shone with light falling over the woman's tanned legs.

"Come on," she said, leading the way.

"Where's your father Donnie?"

"I didn't see him get away. Did you see it?" Donnie asked, in an excited whisper.

"The bear. It was a bear, wasn't it?" the kid asked.

"That wasn't a bear. It stood on two legs. Looked like a person..." Donnie explained, before being interrupted.

"It *was* a bear." The woman quickly corrected him.

"I saw it with the torch Mum..."

"That's enough, Donnie. Now we have to get help and find your father."

She tried to scan through the darkness. Which way was the camp? The main Forest Road ran to the west of their campsite. Which way was West? God it was dark. She took hold of Donnie's torch.

"Which way is the Forest Road?" she asked.

Deep down Donnie didn't know. Even though he had a torch, most of the time it didn't work; especially whilst trying to run away. The darkness had disorientated them all and now pointing in any direction would be a wild guess.

"That way?" he guessed.

3

"Are you sure?" the woman asked.

"Not really."

"Well, we can't split up and I'm sure we came from that way, so the road has to be this way. Come on." The woman led them away and again they were plunged into blackness.

"You gotta give it a whack," Donnie said, and again there was light. All around a mist covered the thick tree trunks and ferns, it covered the lower parts of the ground with a creepy smoky essence.

"There's got to be a way out of here eventually," the woman added.

For some time, they walked, and although the torch managed to hold out, not one of them realised they were walking slightly uphill. On they went, further into the Darke Forest with the mist growing thicker and their bodies getting colder.

"Mum, I'm cold," the kid said.

"Same," added Donnie.

"It's not much further. When we get to the road we'll be nearly home free."

"I want Dad to carry me," the kid said in a moan.

The woman then felt a drastic change in temperature. Suddenly it had got a lot colder. What could that mean?

Was dawn approaching, or had they just gone deeper into the woods than she'd realised? It would probably get colder before it got warmer she guessed, but she didn't really know. Putting her concern to the back of her mind she trudged onwards. The small light revealing nothing but more trees ahead.

Donnie had begun to straggle behind. The damp air had triggered his asthma and he wheezed gently. As he stepped forward his whole lower body abruptly crashed into something solid, knocking him back as he tried to grasp at something to stabilise his footing. Clumsily he crashed to the soft damp floor.

"Donnie?" The woman called out rushing back. She shone the torch at him for a moment, then at the obstacle that stood in the path.

"Oh god. We are lost," she said, looking at the solid stone slab. It was sticking out of the ground at an angle, and in the light she could make out that it had a curved top, capped with green moss.

"That's a grave stone," Donnie said, gradually getting up.

"Oh god," the woman repeated, and tried scanning the whole area. They had found some kind of old cemetery. Looking up they could finally see the sky, but it was making no difference below; everything seemed ominous and still.

Behind, from where they'd emerged, the sound of a twig snapping echoed out to them.

"What was that?" the kid asked.

"Let's go. Now." The woman clicked off her torch and led them away. She grasped the kid's hand and Donnie strode with them.

They walked past more and more gravestones and didn't look back. They all felt something, a presence of some kind. You know that old unaccountable feeling of being watched? This is what they felt, and at first it bugged Donnie.

His breathing came louder than ever, and he started to slow down, the other two were at least three gravestones out in front. Then as he steadied himself more a sound came from behind; loud thumping, like footsteps along hallowed ground. They came within Donnie's grasp and so in a panicking knee-jerk reaction, he turned out of the path and ducked behind a large memorial stone.

'Just stay still in the dark. You don't move; it can't see you.' He thought to himself.

Through the darkness he saw a movement glide past; the outline of a wispy cloak floated by. For a moment he guessed it was a ghost with the way it moved in the still cold air, but he couldn't be sure. Should he shout a warning for the other two? He decided not to and cautiously followed.

'Whatever had created the disturbance tonight, continued to do so.' He reflected.

He headed forwards with the soft ground at his feet aware of the still but murky air around him. His breathing was deafening, especially as there wasn't any other sounds, and because of the dark he couldn't walk any faster than at a stumbling pace. So that was what he did.

Unexpectedly a tree root, or something sticking out of the ground, tripped him forward. He gasped and fell awkwardly to the forest floor once again; this time he grunted in slight pain.

The soft ground felt freshly dampened from the condensation. Exhaling loudly, he got up and looked ahead; somehow his path seemed darker than before. Trying to adjust his vision he had the frightful realisation; something was standing inches in front of him and staring down. He remained frozen on the spot as a strong icy force gripped his senses; it wasn't a bear and it was standing on two legs. He felt fingers take a grip around him; they were beyond cold for just a person, so cold that he felt its bitterness through his t-shirt and straight onto his bare shoulder.

"Donnie," shouted the woman distraughtly, as she shone her torch. A beam of light silhouetted the figure with this grip; he looked up to a shadow filled hood.

In one motion the hood and figure turned. They heard the slightest of hiss, like a cat. The cold hand left Donnie's shoulder and moved towards the woman. She shone the light forward, as the figure closed in and the torch flew away. The kid next to her screamed, but remained untouched as the woman fell to the floor. The shadow on top of her moved.

Donnie marched forward and grasped the kid's hand.

"Run," he shouted. Something told him inside that he couldn't fight whatever this thing was.

"Just go," Donnie commanded, and they ran past several of the grave stones and memorials. They came to thicker woods and neither of them looked back.

"What do we do, Donnie?"

"Just keep going," Donnie said turning. He could see the discarded torch far away on the horizon and came to a slow. He wheezed louder and let out a sharp cough.

"Use your pump," the kid said.

"I left it, back at the damn tent."

"That's no good. Let's go back and get it. Maybe we will find Dad."

"I don't know which way it is." Donnie looked around in every direction. From behind was the cemetery. No matter where the two glanced, neither of them could gauge their bearings.

"This way," Donnie said, and again he had that feeling, just like moments ago, telling him to run.

"It has to be this way, come on." He surged forward pulling the kid along. They continued though darkness, the ground beginning to slope upwards once more.

"I want Mum," the kid whined.

Donnie had no idea what to say. He didn't know if she was gone, and he didn't want to know. Just being able to take his next breath was more of a worry right now.

"Let's just get there first," he said in a slight haze. Donnie was beginning to feel distant, like he wasn't in control, maybe it was the lack of oxygen combined with the cold.

"Where are we going?" the kid asked, and then it became apparent; on the horizon stood the shadowy outline of a large house. A soft glow of candlelight danced from inside a few of the ground floor windows.

"Is that a haunted house?" the kid asked, as he was dragged forward. "Donnie? I don't want to go in there."

"But why? This is our new home. Come on." Donnie said in monotone. He let go of the kid's grasp and skipped forward.

"Donnie," the kid cried out, but it was no use.

"Come on."

The kid had no choice, it was follow or stay out in the dark alone.

As they got closer to the old house they could see that it was painted all white, but seemed run down. Wooden slats on the outside were half hung or completely missing. Window frames were peeling paint and the front decking had partially collapsed. The damp forest environment had left moss scattered all around the once whitewashed wood.

"I don't want to," the kid said again, as Donnie stepped towards the large door. As he did, it creaked loudly and slowly opened inwards.

He walked over the threshold and into flickering candlelight. Quickly Donnie was out of sight.

"Come back Donnie," the kid whimpered.

"I want my Daddy," the kid added, and began to whimper.

The door creaked open a little more, and the kid unwillingly followed Donnie in.

You're thinking that after walking inside the door it slammed shut and they were never seen or heard of again, right?

Wrong.

This isn't some crappy camp fire tale. This is my story, Darke Blood.

In order for me to tell this thing right, perspectives must change. Just remember, coincidence under all circumstances should be embraced.

My name is Blake Malone, and I do hope you will join me on this journey as I relive each moment in an effort to remember what happened. I'll try not to patronise you, but there are no guarantees.

Guess that's the Introduction taken care of. So cue the first chapter.

Part One: Arriving at the Heath

* 1 *

The bus vibrated and shuddered as it came bounding down the off ramp. The dated plastic interior squeaked dangerously and I braced myself as the driver slammed on his brakes for the imminent red light ahead. For a moment I felt weightless in my seat; metal ground on metal bringing the barely populated and musty smelling vehicle to a complete stop. I powered off my cd Walkman and Michael Jackson finally stopped blaming it on the boogie.

Anyway, in between stuffing the Walkman into my rucksack and staring forward, this place must have been my stop. I took one last look at the girl who had been exchanging glances with me throughout the journey. Maybe we could strike up a conversation, if she gets off here as well. Ambitious if I do say so, because one thing I pride myself on is being a terrible judge of character, so my hopes for anything more than a pity filled glance were low.

From my window I could see nothing but a desolate flat car park shrouded in near darkness. The sun must have recently gone down, but oddly I couldn't remember. This had to be my stop. Was this some kind of Park and Ride for the town of Darke Heath? From what I'd heard the place was a typical small town, neighboured with lush surrounding woodlands; a place to spend a summer by the lake, or even a winter escape. What stared back at me now seemed to be a pure concrete wasteland.

After a loud hiss and violent shudder, the bus came to stop in what appeared to be a highway truck stop.

"Glenwood travel interchange. Darke Heath pick-up point," the portly bus driver announced, clambering out of his beaten seat. He seemed like one of those trucker types.

I grabbed the rucksack and made my way to the front. To my luck the girl I had my eye on was sliding into her leather jacket and readying to leave; a perfect opportunity to talk. She began to edge out in front of me.

"After you," I said with an intrigued smile, and a hope of something more.

As I looked directly at her nose stud she didn't even acknowledge me and headed out of the bus. She seemed to have a 'this is bullshit' look on her face as it flashed past me.

'Gee... you're welcome.' I mentally grumbled.

As I said, shit judge of character. Maybe I gave this new start too much respect. Already you're thinking I'm an asshole; this girl just clearly ignored me, so maybe I do look like an asshole. You can keep thoughts like that to yourself, thank you very much.

Taking a deep breath, I decided to draw a line in the sand and carry on. This is just the pick-up point for Darke Heath anyway, and my ride should be out there waiting for me. I took some more air in through my nose this time; I was standing on solid ground again. There were moments when riding this faded silver rust bucket, I thought I might not make it.

The smell around here could only be described as strong pine. I stood idle for a moment, looking in every direction; I couldn't see any trees at all.

"The Heath is ten kilometres west of here kid. This is yours, Jesus what you carrying - a body?" The bus driver asked, as he lugged my large trunk from the underneath bag hold compartment.

"Just a few tools, thanks. My ride should be meeting me here." I said dragging the trunk awkwardly away from the bus.

"I wouldn't hang around here after dark. The sun's already down," the driver added. I looked back at him and nodded.

I sat on the trunk to gather myself. The other passengers who'd got off the bus had all trailed away in different directions. Reaching into my jacket pocket I took out the printed email sent to me last week; the time and place were exactly where I sat now.

"I'm sorry about before," a voice said in front of me.

In my train of thought I hadn't realized the blonde from the bus was standing in my view.

"That's... okay?" I said, in that lower volume of uncertainty, as I didn't really feel certain she was addressing me. It was only then I slowly began to stand.

She smiled from ear to ear and ran my way.

'What really? I'll just go with it for now.'

With a frown and a smile, I stood fully on my feet and readied myself for an embrace. More like readied myself for sheer embarrassment; I watched the girl run past me and straight into the arms of some guy who happened to be standing right behind me.

Did I just use my own strength to stand up simply for that? I mean I'm able bodied and all that but, oh never mind.

I quickly sat back down hoping nobody saw. Exceptional start I thought, as I reread the folded piece of paper.

Behind me the loud revving of a motorbike echoed across the empty travel interchange; it was her and that guy, probably heading somewhere cool to be with more of their friends. Yet here I sit on this shitty concrete plain watching a fat man trying to get back up on his bus.

It was getting dark and very soon I would have to do something if my ride didn't arrive.

"Mr Malone," a strained southern accent called from behind.

'That's me. Yes, he's here.'

"Hello. You must be...?" I said looking up at a weathered looking man standing taller than me.

"Angus Greene, good to meet you Mr Malone," he said, and we firmly shook hands.

Angus looked me up and down in silence for a few long drawn out seconds. He muttered something to himself before shaking off whatever daze I had put him into.

"Sorry I'm late, there was another call out I had to answer. Somebody jammed a tape in their recorder." He drawled with a country style accent. Everything about him seemed country, from his thick flannel shirt to the dirty jeans he wore. This guy was a worker.

"Call me Blake," I said, shouldering my rucksack and lowering to take hold of the trunk.

"Let me give you a hand there, Blake. Malone suggests you got some Irish in ya, that and the lack of a tan."

"Yeah, my mother's family are from the old country."

"Come on, the truck's over here. You'll feel right at home in the Heath, we got plenty of Irish descendants' scattered around and not much sun," Angus said, as we lifted the trunk into the back of an old green pick-up truck.

"Hop in kid. I'll just throw a rope over your trunk."

So far so good. I did feel a little bad for him helping me carry this heavy trunk, but he had insisted. I was now sitting in an antique of a truck ready for the final approach to Darke Heath, where hopefully something meaningful awaited me.

Angus grunted as he stepped up into the driver's seat. He turned the key and the green beast came to life. The radio played country music in the background and we headed out of the travel interchange.

"It would have been nicer if the bus company had kept a service running into the Heath itself, but they haven't for years, and as for the railroad? They might as well just rip up the track; used to be a real tourist haven all year around. Now, we get less of those folks coming by," he said.

"Why do you think that is?" I asked.

"You probably know the Heath has a bad rap for as long as anyone can remember. I don't wanna scare you early on Blake, but there have always been stories. People going missing, mainly tourists mind. Most of these kids head out into the trees without a damn bit of survival knowledge. That's how I see's it anyways," Angus explained.

There had to be a valid reason for the people disappearing, but I wasn't going to pry this early on.

"I'm gonna be honest with you now, Blake. I know the emails we exchanged were brief, but I may have spoken a few half-truths with you," he added, glancing at me.

"Okay?" I asked, now feeling slightly edgy. Should I have got in the truck with a person I didn't know? Again, the lack of character judgement sprang to mind.

"Now I advertised the technician job post with a view to spending less time at work and more with the family. The truth is kid, my wife and kids are gone. They skipped town recently. Without depressing ya that much, I just want to spend more time by myself and get my life back together. I know that sounds heavy, but that's the truth."

"No problem man," I said, trying to sound understanding. The guy seemed good on the surface.

"Break-ups can be rough.," I added, feeling that Angus wanted me to say more.

"You'll fit in well around town, plenty of kids your age about. There is something else I wanna talk about," he said, as we continued along a nearly dark road.

"Sure. Go ahead."

"It couldn't possibly be worse than talking about my marital situation," he said, chuckling to himself and then continued.

"The last kid I took on wasn't what he said he was. It doesn't bother me much if you're not up to scratch with the work knowledge because you can always learn. This kid before, he was writing stuff about the town in those internet chatrooms. He did a number on the town's rep and stirred up some major conspiracies about things. Then he just took off. You ain't got an agenda like that do you?"

There was an agenda, but what I'd chosen not to mention is that I knew a lot about this 'kid' Angus had previously employed. He went by the internet alias name of 'Darke Crusader', I know right? The name says it all. He spent his short time in Darke Heath reporting on what he thought were weird goings on; people disappearing, people he had personally became acquainted with. Then he'd found some would return but with no recollection of where they'd been. He deemed the forest as a 'no go' zone even in the daytime, for reasons he never said.

19

Either way, there was a lot of mystery surrounding this place and to me that seemed interesting. When I researched the town, the 'Crusader's' online forum sat at the top of every search engine.

Something is going on in Darke Heath and I'm going to find out what. So, my answer to the question Angus gave me was simply this;

"No way. I don't use computers that much."

"That's good to know. So why come to Darke Heath?" he asked.

"I felt like starting over. Truth is Angus; I've never really had any true friends. I'm trying to find a deeper reason, but…"

"Then you found the Heath," Angus said.

"I did."

Deep down my memory of before the bus seemed to be a blank. All the 'furniture' memories remained like my name and birthday; even the 'Darke Crusader' stuff was still in there. Everything else however, seemed blurred. This was the first moment I drew a line under all my inner-self doubts because something was blocking my memory.

"You'll find out soon enough whether you made the right choice. Me? I've never made one good decision in my whole life and I'm still here," Angus said, and laughed to himself again.

I looked out of the window. Quickly we had come away from the fading light into complete darkness; facing me was pure black. We must be in the forest.

"Yep. Not much to see out there at night. Most of the forest is pine and so there's no leaves to fall; keeps the innards of that place real dark. Guess that's where the name came from. Some people say there are parts of it still unexplored. Don't go in too deep, or when its sundown, and you'll be just fine. We're nearly there," Angus said, as he put his foot down a little further.

For some time, the truck climbed upwards in the darkness then ahead on the horizon we both saw the faint glow of light. The horizon became the brow of a hill and we steadily made our way over it. Facing us now was the glow of the streetlights below that spread throughout the town.

"There she is," Angus said.

Headlights shone momentarily at a green sign, it read 'Darke Heath' and as we flashed by the truck headed lower down into the town itself which sat cradled in the valley. Surrounding it on every side was the pure black of the forest.

"You'll get a better appreciation for the views in daylight," Angus said, and turned the wheel left as the main road banked off into a curved street.

"Cool," I said, with a slightly excited tone. This place looked alright so far; good looking houses and smart streets.

We came onto another street wider than the last. Reading the sign, I realised this was the Main Street of Darke Heath.

"You get to live right in the centre of town; your apartment is above the store." Angus pulled up along the sidewalk.

"And there it is." He pointed up to the sign above a store which read 'The Electrical Workshop'.

"Come on in, Pam will be getting ready to head home soon. She works the front." He stepped out of the truck and towards the glass fronted store. In the window were various lighting displays; a neon sign hung on chains displaying 'VCR repair' and a smaller cardboard notice below read 'DVD player repairs'.

So this was it. For a rugged looking older guy, he kept the place looking smart; a bell above the door rung as he held it open for me to go in.

"Yeah, you'll find it colder around these parts. All that fresh air," Angus said.

I had noticed it was considerably colder within the forest town. My open shirt and under shirt weren't doing much to keep me warm.

Inside the shop, shelves were organised in three lines and stacked with all things electronic or electrical; towards the outer edges there were more component type stuff, such as cabling and light bulbs. Hanging from the ceiling above were more display type lights. The place smelt of carpet and looking down I could see that it seemed brand new.

"Yeah. We just replaced all the carpet tiles. Pam, come and say 'hi' to our new employee," Angus called towards the counter and from behind a large computer screen a head of dark hair emerged; staring my way was Pam. Her head disappeared again and then she stood up.

"You must be Malone," she said.

I could only see the top of her head move past the monitor as she jumped down and emerged from behind the counter top.

"Hi. Call me Blake," I said looking down at the oriental looking girl who approached. She wore a black shirt with a white line drawing of a dragon's head breathing fire.

"Nice to meet you," she said, looking up at me through thick glasses.

"When Pam isn't playing with her dragons and castles, she's serving customers in here..." Angus smiled.

"It's dungeons and dragons. Plus, many other RPG games," Pam retorted, defensively.

"Pam designed the current layout we have of the store. Not too bad if I say so myself. I'll grab your trunk. Pam give our newcomer here the tour," Angus said, as the doorbell went.

"Well, Mr Malone. Welcome to this strange place. But strange is good, everything you see here is my domain," she said, carelessly waving her hands around.

"Your domain and first quest awaits." She turned and signalled for me to follow.

We headed behind the counter and through an open doorway.

"Introducing the actual electrical workshop; what an impressive mess it is!" She approached a workbench with a stack of TV's ranging in sizes. Most of the surfaces in this place were taken by something half assembled or repaired. If tidy, this place could look quite cool.

"Impressive," I said.

"If you say so. The apartment is upstairs. Angus can show you that. Tour complete." Pam's eyes looked up at me through the thick lenses. For a moment, she stood expecting me to say something; so I did,

"So, Pam. What brings you to Darke Heath?"

"My parents and their American dream. We moved here from Chicago two years ago. They insisted I get a job if I wanted to live in their basement. So that's what I did."

It felt like every time Pam spoke, it was to abruptly end the conversation. Again, we both stood in silence.

"Here we are," Angus said, carrying my trunk into the workshop.

"Yeah, the workshop needs some attention in terms of housekeeping. Speaking of houses, the apartment is upstairs. Here's the keys. I gotta run. Another repair job. I won't be back tonight Pam so lock up. Show everything to Blake and I'll see you both tomorrow morning."

He handed me a large set of keys and then left. Again, the bell rang from the front and he was gone.

"Just so you know, he isn't going to a repair job, but that's a story for another day. I am going to lock up and go home. If you want to get outside use the back door over there. The code for it is 1, 3, 7, 9, or think of the four corners. You need to set the alarm before you sleep tonight which is the same code. See you tomorrow." Pam said dismissively, and headed to the front of the store.

I found it strange that both of them had just decided to leave so abruptly. Well that is why I am here, to find out stuff. The main thing was I had arrived. Now for my first night in Darke Heath.

* 2 *

Having dragged my trunk up the workshop stairs, I now stood facing a half-open door to the apartment. Well, I presumed my apartment, and yet the door was fricking wide open. Ignoring the current security arrangements of a flimsy lock, I pushed at the light door and it squeaked in reply before hitting the interior wall.

"Whoops," I said, not expecting it to be quite so flimsy.

As I stepped over the threshold my nostrils were invaded by the distinct but fading smell of paint. Magnolia dominated every vertical wall, and I walked through a narrow hallway into an opening.

"Nice what they've done with the place," I said, dropping the trunk down onto a creaky but newly carpeted floor.

A metal framed bed sat in the middle of the cosy room, it was sized somewhere between double or single with the mattress still cloaked in polythene. The room only contained one other thing, and that was a wide sideboard consisting of drawers and cupboards. The window above this varnished surface called to me, so I slung my rucksack onto the bed and looked down into Main Street.

For a moment I stared out onto the black road surface. Every so often a vehicle would pass, but

26

nobody seemed to walk along the sidewalks. The place seemed awfully quiet, maybe too quiet, as if the town didn't like going out in the evening or something. I turned back and stared at the dank and somewhat confining apartment. Had I made the right choice to come here?

My memory, or lack of it, continued to interest me. Maybe the tiredness of a long journey had something to do with my amnesia. All I could really think about was making this new start, and so here I stood ready for it.

I unlocked the trunk. On top of all my possessions sat a folded and crumpled sleeping bag. Not knowing the policy with the polythene, I chose to keep it for now and sat the bag on top of the mattress. Next I took out my leather-bound diary. This was where all my information and leads about the 'Darke Crusader' were kept. I placed it on the bed in preparation to read later before going to sleep. The rest of my trunk contained unimportant stuff like clothes and tools. They could wait for now. I stood up again and noticed another narrow hallway leading from the bedroom. Guess that's where the rest of the apartment was.

In curiosity, I followed the small passageway and came to two doors. Opening the first led to small square kitchen. Cupboards at head height hung over a countertop. It was fully furnished and even had a microwave which sat on a separate table with a couple of folding chairs. A small square window looked out into the darkness behind the workshop. I noticed it was slightly ajar, so I pulled it shut, noting that the lock didn't seem to connect, but then looking around out there it would take some agility to break in.

"Cool," I said in admiration of my first real kitchen and then turned back to the other door.

The bathroom also looked new. Fresh white tiles spread across all four of the walls and in pride of place a large walk-in shower. This place had definitely had work done recently. For some strange reason this small square room made me feel at ease, like I had stood in a similar room before and spent time there, maybe that's what my last place was like, then again right now I couldn't remember.

Going back to the bed, I sat on it and for the moment decided to chill and just process the move. Then I would have to venture out and find food.

Taking hold of my diary I sat back and opened the first page. The polythene below me crumpled loudly.

"Where did you go Crusader?"

And like that a wave of exhaustion hit me. Before I knew it I was dreaming.

I was sitting in the passenger seat of a truck looking into the abyss of darkness, it resembled the journey with Angus, but this wasn't his vehicle. In a flash I had moved from inside the vehicle to standing amongst the shadowy trees. A beam of light on the horizon moved from right to left, was that the truck on the road? Why the hell was I now standing inside the forest?

My feet began to trudge forward towards the very distant light. Something didn't feel right; like I was having an all-out of body experience. Then as my voice spoke, it gave me the realisation that I wasn't me at all. I must have been someone else.

"Just move. The Forest Road is on the horizon. I'll get help and the Sheriff. He'll know what to do," I said, with heavy lungs that ached as they did their best to take in as much air as possible.

Turning my head round, the upright solid shadows of trees faced me. Did one of them move? Was there a face staring back at me from the black?

"Shit." I said gulping, and sidestepped around a thick tree trunk.

By now the beam of light out front had passed by but I could still gauge where the road stood.

'Just get there and someone will pass. They can help.'

A twig snapped behind me. It was close by. Something was stalking me in the dark. Whispering or breathing filtered into my ears and that's when I semi-woke up, but the dream kept me back from the reality of consciousness.

'Steal her heart.'

The voice that spoke to me was hypnotic and dreamy. For a second my right shoulder ached and as soon as the pain went, I was pulled all the way back into the dream.

Thoughts flooded through me from the character I now played again; this didn't feel like me.

'I have to keep going. The others need my help. We got split up at the camp. God I hope they are alright. Whatever disturbed us was chasing me and not them, so they had to of got away right?'

With straining lungs I climbed up a steep bank until my bare feet stepped onto solid road. Placing my hands on each knee, I lowered myself down in exhaustion. Coming out of the trees had given me more light and I turned to see if anything was coming out towards me.

Looking closer, I suddenly saw it. A shadow drifting through the trees and towards the steep bank. Out of the corner of my eye something shone; it was a car, thank god. From the horizon, light beamed towards me and I watched the gliding shadow stop. Light passed over the shadow filled hood as it ominously watched over me before slowly moving back and away.

"Come to the bar," a loud whisper said from behind.

"Across the street," the whisper added, it sounded like a woman.

I turned erratically as yet more light approached and I glanced down into the forest on the other side of the road. Another shadow stood there, but I saw something at chest height that glowed.

'Steal her heart and bring it to me.'

I headed towards the shadow holding the glowing heart, that's what it looked like. My footing abruptly gave way and I slid as I stepped down.

Everyone has felt the motion of slowly trailing off to sleep; that feeling of your body drifting away in a floating sensation. Unexpectedly something wakes you and that floating sensation comes crashing down as you jolt awake. That was my deal. I actually fell out of bed with my sleeping bag and diary in tow, my body thumped onto the creaky floor as I came to.

"Holy shit!" I said, out of breath. Maybe that whole idea of your mind thinking it's real makes things real.

For a moment in that dream I was someone else, running away from a camp having been split up with people I couldn't quite put my finger on.

'Come to the bar.'

I untangled the sleeping bag from my legs and slowly stood up. What time was it? In a slight daze, I headed over to my trunk and took out my small alarm clock.

"Ten thirty," I said, and carried the clock over to the window adjacent to the sideboard.

So I had been out for a few hours. That journey sure took it out of me.

Looking out of the window, a place across the street caught my eye. I hadn't seen it earlier. Dim overhead lighting shone bleakly on a sign that read 'The Darke Bar'.

'The bar.'

I hadn't noticed the place before. Maybe it hadn't stood out to me then. Something was drawing me there, so I plucked up some courage and decided to go for a drink.

'Steal her heart.'

On the way out of my apartment door I quickly checked myself in a full-length mirror hanging in the hallway. Another thing I hadn't noticed before.

I ran my hand through my just above shoulder length hair and then adjusted my open shirt. For a moment I stared at myself, and then straightened up the under shirt. At the very corner where neck met fabric you could just see the scarring.

I pulled the shirt over to cover the markings.

How did I get that burn? I remember the smell of smoke and burning, the heat near my face from a fire long ago. Ah, who cares? I'm here now and the promise of beer sounds good to me.

'Put it to the back of your mind and go get 'em, Malone.'

"Let's rock," I said, nodding to myself and headed down into the workshop.

Walking across to the bar, I couldn't see through the blacked-out windows that banked either side of the equally dark door. There came that uncertainty and slight thrill of what I could be getting myself into.

'What the hell,' I thought, 'right, new start and time to meet new people.'

I pushed the door open and strolled in. My feet stepped onto the wooden floorboards and the noise of a busy bar hit me, what followed was the acrid smell of stale cigarette smoke. To the right of me was the counter with bright spotlights above, to the left were a range of booths and couches. I reckoned most of them were taken, but I couldn't get a good view as the light was pretty dim. A cloud of smoke covered a larger table to my left where people laughed and joked as they drank. Others stopped as I came to the bar counter.

That's when I noticed a couple were playing pool towards the right of the counter.

"What will it be newcomer?" the bar man said. He wore a black sleeveless shirt with 'Offspring' written in flames across his chest. The only other notable features this guy had was the pale bald head coupled with a series of piercings in his right ear. Bright light reflected off him slightly and he didn't look particularly friendly or warming to me.

"I'll have a beer please," I said, leaning on the wooden surface.

"Coming right up."

He turned to a fridge at low height and took out a bottle of beer.

"So, you new in town?" he asked, placing the bottle in front of me.

"Yeah. Got here tonight." I took another look around, it felt like there were several eyes on me, especially from the long table with several couches and chairs around. All of them filled with someone, and they sounded loud.

The bar man noticed me looking.

"Yep, that's the regular demographic; noisy bastards," he said, and then turned towards them.

"Hey, you cool kids. Do you wanna adjust the volume a tad? We got other people who want to have conversations in here."

The table simmered down slightly and again I felt a wave of eyes on me.

"Sorry about that. So, you got in tonight? This is pretty much the place in Darke Heath at night. Lucky for you I ain't like the normal stereotype you get in here, if you get my drift? It's pretty luck that you, a new comer, found this place so easily."

I sensed a small essence of suspicion from the man.

As I was about to explain my living arrangements across the street, a commotion erupted from the other side of the bar. It looked like the couple playing pool were in some kind of disagreement.

"Damn it, pay up," the brunette girl said, clearly being the dominant of the two. She pushed the guy against the bar.

"You wanna take that anti-social activity outside Caitlyn," the bar man interrupted, and she pushed the guy away.

"He ain't worth it Splint. Get outa here," said Caitlyn, as her victim scurried away and out to the door.

"I hate it when they don't pay," she said, to the bar keep Splint.

Then she turned towards me, and our eyes locked from across the bar. That was before I looked away. She squinted momentarily as I tried to play it cool and swig my beer.

"You know most of them ain't worth shit. Want another coffee?" Splint asked, as Caitlyn continued to watch me.

"Nah, I'll take a beer," Caitlyn said, keeping one hand on the bar as she walked around towards me.

I looked at her approaching in tight dark red jeans and knee length boots. Her toned midriff was exposed from the short sleeveless leather top she wore. For moment I couldn't take my eyes away.

'Come on Malone, be cool damn it.'

"Are you sure about the beer, Caitlyn? I don't think you remember the last time you drank beer, but I do," Splint said, and for his trouble received nothing but a spiteful grab as Caitlyn took the bottle from his hands.

"Hi," I said, as she took a swig from the bottle before placing it down.

"This is the newcomer. Got in tonight."

"It's Blake," I said, nodding to Splint.

"I'm Splint. Your good bar keep for the Darke Bar. When I'm not here, I'm here, get my drift? This is Caitlyn. She likes to express herself with violence sometimes."

Caitlyn cracked a one-sided smile and looked me in the eye again. Her dark eyes seemed to burn through me, she scanned the room and then spoke,

"I only do what's necessary to take what's rightfully mine; normally violence comes second. So, does Blake wanna shoot some pool?"

"Only if there's nothing at stake?" I said, trying to be funny. She cracked a smile again and nodded.

"He's witty," Splint said, turning away to serve someone else.

"So what brings you to the Heath?" Caitlyn asked, and I followed her lead towards the pool table.

I'm going to be honest with you right now. This woman seemed hot. Like really hot. Not some low class hot, we're talking old Hollywood black and white movie class. Thinking about that distracted me from giving her an answer, so quickly my words scrambled their way out from my weirdly empty mind.

"I'm just looking, for a fresh start."

"We don't get many of them. You want to break?" she asked.

I don't ever remember playing pool once, but then I'm not remembering much at the moment. I suspected this could only go one way.

"It's been a long time since I played. You break," I said, taking a swig of beer.

"Now that sort of talk I hear too often, but I'll allow it as there is nothing at stake," Caitlyn remarked, and slowly bent down to take aim. She forcefully pushed the cue and the pool balls clapped loudly from impact.

"The only thing at stake here is a reminder as to why I shouldn't play pool," I said, taking the cue from her.

Awkwardly I lowered and took aim for the white. Without any real skill, I hit the ball and it knocked a red into the far side pocket.

"You're looking more and more like my last punter right now," she said, with a concentrated smile.

"I may look like a hustler but you will soon find out I'm not," I said, swigging my beer again.

"Guess I'll have to keep my eye on you then, Blake," Caitlyn observed.

From the first lucky shot my ability to play pool went downhill rapidly, and that's even after the courage the beer had given me on an empty stomach. Now I began to feel a tad dizzy. Caitlyn made short work of me and at least four red balls were left on the table as she sunk the black.

"Guess you were right," she said, placing the cue onto the table.

"I never lie about how bad I am at something," I said, and my stomach turned a little. I was hungry and needed food.

"So is there anywhere around here I can get fed?" I asked, and Caitlyn glanced at me with that squint again.

"I guess this is happening. You want to head out?" she asked me.

"Sure," I said, thinking we were simply heading to a place where we could eat. Again, my judge of character was well beneath all expectations of that night.

"Splint, I'm heading out." Caitlyn called back, as she took hold of a long dark purple coat hung up by the bar.

"Already? Guess you can't fault instinct," Splint grinned.

At the time I never thought about what he meant; it went straight over my head as I walked out holding the door for Caitlyn.

Here I was leaving a bar, with someone. Considering how my arrival had gone, it looked like my night was redeemed, at least for a few moments.

Just to clarify, I'm not that type of guy who heads into bars and picks up women. My intentions were food based right now. And to further clarify? This girl was the classic type of good-looking you don't pass up.

* 3 *

"After you," I said, suggesting that Caitlyn led the way. Well, I didn't know my way around the town and it seemed right to be polite.

Even though my efforts to show off my good manners had been implemented, she seemed off compared to when we were inside the bar. Marching forward I had to make an effort to keep up with her Victorian style purple coat that seemingly trailed away. We headed left out of the bar and along Main Street.

"Cold out here," I said, trying to tackle the apparent gap that stood between us.

"It's about to get a lot colder for you," Caitlyn said, and spun towards me. She gripped my open shirt and with an unquestionable force I was thrown into the darkness of a side street. Nothing stopped me from falling and down I went.

"What the hell?" I yelled, from the cold floor in shock. It had taken me by complete surprise, so maybe that was why I fell so easily.

"Get up," she commanded, pulling me to my feet. Stumbling forward, I was met with the angry pale face of Caitlyn.

"Alexis hasn't sent many newcomers my way for a while. Guess the herd is thinning a little," she added to my confusion.

"What are you talking...?" I was shoved with some force against a wall behind me. A sharp searing pain came from my lower back as I felt something crunch and the air was abruptly knocked out of me as I turned to see what stabbed me; nothing, just plain brick wall. Had I struck it that hard?

I sucked the air in painfully and found standing up an almost impossible task. I was in trouble, I'd been blindsided by a pretty bar vixen.

"What, do you... want?" I asked trying to get up, but both my hands shook as I held them out in some semblance of defence.

Again she took hold of me and up against the wall I went; the pain of my back growing evermore.

"I want this shit to end once and for all," she said, keeping me pinned with one hand and reaching into her purple coat with the other.

"Just... just take my wallet and go."

I slowly reached into my jeans back pocket. Maybe this was just a high class mugging and perhaps she could be reasoned with.

"You can't pay for this, it's over," she stated sharply. I felt her placing something cold onto the side of my neck.

In a surge of adrenaline, I broke out and she reeled back. The object she held sparked for a moment.

"A stun gun?" I questioned, as Caitlyn angrily glared at me. She was poised to send a pulse of electricity into me, something I could do without considering my current condition. No pun intended.

"Look you don't need to use that. What do you want?" I asked, trying to compose myself and introduce some level of reasoning. Again, the wallet was offered.

She came forward, and as she did I gasped in pain and reached for my lower back.

"Hold on..."

My attacker then stopped and looked down on me intrigued.

"Ah... I think you broke something." The pain continued to shoot along my ribs. Breathing hurt, so I tried to take shorter gasps.

"Brittle bones? Another first," she remarked bluntly, and came into grab me.

"No way, you pushed me hard," I said, doing my best to cower away, she stopped again. I must have looked like such a puss right there, trying to kick myself away from a girl who had pretty much incapacitated me.

"Wait a minute. You are genuinely in pain? They don't feel pain," Caitlyn said, as if she was reasoning with herself.

"Well I do!" I said loudly, causing my body to contract in pain.

She stepped back and looked me up and down.

"So let me just ask; you turned up here tonight and happen to just stroll into the Darke Bar?"

"Yep, I said earlier." I slowly rose.

"And you're as pale as the moon and, hold on." Caitlyn stepped up to me and took hold of my chin. She poked her finger into my mouth and forced my lips open. Whilst the amateur dentist did her examination, I tried to explain my Irish descent. I then tried to ask what the hell she was doing with her hand in my mouth.

"No shit. You're telling the truth," she said, finally taking her hands off me. The stun gun went away allowing me to drop my guard slightly.

"Of course I am. Who did you..." Another sharp pain ran down my side and I gasped loudly. This was bad.

Caitlyn then awkwardly tried to aid me.

"I've made a genuine mistake," she said, appearing to be quite embarrassed.

"I think so too. Look I'm okay I think, just need to sit down and be still for the next few weeks," I mumbled, slowly lowering myself back to the floor. Gently I leaned back against the wall which had inspired all my pain.

Caitlyn crouched down beside me, she now appeared genuinely concerned. Taking a look at her, I could see she was on high alert. Her behaviour resembled something of a predatory animal, and before I could ask she sprung up; her senses had picked something up, and then I saw them.

Approaching from the other side of Main Street were three figures.

"Not now. Shit," she said.

Immediately I got a vibe that these three figures weren't going to be friendly.

"Come on, I've already been beaten up once tonight," I moaned from the cold floor.

The three prowlers spread out into a triangular formation as they came closer. In the minimal street light, I couldn't make out who they were, even though most of their bodies were covered by dark clothing.

"Alexis wishes to discuss new terms for the Heath," a voice came from the middle shadow.

That name 'Alexis' again, just like Caitlyn mentioned.

"Tell him to make a personal visit," she said, and reached for her stun gun whilst turning to me.

"Blake, stay back. This is going to get violent very quickly."

Was she being protective? Or maybe she'd finally got the message I was in genuine pain.

"Who's your boyfriend?" another figure sneered.

"None of your business. This isn't his fight," Caitlyn added.

"It's okay, I can handle myself," I said, plucking up some courage. The flow of adrenaline took away my pain temporarily and I got up.

"Looks like we got a new player in town," the middle voice said.

"Just stay back, Blake," Caitlyn ordered, but I was foolishly protective. I mean anyone would be if three guys wanted to take on one girl. Stun gun or not, I was still male and stupid.

"These new terms? They don't include your existence anymore Caitlyn," the middle figure added and came surging forward. The other two followed as Caitlin stepped in.

She lunged forward with a powerful uppercut into the stomach of victim number one. Quickly she spun and threw him into one of the others. They landed on the floor in a flailing pile. Jesus, she could fight and right now it made her a hell of a lot more attractive.

"Just you and me." Caitlyn engaged the only standing attacker.

"You sure you want to do this?" she asked, powering up the stun gun. A small blue spark flashed in the shadowy darkness.

I watched as the other two jumped up and charged.

"Behind you," I shouted, and again my back speared in pain.

Caitlyn turned with the stun gun first and drove it into the nearest approaching neck. A huge spark filled the shadowy street and the victim flopped to the cold floor. As he did the other one pounced and jumped onto her. She quickly became overwhelmed as the third guy jumped in. They grunted as arms and legs were thrown around.

I had to act.

'Come on Malone she needs help.'

I jogged over to the melee and grasped an overcoat. Heaving, I pulled one attacker free from Caitlyn and reeled back in the continued pain. This only pissed the guy off who now focused his attentions on me.

"Shit," I said, backing away with both hands held up. He stared down at me and cracked a small grin.

"Yeah... shit," he agreed, with a sinister nod.

"Come on," I groaned out loud, as my opponent twitched robotically. Trance-like he stood there for a few long seconds. My hope was to hold him off until Caitlyn would swoop in, but it all happened too fast.

I crashed to the cold floor once more as he jumped me. The full impact felt by my back. I tried to push and grasp at something to get this man off me.

From the corner of my eye I saw yet another bright flash but that didn't help me right now. Sharp teeth snapped as this freak tried to take a bite out of me. He inched closer to my neck and globules of drool dripped on to me. This guy snapped at me like a wild dog, his canine teeth looking pretty sharp, maybe the sicko sharpened them or something? I've heard of people like that.

Then came a thudding crunch. I closed both eyes as a great weight lifted from my body.

"Homerun," said a familiar voice, as I looked up to see Splint the barman, and he held a damn baseball bat. His free hand came down my way to grasp my arm as he pulled me up.

I awkwardly rose to see Caitlyn approaching my now downed and confused attacker.

"Damn amps," she said, turning back to us.

"Looks like I showed up in the nick of time," Splint grinned, admiring his weapon. "All thanks to old hickory here," he added.

"Thanks man," I said to him, and tried to gather myself together again.

"I did say he ain't like one of them. Guess your instincts were off Caitlyn, about this one anyway. He ain't what we thought he was." Splint explained as Caitlyn came closer.

"Looking at him, do you blame me?" she asked.

"He does look like one, I give you that much. Guess you survived long enough to earn yourself a date with the lovely Caitlyn sometime. I, on the other hand, have got 'people' to serve if you get my drift. Thank me later, and Caitlyn get that last amp before he splits." Splint shouted, as he headed back towards the bar.

"What was that all about?" I asked, as Caitlyn focused on me.

Before I could say or do anything else, she gripped either side of my head and pulled me in. Her lips locked with mine and we kissed. Momentarily it took me away and all the pain drained off; this girl was walking anaesthetic. She slowly lifted her lips from mine and withdrew as our eyes met.

"Maybe some time I can explain things," she said. There was something about her manner or demeanour that I just couldn't quite put my finger on, but I watched curiously as Caitlyn scanned me like prey.

"But right now," she murmured, "duty calls." She lowered herself down to one of the fallen attackers.

49

"You probably wanna give him another buzz," I added.

"They only need one. Watch," she said.

"Up you get. You fell hard on your head, but you'll live."

She helped the now dazed and panicked man to his feet.

"Get on home," she said, as the man looked all around. He then jogged away.

"This is getting weirder and weirder," I said.

"Maybe we can see each other again and I can explain. Ah shit." Caitlyn watched as the third man got up.

"Yeah, you should go," I said waving her off, but she came to me again and placed her lips on mine momentarily.

"See you around," she said, and I watched as she dashed away into the night.

Well that was a turn of events. A night best described as random and oddly painful, but I'm alive I guess. This girl who came out of nowhere kissed me, twice. I'll ignore the back pain right now, as I write this sitting on my polythene covered bed; tonight was a genuine success. Yeah, there are currently more questions than answers. Like why is Caitlyn so strong? Who were those three 'people' as Splint says that attacked us, and why does a stun gun break them out of whatever trance they are in? And what did that kiss really mean?

'Don't fear 'Darke Crusader', I'm making progress. With Caitlyn on my side and hopefully Splint, the truth of your whereabouts can be found. I may actually have made new friends tonight.'

After the initial pain of standing I closed my diary and placed it on the sideboard. Looking across the street I could see the Darke Bar sign had disappeared. The place must be closed for the night.

"Until tomorrow," I said, reaching up and pulling on the blind. It covered the whole window and the world outside.

What a night.

Slowly I tugged on each of my sleeves and eased my shirt off. Gasping every so often at the recurring pain, hopefully nothing was broken. It took longer than I thought to take one layer off, so I decided to leave the under shirt on for now, even though it had ripped in the commotion of being bundled up by some bite crazy guy. Now my shoulder and its burn-like scars were on show.

Lowering myself onto the bed, I was relieved to see it supported my weight as I kicked off both of my boots. My toes curled over into the new soft carpeting, creating a comforting feeling. There have only ever been a few moments in my life when I had completely forgotten the concept of time and this was one of them.

My small analogue travel clock read just past midnight. That was when I noticed the blind I had just pulled down moving in a light breeze.

Cold air crept across my bare shoulder. Did a door just open? A distant crashing thud came from somewhere nearby.

"What the shit was that?" I whispered to myself. My stomach began to turn as whatever made that sound was in my apartment.

* 4 *

I scanned the room frantically for any type of defensive weapon. My trunk. Inside there was a tool kit, but then again nothing in there was really that intimidating. Plus, it was buried beneath all my clothes, no time for that. Maybe if I shouted they would go away? Peering into the small corridor with two open doorways at the end, I shouted half-heartedly,

"Who's there?"

No response, but I could feel somebody's presence, probably one of those guys who attacked us earlier coming to finish me off.

From the kitchen, there was another crash.

"I said who's there, dammit," I shouted for the second time. I used my words to grow a little anger and courage.

You know what? This asshole is in my house. I have a right to be angry and defend myself. It had been a long day, and tomorrow I started my new job.

Taking a deep breath, I marched forward and headed for the kitchen doorway. Turning into the well-lit room I spoke before seeing,

"What are you fu…"

Facing me was the purple felt coat that formed itself around Caitlyn. Her dark hair flowed over her pale face as she looked down at the floor. The kitchen had somehow become a mess from her arrival; one chair was knocked over and the small plastic table was askew.

Slowly she looked up to me, but something didn't seem right. I backed off a little as my eyes met hers. Two dilated pupils stared back at me with a firm primeval glare, a huge sense of dread hit me like a tidal wave.

"Jesus," I said, continuing backwards and until my shoulder struck the light switch. The room was plunged into darkness as I dashed out.

"It's just me Blake," she said, as I saw the kitchen light come back on. Her head peered around the doorway and my eyes met hers, but this time they weren't dilated at all, there was no sign of the grimace now.

"I got you a grilled cheese sandwich." She held out a square brown bag.

I cautiously walked back towards the kitchen and took it. She smiled at me and said,

"Sorry about startling you like that. I didn't see a door bell down there so I climbed up to the window."

'Because that's the natural thing to do, right?' I thought.

Opening the bag, I could see it contained a sandwich and that it was still warm. I didn't hesitate in taking a bite. Having not eaten since I couldn't remember when it felt so good, even though this visitation weirded me out a little.

"Nothing's broken so it should all be okay," Caitlyn said, as I followed her back into the kitchen. She picked up the scattered chair and straightened the table.

"How's the back?" she asked.

Even though she had fed me I continued to stand off, especially from what I'd just seen.

"Are you okay, Blake?"

I nodded and turned to avoid the awkward eye contact.

"It's okay to be freaked out by somebody coming in through your kitchen window in the middle of the night," she smiled.

"I'm not weirded out at all," I said half-heartedly, "you made up for it with the sandwich. Please come in," I added, trying my best to be inviting. She followed and I could feel eyes on me like she was trying to work me out.

"Is there something bothering you?" she asked.

Walking to the bed, I finally turned to her and decided it was probably time to make eye contact.

"Did this freak you out?"

She stood and hung her head at a downward angle; dark hair draped over the pale skin of a face that resembled more of a frowning primeval demon than a classically hot girl from an old school cinema. Two dilated eyes stared back at me with the darkest of glares, she was the predator and I was the prey.

My fear rooted me there like a statue; I had no idea as to what my next move was going to be.

I mean, holy shit, it really was terrifying at first, my whole body froze and locked at the sight of her two pure dark eyes glinting at me, with just a hint of animalistic orange surrounding the pupils. Her whole forehead hung down with that frown, but worst of all it went all the way to her mouth as well; from her near perfect red lips were two long sharp fangs.

"It's okay, I won't hurt you," she said with a slight lisp from the teeth. It lightened the somewhat terrifying mood actually.

"This is what I am and it's okay," she tilted her head slightly and stepped closer to me. Her hands steadily reached out to mine, they were warmer than ever. I thought creatures like her were pure cold.

She pulled me closer and placed my hand in the centre of her chest.

"Do you feel that?"

I nodded as I felt a solid heartbeat.

"Just like you, I have a heart also. We managed to restart it a while back," she said, but I couldn't really focus. My mouth was dry and I was probably giving her that wide eyed death stare.

'Real cool, Malone.'

Finally, I broke my fear stricken silence,

"You're, you're a..."

"Say it. I don't mind." A beaming smile faced me with those pure white fangs.

"A vampire?"

She nodded. Her face transformed back to one of a human. The smile continued as her two fangs slowly receded into normal sized looking teeth.

"Partially, anyway."

'Whatever that meant.'

As her face fully resumed to normal, I felt more comfortable and dropped to the bed. I winced as my spine hit the mattress a little too hard.

"There are, so many questions I have right now," I said, as Caitlyn took off her purple coat. She knelt and placed her hands on my knees.

"Shoot. What do you want to know?" she asked, continuing to smile up at me.

"You suck blood, right?"

"Used to, blood is just a bunch of chemicals mixed the right way. A decent biologist or chemist could tell you that, so we produced a substitute. There's a science to vampirism. So no I don't suck people's blood anymore or not much anyway. Too many diseases, we also get sick, you know," Caitlyn explained, she spoke with such pride and assurance.

"Science? I thought this stuff was just..." I tried to think of a word. Then she said it for me,

"Fiction or mythology?"

I nodded.

"Nope. Some of the stuff in the TV shows and films they get right. Where do you think they get it from? Then again, a lot of stuff they don't know. Like the human brain has a whole section designated for vampirism. We are a side-step in evolution because being a vampire isn't exactly practical. Look it's the middle of the night and I am wide awake."

"No sunlight. No tan like me. That's why you attacked me earlier. You thought I was one of them didn't you?" I asked, whilst slowly rising, and she gripped my hands as I did; this girl was attached to me.

"Sort of. Actually, I thought you were an 'amp'." Caitlyn got up and let go of me, "very similar to a vampire, but not the real thing."

She turned to look around the apartment.

"How so?"

"It's a long story, Blake," she added, scanning my trunk, then slowly she lowered herself onto it and sat. Her dark red denim covered legs crossed one over the other.

"Hey, you brought me a grilled cheese, the least I can do is listen to you for a while," I said, taking another bite of the sandwich.

"Haven't you got to be up in the morning?" Caitlyn asked, taking out her stun gun from the jacket.

"Yep," I said, sitting back on the bed. I shuffled up the headboard and continued eating. My legs making that crumpling sound from the polythene that covered the mattress. Caitlyn looked at it with intrigue.

"Yeah, I know. I wasn't sure about the policy of removing the packaging to the mattress. So, what's an 'amp'?" I asked.

"The cheaper version of a vampire, created by electrical stimulation to the brain. Hence unlocking the vampire function without a need for siring," she explained.

"Did you get any of that?" she asked, smiling at me. I must have looked so dumb at that moment, with half a cheese sandwich in my mouth as this girl talked technical to me.

"So you can make anyone an 'amp' I guess?" I asked with a half full mouth. Animal.

She nodded and put her stun gun back in the coat.

"The whole vampire scene in Darke Heath has changed recently. These amps were created to be used as blood mules for the actual vampires. The sick bastards found a way around of not coming into my town, and now they prey on the innocent and get them to do their dirty work."

"Wait. There are more vampires and you're not on their side? And you stop these amps by snapping them out of whatever thing they got going on with that stun gun?" I asked, beginning my interrogation.

"Yep. They live in the woods and are led by Alexis. He's a real asshole, we go back a few years. Look it's a long and complicated story. You don't need to hear most of it..."

I sat forward and interrupted,

"No please, go on." Edging forward my back seared in pain again and I winced.

Caitlyn sprung up and came to me.

"Your back? Look you need to rest. I pushed you pretty hard out there. You should sleep," she said. There was an element of mistrust in the back of my mind about her, but something urged me on.

Was she just trying to get me to sleep so she could take my blood in the night? Either way I didn't really have a choice but to trust her. At least she did seem apologetic for my condition. There was something else, a force or aura which seemed to surround her, it felt like she could probably get whatever she wanted just by looking at me in a certain way. My eyes were peering at her through a soft-focus camera.

I took a closer look at my ripped shirt and then tried to take it off.

"Let me help," she said, and drifted towards me. Her hands gently gripped the shirt as she lifted it off me.

"How does it look?" I asked, turning my back to her. This would normally feel weird, but again that aura from her seemed to control me.

"No visible sign of any damage." Her warm hand graced my lower back. It soothed the pain temporarily. She then moved up to my right shoulder.

"You have an awful scar here, a burn?"

"Yeah, happened a while back." I think.

Her lips softly brushed my upper back as she kissed me.

"Creatures like me have a certain effect on mortals like you, Blake. You can probably feel my presence take over your urges already," she said.

"I can feel it," I agreed. "Now if I go to sleep, don't get any ideas about sucking my blood. I like my neck how it is," I added, and pulled my hair aside to reveal my pasty white neck.

"I would only bite you there if I wanted to sire you." Caitlyn smiled putting both her hands around me, she moved towards my neck and kissed it.

"Sire?"

"Make you a vampire, but If I was hungry and wanted a meal, I would bite you here on the shoulder," she placed her open mouth on my left shoulder. Her teeth gently clamped down on me just enough to know they were there.

"That way you aren't sired, or…" she slowly turned me around and took my arm, "the forearm," she added, placing her finger on the inside crease of my elbow. "You don't think this is weird, do you?" her eyes met mine.

"Not at all," I said, not wanting this to end.

"I'm starting to like you, Caitlyn," I added, thinking what the hell. She was the one kissing and putting her hands all over me.

"When I first saw you in the bar, my heart sunk at the thought of you being an amp. I'm glad you aren't," Caitlyn said, moving in.

Our lips met and her hands caressed my skin; the girl was damn passionate about this stuff.

She pulled away then, slowly.

"You must sleep. I will lie with you but that is all," she said with concern.

"Sure, you'll have to excuse the plastic" I said, and slowly edged back on the bed.

Caitlyn slowly removed her top and sat on the bed next to me.

"Do you mind if I keep my jeans on? They are somewhat a pain in the ass to get out of. Literally," she asked.

"I'm good either way. You look good in them," I said, just happy with the fact this girl was in the same bed as me.

She turned and slowly draped herself over me.

"Nice to meet you by the way," I said, as she nodded.

"Likewise."

For a few moments, we lay there in silence. Was it right to be in bed with someone I barely knew? Who the hell cares right? Make hay while the sun shines, whatever the shit that meant.

Before long my eyes became heavy as a great comfort set in.

"Why did you come to the Heath?" she asked, startling me slightly.

"I'm sorry you were falling asleep. I forget, I'm nocturnal, you're not."

I opened my eyes again and softly spoke,

"I wanted a new start. Things didn't work out back where I came from."

"You carry a lot of conflict and tension; I can sense it, I can smell it," Caitlyn said.

'Maybe that's why she found me attractive' I thought; *'I'm the new mysterious guy in town who's also a mortal, Then the guy gets hurt so she becomes sympathetic and begins to fall for him, that makes a good project for her. Why do I all always try to rationalise things?'*

"There's something about you Blake that I can't quite put my finger on, but I'll find out," she added, and at that very moment a chill ran down my spine. I looked over to my alarm clock and although the late hour didn't bother me, the fact my diary was sitting there did.

My conscience begged me to say what I had really come to Darke Heath for. The answer sat glaringly in that leather-bound book, but I was too hypnotically tranced out by her to say anything right there and then. Even though there is this girl stripped down to her bra with me in bed, this was still my first night here. I'm gonna have to keep my cards firmly close to my chest.

After all Caitlyn is a vampire, and from most fictional characters' experience, and in truth can they ever really be trusted?

* 5 *

The morning light shone in through the thin blind that wasn't doing much to hold back the sun.

'Probably one of the reasons Caitlyn had left', I thought, as I woke to find just me in the bed with an aching back.

The time read 7.30am as I squinted over to the clock. Slowly I stretched out and felt the full dull pain shoot through me, still it wasn't as bad as last night, certainly nothing a hot shower couldn't soothe and so that's where I headed.

As I stood in the claustrophobic prison cell type bathroom, it felt good to have hot steaming water flow over me. I smiled slowly whilst reliving some of the best moments from last night, and most of them were Caitlyn related.

With a proverbial spring in my step I felt ready to face anything that came my way today, but before heading out I threw on some clothes and scanned the apartment. It was then my eyes widened at the empty space on top of the sideboard.

My diary. She had taken my diary.

"Oh shit," I said, quickly rushing to the window and checking all around the sideboard.

Would she have taken it? Jesus, what if she had read it and found out what I was really doing here? Even after I had already given her my version of why

I had come to Darke Heath? That new start of mine may have taken strides to being a complete failure.

'You lied Blake. You aren't here for a new start; you've come to snoop around. I thought we had something. We shared a bed.' I could just hear it now. That's pretty much what I envisioned Caitlyn would say to me.

Ah man, to have a pissed off a vampire that's after you is one thing, but to have one you kissed and shared a bed with is another.

After turning over everything in that bedroom I still didn't find the damn diary. She must have taken it, and now my cover could be blown wide open. I'm not talking FBI cover, but more like the real reason I am in Darke Heath; investigating the weird happenings and where the Darke Crusader had gone. Shit my head ached now and as I looked at the time I saw that it was after eight; the Workshop opens soon.

'Put it all to the back of your mind for now Malone, if there's space. It's work time.'

I headed down the stairs from my apartment and as my feet touched the floor, Pam emerged from the back door holding a takeout drink.

"I see you survived your first night in Darke Heath, plus 'exp'," she said, continuing straight past me.

"How's it going Pam?" I asked, following her through to the shop front.

She took off her two-strapped ruck sack and sat at the counter top computer.

"It could be worse, Mr Malone. Then again, I could be elsewhere," she said.

"Nobody likes to work," I said with an attempt at humour. Again the conversation with her felt awkward.

"Umm… yes," she added as her monitor powered up.

"What time does the boss normally get in?" I asked as she took a sip of what appeared to be tea.

"No particular time, recently anyway. Something strange is happening with Mr Greene at the moment."

"What makes you say that?" I asked, trying not to pry.

She turned her head towards me and looked up like she was working something out. Two small eyes peered through thick lenses and stared back at me for a moment, and then she spoke,

"I have two theories right now. One is a little shadier than the other," she said, and paused for a moment.

"I can trust you. You are new in town, so who are you going to tell?" she asked rhetorically, but I answered anyway.

"I know, right?"

"Theory one suggests that Mr Greene is involved in some kind of illegal activity, most probably drugs," she said.

"Seriously?" I asked, stepping closer.

"Maybe. It's more common than people think," Pam said, and then tapped a few times on the computer keyboard.

"What about theory two?" I asked again, trying to appear only vaguely interested. I backed off and looked at a bunch of power adaptors on the shelf behind me.

"This theory is more realistic, but has several holes. After spending a night in this town, you would agree it's strange, yes?"

"Well yeah, kind of," I said, with effort to cover up my experience of last night.

"There are all sorts of stories and rumours in Darke Heath, legends of a dragon residing out in the deep forest, or the native American girl who rides a ghost horse around the town. Some even talk of 'Peoples of the Night' but, I haven't quite worked it all out yet, but I reckon Mr Greene is involved in there somewhere."

"Maybe," I said, beginning to lose interest. She had a point about this town and maybe she knew something about the 'nocturnal' types that shared this place or 'Peoples' as she called them.

Having learned not to trust anyone, I poked no more at the thought of Angus behaving weirdly. He had given me a job and put a roof over my head, even if it could potentially be drug funded.

Pam was busy surfing the internet, so I left her to it and headed back into the workshop.

Again, more questions than answers. As I looked at the junk filled workbench, the back door opened.

"It's a cold one," Angus said, as he walked in.

"Good mornin', Blake. How was your first night in the Heath?" He asked, and took off a cowboy type hat as he navigated his way around the various large appliances.

"Not bad," I said, with a half-smile.

"Well that's better than bad. I'm sorry I had to shoot last night, repair job an' all. I forgot to mention, there's bedlinen in the sideboard upstairs and the kitchen cupboards are stocked with snacks and what-not. That should set ya straight for a while. As for the mattress, go ahead and get rid of that polythene packing, if you haven't already. We had to repaint the place so the packing got left on," Angus explained, continuing past me.

"Okay. Thanks," I said. Now he tells me.

He then glanced through the doorway to Pam.

"Morning Pam."

"Mr Greene"

"You can probably guess what your first job is gonna be here Blake? Restore some kind of order to this place," he said, and positioned his hat down on a washer.

"This here washer is in for repair." He peeled off a post-it note.

"Usually they have a ticket like this, tellin' ya what's wrong, who it belongs to and anything else. If you take a look around the place it's crammed with all kinds of crap people want repaired. Your job is to play electronic triage; take a look at everythin' and see if it's worth our time, or your time for that matter."

I can do that. Scrap anything that isn't worth repairing; TV's and washers from the mid-eighties and before for sure, because that's what most of it was.

"I can do that. No problem," I said out loud, as Angus unlocked a door in the corner.

Hidden behind a rack full of junk was an office with blinds on the inside windows. A light came on as Angus went in.

"You'll find any tools you need about the place. I'll be in my office if you need me," he said, closing the door behind him.

"And that's where he will stay. Until tonight anyway," Pam said, from the front.

"Told you he was weird," she added.

I put thoughts of last night and Pam's 'theories' to one side and lost myself in my work for the rest of the day. Slowly but surely the junk filtered out from anything of actual value. It seemed strange to me that people really wanted to hold onto old stuff that would be cheaper to replace. Even someone with as little electronic knowledge as me knew most of this stuff had replacement components discontinued years ago.

As I shuffled out an awkwardly shaped radio from the workshop I caught the sound of Angus speaking from the office. He sounded panicked and distressed.

Stopping for a moment, I looked towards Pam who was selling a light fixture to an old couple. Wondering whether she was right, and with the radio in both hands, I covertly moved towards the office door. Only a muffled voice came out from the well-insulated office and he definitely sounded uneasy, but about what?

Just as I stepped closer, the talking stopped. Shit he was off the phone; I was standing too close and it looked too damn obvious.

I dropped to the floor and lowered the radio down. With my back facing his office door I pretended to examine it.

'Shit, that hurt.'

His door flung open and I felt his eyes on me. The office door slammed shut and Angus hastily locked it.

"Damn callouts. Got another one Blake, I might not be back 'til late, or even tomorrow. Don't wait up," he said, and with that he took off.

"Sure, see you later," I said, gently rising as he left. My backache protested again as I moved.

That radio was staying there tonight and if the boss was gone, that would be me done for the evening.

Pam had finished selling the light as I headed out into the store.

"Angus had to take off," I said, looking out through the front. It had suddenly got dark out.

"Uh huh. Just like yesterday and tomorrow probably."

Another weird pause came and went as Pam glanced up and then pointedly remarked,

"There's the boy that I like."

"Huh?" I asked.

Across the street stood the barman Splint, he was sweeping outside the Darke Bar, maybe he knew where Caitlyn went. My feet began to move before I could think.

'Quick think of a reason to go out there.'

"Who is that?" I asked, pretending to look at something inside the store.

"He works the bar across the street. I wouldn't be seen in there, but he's cute," she said, showing a side I didn't think existed.

"There's a bar opposite here? Cool, I'm gonna go and say hi," I said, much to Pam's protest.

"No."

"Don't worry. I'll big you up," I added, and walked out into the cold evening.

Splint's back was turned as I spoke,

"Hey, Splint."

He faced me and immediately became defensive.

"You got some nerve coming over here," he said, clutching the broom.

"What? Why?" I asked, unsure of what was happening.

"What have you done with her?" he asked, angrily, "I ought to drop you right here. Caitlyn was one of the good ones. She was on our side damn it," he added, before I could edge a word in.

"Splint, I have no idea what you are talking about. Where's Caitlyn?" I finally asked

"Huh? What do you mean where's Caitlyn? Probably a pile of dust somewhere up in that apartment of yours," he pointed up to my window and then headed for the bar's front door.

"Tell me what's happening, man. Last night Caitlyn came to mine. She stayed for a while but when I woke up this morning she had gone. Disappeared without a trace," I explained as he stopped.

"Again, I am not what you think I am. Seriously." I added.

"So she left yours last night?"

"Yeah, or in the morning. Do you know where she could be?" I asked.

"No, but I have an idea. She checks in with me every morning, but today nothing. Odd." Splint said. For a moment, I wondered if she and him were involved.

"Are you and Caitlyn, like, seeing each other?" I hesitated.

He frowned at me for a moment and spoke,

"Nah man, she ain't my type; I run the bar and she runs security for me. Look, right now we can't do anything. My bar opens tonight as usual for a bunch of loud pain in the ass amps, and any other weird types who live around here. Caitlyn would normally keep them in check, but without her it could get interesting. You get my drift? But I have a key to her apartment, so we'll check it out tonight." Splint said.

"Okay." I agreed.

"Meet me around back just after midnight. Jesus that crazy Dungeon's and Dragon's girl is looking over at us." Splint added. He looked down as I turned to see Pam standing in the store front window.

"That's Pam. Don't worry she won't come in the bar." I waved at her which was a mistake.

"Ah, don't wave. Look now she's coming over here." Splint smacked the palm of his hand to his forehead.

Pam crossed the street after a large truck rushed by; with both arms folded she shuffled towards us.

"Hi," she said, looking up at Splint. He briefly glanced at her with a temporary smile.

"Pam, this is Splint. Splint meet Pam," I said.

"Yeah I know. Hi," Pam said, again she was seemingly hypnotised.

"Pleasure as always. Well if you guys will excuse me I gotta bar to run," Splint said, he disappeared hurriedly into the bar.

"Did you see the way he smiled at me?" Pam asked.

"No," I said, as we crossed the street.

"It was definitely a smile," Pam added.

"If you say so."

"What did he say? You were talking about something," Pam asked.

'Just lie. Try not to say anything to give yourself away.' My brain demanded.

"Nothing much, just talked about the bar and beer, maybe I'll go and check it out tonight," I said, holding the door open for Pam. "But I'm still a little tired from yesterday's journey, maybe you should be the one to check it out?" I said. Wondering again if it was probably a mistake.

6

After another hot shower followed by pop tarts for dinner, I found myself horizontally spread out over a freshly made bed complete with linen, and no polythene. For the first time in at least three sleeps I didn't dream about anything; just plain blackness; The perfect recharge for my mind. The missing diary still worried me, along with the seemingly disappearing Caitlyn, but I was tired enough to grant myself some shut eye.

My alarm clock buzzed sharply at a quarter to midnight, and energetically I sprung up and thumped off the piercing sound. My back felt good to my surprise and after stretching; everything felt refreshed.

From behind the drawn blind I could see the lights on in the bar opposite. They shut off suddenly meaning it must have been closing time. Peering out and looking down I saw Splint appear from the door and nod towards me. Guess that was his signal that he'd survived the night.

After throwing on a leather jacket over a hooded jumper, I made my way downstairs and across the road; it was real cold tonight. My breath could be seen as a plume of vapour rising in front of me. Continuing past the bar I turned into the side street where Caitlyn had pushed me. There stood the solid wall I had crashed into. I passed it and headed around another corner.

The back of the bar was in a shadowy side street and in the dark I could just make out a bunch of garages, dumpsters and a parked delivery truck of some kind. I followed the light up ahead as a shadow came towards me.

"Ah right, you showed up my pretty fly white guy, good." Splint said. I couldn't see his face as the light behind was shining over him and reflecting off his hairless head.

"Yeah, I'm here." I looked past him as another shorter figure approached.

"Yeah, we got ourselves a plus one with us tonight," Splint said, and faced the shadow that slowly stumbled our way.

"Pam?" I asked, as she drunkenly staggered towards us.

"Mr Malone. Nice to see you outside, of a work environment," she slurred.

"Really? She's drunk," I said to Splint.

"She came into the bar. What can I do, man? It's a public bar and she wanted a beer."

He reached over to Pam and stopped her from stumbling away.

"How many did she have?"

She looked up at me and defensively said,

"Five." Her small hand was held out in front to count the amount of poison she had consumed.

"I like you, Blake. High five."

She then attempted to make contact with my hand, but to no avail.

"I couldn't let her leave in this condition. Especially with the 'types' I serve in there," Splint explained.

"Yeah, he's a good guy, Splint. I like him, very much." Pam stumbled again as we both stood either side of her.

"Two sober guys, one wasted Asian girl and a dark back street, this can't look good," I said.

"I'm, south Korean," Pam said in defence, and hiccupped loudly.

"You're right man, let's get her back inside. Caitlyn's place is down here, come on."

We partially carried Pam towards the bar and down a set of stairs. We descended cautiously, and every so often stopped for our drunken guest to either laugh or say something she would regret in the morning.

In her defence, Pam seemed like the nerd type. Maybe she didn't get out that often and loosen up with a beer or two. In this town, I didn't blame her.

"You know she likes you right?" I said to Splint as we came off the last step.

"Yeah. I like you," she added, her slur was becoming more apparent.

"Let's sit her here." Splint began to lower her down onto the steps.

"Will she be okay out here?" I asked, as Pam leant against the wall.

"This shouldn't take long. Plus she's practically asleep. Now come on."

Splint led me forward in near darkness. We walked along a subterranean alleyway and to a single door.

This must have been Caitlyn's place. Splint reached up above the door and grabbed a key, he put it in the lock and the door opened inwards to reveal more darkness.

Just before we walked in there was a movement behind. I jumped out of my skin as someone approached.

"What you guys doin'?" Pam asked, as she bounced off the alley wall and into Splint's arms.

"I like this spot," she added, as he tried to stabilise their footing.

"I'll keep her out here. Go in and check it out," he ordered, nodding to the open doorway. "Come on, man. We need to find her," Splint added, as at first I hesitated.

He was right, this girl had gone missing, the girl who'd kissed me. Now it was up to me to find out what had happened. After a deep breath, I turned and walked through the open door.

Her apartment was a mass of darkness. It smelt of her, or the perfume she wore, anyway. With closed eyes I Immediately saw her face in front of me. That vulnerable look she gave back when she wanted to lie beside me.

"Why didn't you tell me why you really came to the Heath?" she seemed to ask dreamily.

I trailed back into the reality of a dark basement apartment and stepped forward with some reluctance. My hands reached out and felt around for a light switch of some kind, and the further I went in, the more uneasy I felt. That was until my knee crashed into a small low level table; something began to fall and I quickly grabbed at it, feeling my hand grasp around a table lamp. A glow of light burst from the black and my eyes ached momentarily.

There I stood in an open plan area the size of the bar above. All of the high-level windows were curtained off and nobody seemed to be at home. In the near corner was a seating area, a corner piece leather sofa and an armchair that stood around a large glass coffee table. Looking around I saw another lamp and headed over to it. More light filled the apartment which showed itself to be tidy and fairly modern.

Next to the seating area was a small kitchen followed by a long shelving unit packed full of books. Past that was an archway which must have led to the bedroom.

"Anybody here?" I asked, and received no reply.

So, this was the apartment of a vampire? Not bad. Better than mine anyway, but where was she? Using some stealth I approached the archway and felt around for a light switch. As my hand clicked across something a soft glow of light filled the bedroom and I saw a large circular bed fully made and untouched. Her sheets were made of silk, and dark red. Like the colour of blood.

I carefully scanned the bedroom area. No signs of struggle, or even life.

"Hey. Found anything?" Splint asked, with a half-conscious Pam in tow. They stood in the doorway.

"Nothing. Her bed is still made. Something tells me she didn't sleep here recently," I said, and came out of the archway.

"If something happened, she would leave a sign," Splint said, he shuffled Pam over to the corner sofa.

She wrapped her arms enthusiastically around him and the force saw them fall onto it. It amused me to see Splint struggling uncomfortably in the awkward situation he'd gotten himself into.

"Come on, man," he said, breaking free. In doing so he fell off the sofa and onto the carpeted floor.

"Just lie back and sleep, Pam." He placed a cushion under her head and eventually stood up.

"Anything?" he asked, as I approached. Then on the glass coffee table I saw my diary.

As Splint headed to the book shelves I reached down and took it back. I stuffed the leather-bound book into my jacket without Splint noticing.

'Good I got it back, and she did take it. Whether she read anything is another matter, but it was a small victory to me.'

There's nothing here man. She's gone," I said, and sat in the armchair.

"What's with the books?" Pam asked, trying to sit up before lying back again. She'd seen Splint examining the shelves closely.

I looked over at him. There were a lot of books. What could she be keeping them for?

From where I sat there seemed to be one book sticking out further than the others. It was tilted at an angle, like someone was about to pull it out with the intention of reading it.

"That's odd," I said, and moved to the shelves.

"This book is out of place," I added, and Splint saw what I meant.

"It's her. It's Caitlyn. This is her way of sending us a message," Splint said.

"Well, what does it mean then?" I asked, and pulled on the book. It eventually came free and looked real old.

The shelves smelled of old books.

"Tales of the old Darke Forest- A walker's guide." I said, handing it to Splint.

"That's where she's gone then, into the forest," he said.

"Are you certain?"

"This has got Caitlyn written all over it. She would never go into that forest alone. You get my drift? She always talks about them amps waiting for her in the apartment. Guess they finally did."

"Yeah I guess so. The forest it is then, but why would they take her?" I asked.

He stuffed the book back and surged towards the front door.

"Probably to discuss 'terms'. Come on. We have to go and get her," he said.

"What about Pam?" I asked.

"She'll sleep it off for now. We'll be back before sunrise. Now let's roll," Splint led us outside into the cold air.

I shut the door behind us.

"Where exactly are we going Splint?"

"You're about to lose your Darke Forest virginity, boy."

He looked at me with concern, and I nodded slowly.

If it means getting some answers about this place, then so be it.

We climbed the steps back up to the side street. Splint led the way and we came to a garage. In the dark he fumbled with some keys until he'd unlocked a garage door.

"Are you like, completely sure about this, Splint?"

"Yeah, yeah. You'll like this," Splint said. He heaved the door upwards.

I couldn't see properly into the shadowy depths of this garage, but there was a car.

"Oh. it's a car," I said, with mild disappointment.

"Not just any car. This beaut's straight outa the seventies."

Splint opened the nearest door and clunked it shut as he got in.

He turned over the engine and it roared into life. Two bright lights glared at me as he revved the vehicle out. It was then the metallic odour of fumes hit me. It was a fricking Mustang.

I hopped in and lowered myself into the leather seat. Inside there was a strong smell of gasoline; this was a speedster's car, straight out of a Steve McQueen film.

"This here car is a guilty pleasure of mine. We don't use it much."

"We?"

I felt the power of acceleration as Splint pulled forward out of the garage and navigated it to the end of the street.

"Yeah, sometimes I head out with Cait on patrol. It's been a while."

He had to speak loudly over the roaring engine.

"It's not exactly inconspicuous. So where exactly are we heading?" I asked, as I was thrown to the side.

Splint turned into Main Street in about two seconds flat.

"You're right about that. We are heading to the one place these blood sucking bastards would have taken her; into the forest."

He punched the car forward and we rocketed away.

It was a rush to be in such a loud and fast machine and neither of us spoke as we soon came to Darke Heath's limits. Taking corners deathly fast, it was the only way you could do it in such a vehicle. We were coming for Caitlyn.

"What did you mean back then about 'discussing terms'?" I asked, in between the loud revving.

He let off the gas and spoke while the car rolled.

"You see Blake, there's a hell of a lot of history going back in this town with Cait and the other night folk, most of which I don't know. What I do know is that she isn't on their side anymore and I'm guessin' they probably don't take too well to that," Splint explained.

"As to where we are heading? According to Cait there's an old house out in the forest, that's where they'll be shacked up. We take the main Forest Road out of the Heath and then there's a turn off coming up. From there on its vamp territory."

"And the plan?" I asked, it probably should be discussed.

"I haven't thought that far yet. We find the house. We park up and check it out," he said as the car began to climb up the main Forest Road.

"That's it?"

"Pretty much. We're going in blind here, Blake, but don't worry, I'm packing." He reached behind to the back seat and grabbed a baseball bat.

The end had been sharpened to a tip.

"Customized equalizer, this should keep any prowlers at bay, if you get my drift. Now let's eat some tunes!" Splint turned a dial and the radio blared out distinctive cords from a guitar.

There is, a house, in New Orleans...

I cracked a half smile as he put his foot down. He didn't seem at all worried about what was coming. I sensed a little insanity from the guy or maybe he just didn't really care about safety. When it comes to fighting, crazy will always trump any other type. And Splint would probably do anything to take someone down. As much as it made me a little wary, he could probably handle himself. Not a bad trait to have when we were heading to a vampire forest.

Ever since smelling the perfume inside Caitlyn's apartment, nothing seemed more important than to see her again. I really wanted to just tell her the truth, but getting to her was the first hurdle and it was coming at us rapidly in the form of a forest turning point.

As the Mustang decelerated, headlights came towards us from the opposite direction, the brightness slowed and came to a halt as we did. I grabbed the radio volume dial and killed the music.

"Shit, I think it's turning in. Keep going man," I said, as we came to the turning point.

"Good call. Don't wanna raise any suspicions just yet," Splint said, gunning the gas. We burst forward as the approaching vehicle turned into the trees.

Our headlights shone across a pickup truck; a green pickup truck.

"Oh shit. I recognise that truck," I said.

"Same. That sure looks like the truck that belongs to old man Angus. Guess our night just a got a little more interesting son," Splint said, as I turned my head.

* 7 *

"What's your boss doing out here?" Splint asked.

"Yeah, I don't know. Look just keep going for a while," I said, and attempted to gather my thoughts.

What was Angus up to? First there was the weird phone call in his office and then his constant disappearance to repair jobs. Maybe Pam was right about him being involved in the weirdness of this place.

"He used to come into the bar sometimes, haven't seen him much recently," Splint said. He slowed the car down into the small roadside parking area and pulled in.

"What do you reckon he's got to do with this?" I asked out loud.

"Only one way to find out, Detective. We handbrake turn this baby around and follow him."

Before I could react, Splint had filled the car radio again with that well-known guitar riff of the Animals and thrown his foot to the floor. The Mustang spun out onto the road and surged forward. He began to turn the wheel and reached down for the handbrake.

"You probably wanna…"

The tyres screeched as we spun all the way around; both of us violently jolting to one side as it stopped.

"Hold on to something," he added over the music and we headed back from where we came.

"We'll hang back and quietly follow, then catch up and see what this guy is doing."

I nodded my agreement at his suggestion as the car came to the turning point and we disappeared into thick darkness.

My first night in the Darke Forest had begun sitting inside a seventies Mustang next to an earring wearing, Rock music listening, reckless driver. This guy sat somewhere between crazy and bad ass, dipping equally into both personas.

Again, I reached for the dial and killed the music.

"Probably not a good idea to play loud music, Splint. Also, kill the main headlights," I said, as the car bounced up and down on the uneven leaf covered road.

"Good thinking, detective. Are you a cop on the quiet, or something?" he asked, as the path ahead became plunged into pure black.

"Nope, just a guy looking for a new start. Then this happened."

"Yep, life's a weird one. I can't see shit. These headlights have two options; on or pitch ass black. All I know right now is that we are going up."

He quickly flashed the headlights and our path ahead was indeed going uphill. The faint horizon of dark and even darker backdrop looked to be the brow of a hill.

"What type of music you into, Blake?"

He was asking this stuff now? Any moment something from the shadows could jump out or Angus and his truck might come from the other way, and Splint wanted to make small talk?

I hesitantly answered, "I listen to a range of music," I said, my main focus was the path in front.

"Like what? Don't say country, for the love of god." I could feel him glance at me for a second.

"I quite like Michael Jackson."

"I'll allow that. I had you down for more Rock or grunge, considering the hair," Splint remarked, again flashing his lights. I could see that the hill climb would soon end as the horizon grew closer.

"I just decided not to get a haircut one day and stuck with it," I grinned.

"Me, I did the opposite, if you get my drift?"

He eased off the gas some more as I felt us moving up onto flatter ground. Ahead in the distance we could see two red brake lights.

"There's our man Angus," Splint said, as he began to pull over. He cracked the window open a little and powered on the interior light.

"This looks like as good a spot as any." He slowly pulled over, "we'll hide it here and walk."

I got out of the car and into the cold dark night. Through the thick trees above me the soft haze clouded over the moon as it shone down; Jesus this place was dark. Up ahead the brake lights had disappeared, followed by the thump of a door closing.

"He's out of the truck. Come on," the shadow of Splint whispered, as he cradled his pointed baseball bat.

"Can these things see well in the dark?" I muttered, and rushed alongside him.

"Beats the shit out of me, they can smell real good though. You wearing cologne?"

"Nah man."

"Good. A real man like me. But we don't wanna announce approach."

Our feet crunched on the Forest Road over leaves and old twigs. It was clear not many vehicles had come along this path recently. We both lowered down as we came past the truck. The cooling engine clicked and hissed as it rested.

"This way," Splint said, he led us further along the darkest of pathways. Finally up ahead on the next horizon we could see the soft warm glow of light; it was coming from the windows of a big house.

The place stood at two or three storeys high with a width of at least five windows each side of the doorway. A shadowy decking sat out front where anything could lurk.

Something was telling me that this place felt familiar.

"I'm guessing that's the place," I said.

"Bingo, Detective."

Splint passed stealthily between two high bricked standing pillars where a gate must have once stood., and as I followed we both crouched down beside some bushes.

"Let's scope the building, then check out the back. There's gotta be a less obvious way in," he whispered.

"We are going in?" I asked, and thought we were just looking for any obvious signs of Caitlyn's whereabouts.

"This is a straight up rescue mission. Don't be wimping out on me now, man." Splint said.

"I'm not wimping. Do we even know what's happening in that place? We don't wanna be walking into a trap," I said, trying to be logical.

"I hear ya, and that's why we are gonna scope the place out. Right here, right now, we are fish in a barrel to them, son, and we don't wanna be noticed by amps and especially vamps. That's game over, there's no 'insert coins here' for us to have another go. Let's bounce," Splint said. He kept low whilst lightly stepping towards the large house.

The white wooden slats that made up the exterior walls stood out in the dark. Some of them were askew or missing, this place had become a victim of time itself. What bugged me the most was what it could have been, only to become some rich guy's house that had just been allowed to fall into disrepair. As we came closer I got this feeling that it been some kind of Care Home or Hospice.

The building gave off a distinctive type of odour, like a rotting musty smell, probably from the decomposing wood that it was made from; much of the exterior had merged into the forest with a layer of moss covering the once clean surfaces.

The left side of the house had been claimed by creeping vines that all but reached the circular window at the very top, an attic room perhaps.

"Around back," Splint said, gesturing to me as I followed him along the soft verge ground.

I guessed we had passed three vine covered windows before we came to the corner.

Splint peered around and saw it was clear, so I continued to follow.

More soft light came from several windows and the one nearest to us was fully open. From inside we could hear something, and the closer we got we both realised it seemed to be music playing.

It sounded like Elvis, or at least something from the late fifties, and in this setting it seemed real creepy. The sound of the music brought back that all too real feeling of familiarity, something took hold of my mind and drew me nearer to the house.

"Should we take a look?" I asked Splint, who after hearing the music held back. His grip tightened on the baseball bat.

"After you," he grunted, whilst taking a paranoid look in several directions.

Something had sure changed his tune, maybe it was the music or my nature to want in on this place. Here he was leading the way, wanting to get in and 'rescue' someone, and yet now Splint seemed a little uneasy. I found myself being the leader and slowly placed both hands on the peeling window ledge, rising steadily I pushed myself off the floor just as the interior came into view.

Candlelight flickered in what was a small box shaped room, and by the door was a free-standing shelf unit with a turntable playing the music. Scanning the rest of the room carefully, I was certain nobody occupied it within.

An empty bed lay in one corner and next to that stood a desk with a computer placed on it.

"What do you see?" Splint asked, coming closer to me.

I lowered myself back down.

"Nobody in. Should we check it out?"

"I suppose we should. The quicker we get in, the quicker we get out of this place." Splint said, and indicated for me to lead.

Again I pulled myself up onto the window ledge and swung both legs over. I dropped lightly to the floor and stood in the small warm room, the musty smell was even stronger in here.

For some moments I stood and imagined whoever might have lived in here; they had music and a computer. Maybe they were connected with the outside world after all? A feeling of utter sadness momentarily overwhelmed me, me especially as the door to this room seemed more like the entrance to a prison cell.

I turned and looked down at Splint as he offered me the bat, which I unquestionably accepted. I held out my hand to pull him up and waited for him the grip, but it didn't come.

"What?" I asked, as he looked around the corner we had just come from.

"Shit, something is coming. Pass me the bat quick," he said, and I handed it back to him.

"Stick around here. I'll be back," he said, and darted away into the shadows and presumably the garden of the house.

I lowered myself down and listened out for anyone passing by, and sure enough I soon heard faint voices approaching.

"They came this way. I can smell them," a young woman's voice said.

"That's the least of my worries right now," the other said, sounding like a male, but young as well.

"Alexis won't find out about us," she said. They sounded deathly close to the window, so I quietly crawled away, especially if one of them could smell me or Splint.

"I guess it can be our little secret for now then?" the guy said, with a somewhat flirtatious tone.

"We'll find a way through this, as long as it doesn't jeopardise what we have. I mean if my mother finds out? Hell, if Alexis does even; there's a bigger picture here, okay?" The woman led him away.

Their voices carried on past me and away from the window.

The turntable finished playing and silence ruled the cell type room in which I was standing, with caution I headed to the thick metal door.

"This has to be a cell," I whispered to myself.

What the hell was this place? I knew I should have waited for Splint to emerge, but I reached for the door and opened it anyway. After some effort I managed to push it open only a little, there was a big enough gap for me to fit through and so I found myself in a dark corridor.

Most of the nearby doors were all closed and had the same porthole at head height. Candlelight came from a majority of them, but I dared not look in any for fear of being seen.

What the hell was this place? Glancing around the area, this appeared to be the maximum security ward or block. From outside I had presumed it was a mansion, but now I wasn't so sure.

I crept along the vinyl flooring and as I came past one door it rattled hard against its frame as something on the other side impacted heavily against it; a guttural moan replied in response from the door opposite. I made my way forwards trying to find a way out of this asylum type place.

A cold sweat covered my skin and dripped from my forehead as I moved along in full stealth mode. Some of the doors I passed excited a reaction, whilst others didn't.

"What is this place," I said, exhaling. The smell had subtly shifted from a mustiness into an angry mould; something funky was rotting away nearby.

Only my imagination dared to think what it might be and what this place was.

Up ahead flickering candlelight came from around a corner and moving past a few more doors I peered around to see a large furnished hallway area. The vinyl flooring ended here and a luxurious carpet began along with the immaculate looking walls and furnishings. A grandfather clock stood ticking away beside a large sideboard unit that displayed a ranged of framed pictures.

Getting closer, and in the minimal light, they seemed real old, nothing but portraits of women in dated clothes in farmers' fields. Anyone could mistake this section of the place as a farmhouse, especially with the owner displaying his family and lands in in gilded frames. I looked back towards the prison area I had just emerged from and immediately had a feeling this place was much more than simply that.

From above I heard loud talking and then came the creaking of an opened door. Light shone on figures emerging onto the landing above and they were coming towards stairs; stairs that led to where I was standing.

'Shit! I had to hide, but where? Back to the maximum security ward. There's gotta be a cupboard or a crawlspace.'

Footsteps above creaked on the wooden floorboards as I frantically glanced around for a hiding place. In the wooden panelling beside a flickering candle I saw the glint of unpolished metal; a door handle, and it was directly under the stairs. With no time and the voices growing closer and louder, I grasped out to the handle and pulled on it. Quickly I became hidden in the darkness., and as I entered I carefully shut the door behind me, confining me to my close confined hiding place.

'Breathe. They don't know you are here but I can hear their loud footsteps above me.'

Voices sounded muffled as they came down to the hallway.

"She's outside with Greg sweeping the grounds. They've been gone a little too long for my liking," a male voice said.

Another then whispered,

"Alexis has been suspecting them for some time now. We should check it out."

"All she's known is this place and then they sire her before the order. What does he expect?" the third asked. Then she added, "Either way we are just the bods around here, let her mother deal with it. I say we check it out and report back to her. Come on."

Three pairs of feet headed out of a creaking front door. They had gone for now, but what was going on with this place? It looked like some kind of mother and daughter situation bothered everyone. 'Greg' and this 'daughter' must have been the ones to come past the window when I was back in the cell. They were clearly together in some capacity.

At my feet I could hear something. There was also light and in my panic I realised the cupboard I stood in wasn't actually a cupboard at all, there was a staircase that led down to a much brighter light.

Intrigue urged me to step down until I reached the bottom and presumably into some sort of a cellar area. It felt muskily warm down in this place. That was when I heard a gasp followed by struggling.

Peering into the cellar area I could see it was well lit by free standing tripod lights. Cabling snaked everywhere in what appeared to be a kind of surgical set up where there were two dentist type chairs and one in which one Caitlyn was confined to. Her arms and legs were shackled in and she looked like she was attempting to break free. Beside the chairs were a range of shelving units where the wires looped down from the many different racks with different types of power units and computers; it looked like a mad scientist's lair with no appreciation for cable management.

The floodlighting seemed to spread out and shine into what appeared to be a massive cave-like area under the house. In my desperation to rescue Caitlyn I rushed to her without thinking.

Quickly I unlocked her arm shackle.

"Blake? What the hell are you doing here?" she asked, unhappy apparently to see me it seemed.

"Breaking you out," I grunted, trying to sound bad ass.

"Somehow, I don't think so," said a damning voice from behind.

'Crap.'

I turned, and before reaching the full one hundred and eighty degrees my head was struck by something solid; my legs turned to jelly as I stumbled back taking a small table full of surgical instruments with me. Continuing to stagger, my whole weight gave way and I crashed to the dusty floor. My body slipped over the edge into the unknown darkness head first. After a short moment I had struck rocky ground and that's where I lay looking up at bright lighting.

'Shit, that hurt.' Then I closed my eyes.

* 8 *

Everything seemed fuzzy and distant as I came to. The loud voices above me must have done that and then again there was more pain. This time my head ached as it lay against a smooth rock; I hadn't moved since I fell and slowly everything was coming back to life.

"I don't see the logic in what you wanna do here," a voice whined from above; a very familiar sounding voice.

Angus.

"You know the terms Mr Greene. You have always known the terms. We do what I say, then you get your end of the deal," the voice stated in that damning way, it was probably the asshole who'd clocked me around the head.

"I'm a reasonable man Alexis, she doesn't need this. Look I haven't seen them all together in a long while. You tell me what's happening," Angus angrily demanded as I groggily started to stand up.

What was happening? Why the hell was Angus all the way out here?

"I have always been reasonable with you too. Don't make me take away our terms," Alexis said.

Painfully I clambered up the rocky ledge, maybe there was something I could use as a weapon. Reaching around, all the rocky surfaces seemed smooth with nothing loose. My eyes had adjusted well to the shadowy darkness so I stepped carefully down into the cavern below.

There's gotta be something down here I could use. I lowered myself to the smooth floor and grasped onto a loose sizeable rock. As I came back up the blood rushed to my head, it made me dizzy as I approached the stoop from where I had awoken.

"Why are you doing this Alexis? After everything that has happened," Caitlyn asked.

"*My* Caitlyn, and that's what you will always be to me, my Caitlyn. But that was from back when we needed each other. Your love saved me once, but now you don't see the world as I do…"

"We can help you. Bring you back to what you were," Caitlyn added, interrupting desperately.

I heard footsteps slowly move, it must have been Alexis.

'Screw it, I'm gonna take a look.'

Cautiously I looked up and over the solid rock wall that faced me. Up on the well-lit stage Alexis stood looking over Caitlyn.

He wore a dirty white lab coat and I could only see one arm, his other sleeve looked as if it were empty. Alexis was African-American and looked to be about the similar age to me and Caitlyn. In the background Angus stood wearing a concerned expression.

'What was he doing here?'

Alexis moved in closer to Caitlyn and spoke.

"You and that witch of a sister with her potions and spells; you have made yourself an abomination to the people of the night; a warm-blooded vampire? More like a human with sharp teeth. Just like what I use this basement for; to make my 'amps', as you so eloquently call them. Now Mr Greene," he turned sharply and approached Angus.

This was my moment. If I could clamber up and hit Alexis with the rock over his head, we could make a dash for freedom. Angus would be okay down here. After all, he and Alexis were on an accepted name basis.

I hoisted myself up and clutched the brick sized rock.

Caitlyn noticed my emergence as I slowly stood tall with my head aching and the slight dizziness. This was happening.

Raising my arm and ready to swing I marched forward to Alexis. His white coated back swiftly turned.

'Take this you son of a bitch.'

As I threw the rock down, he evaded harm with ease and blocked me. His face quickly changing into the demonic form of a vampire.

The rock flew out of my grasp and into the darkness, where I on the other hand, stood there as Alexis grasped at me with his one and only hand. His superior strength lifted me right off my damned feet.

"Looks like our hero has awoken," he said, from behind sharp fangs. "Now I am going to have be the Master Puppeteer," he added.

His grasp left me completely helpless, and something was stopping me from lashing out or kicking . Finally, he threw me down into the free dental chair beside Caitlyn.

My ass had already landed on the cracked and peeling leather before I'd had time to react. Alexis glided towards me and shackled my arms; he moved fast for a guy with pointy teeth and one arm.

"I think it's time our hero here got to see what happens down here first hand," Alexis suggested, as his face morphed back to normal.

"Mr Greene, if you will, please?" he instructed, and then focused back to Caitlyn.

"What the hell is going on?" I asked, looking up to Angus as he approached and leant over me. He shook his head as if to indicate I should say nothing, so I didn't.

"Let him go Alexis. He is no threat to you," Caitlyn pleaded.

"He means something to you though, my sweet. I can smell it," Alexis said, he moved in and kissed Caitlyn passionately. For just a moment, it looked like she enjoyed it and then her shackled hands began to move erratically, and Alexis continued oblivious.

Angus whispered in my ear as he reached for something behind, "I'll loosen your arm and then you break out of here kid."

I nodded as he placed something cold on the top of my neck just below the jaw. As he did I felt another hand slowly unshackle my wrist; it was free.

"Hit me," Angus whispered, as he reached over my body covering me from view.

"Just do it now, damn it," he added, getting ready to place some kind of metal pad onto the other side of my neck.

"Hit me," he repeated and with my free hand I broke out and swung upwards making contact with Angus. My knuckle cracked against his head and he went down groaning.

Alexis withdrew from Caitlyn to see Angus falling away to the floor and then me erratically unshackling my other hand.

"Our hero is indeed a brave one," Alexis sneered as he headed my way. That was until the sound of snapping metal came from Caitlyn's chair, in one movement she was up and standing as I continued to fumble my way into getting up.

Alexis turned back to Caitlyn just as she swung out and made full contact.

"Get out of here kid. We'll talk in the morning," Angus whispered, as he slowly began to rise.

I looked at Caitlyn who again laid in another punch before taking hold of Alexis. I could see she was pushing him further towards the ledge.

Seeing the girl struggle I had no choice but to try and help. I rushed over and grasped a metal surgical tray. As the instruments fell to the wooden floor, Caitlyn pushed Alexis harder getting him nearer to the edge and then let go, just as I stepped in to swing the metal over Alexis's face. He growled violently as it clanged and he disappeared into the darkness below.

"Come on, let's get out of here," I said, taking her hand and we rushed to the stairs.

"Wait," Caitlyn demanded, turning back for Angus.

"I'm alright. Get outta here," he said, waving us away.

I started to climb up as Caitlyn grabbed her purple coat that hung on a wooden beam. She threw it on and followed me up.

As I placed both hands on the door facing me Caitlyn spoke as she pulled me back,

"It was stupid as hell coming out here," she said looking up at me and then pulled me back further.

"Thank you," she breathed and opened her mouth to lock lips with mine.

My heart raced in excitement, or fear, as I turned and pushed the door open.

"What the hell is this place?" I asked, as Caitlyn headed for the front door.

"I'll explain later. We gotta move."

"I hope somebody does explain this shit, it hurt enough," I grumbled.

"For a guy, you sure act like a bitch sometimes."

We stepped out into mostly darkness. Our feet stepping onto the splintered decking that looked out into the forest.

"I have taken a beating in the last few days you know," I whispered.

"How's the back tonight?" Caitlyn asked, treading down the creaky wooden steps.

"Better, actually." I followed.

"Splint is out here somewhere. I can smell him," Caitlyn said.

By now she had walked further ahead so I could only see her shadow. From where we were both standing we heard a roar that only one thing could make; the revving sounds of a Mustang.

"He's getting out of here?" I asked, not believing he would leave us.

"So are we," Caitlyn snapped.

Just as I began to step off the decking something urged me to turn back.

"You'll be back. They always return," echoed a hypnotic female voice, it came from a figure standing there behind me, almost stalking me.

My vision seemed to blur into a tunnel towards the figure. For that brief moment I was powerless.

'Take her heart.'

The tunnel vision drained away as I panicked and jumped out of my skin. One foot fell over the other and I hit the floor hard. The shadow floated forwards slowly and then stopped at the edge of the decking. Projected by the candlelight from behind, it stood there watching me for some moments.

"You'll be back. I guarantee it," the figure said in a breathless type whisper.

My feet quickly kicked out as I frantically clambered up off the gravelled ground and stood up.

"Oh shit, that was messed up," I said, catching up with Caitlyn.

"Some woman just appeared; I almost had a damn heart attack. Wait, what are we doing?" I asked, as she stopped and turned.

"That's the Mistress. His mistress," Caitlyn said, staring out the shadowy figure.

"Maybe we should go?" I asked, continuing forward and past Angus's truck.

"Yeah," Caitlyn appeared in a slight daze.

The figure of this 'Mistress' turned away and disappeared into the house. She shut the front door behind her, and it creaked to a close.

Up ahead red lights came from the Mustang. and the ground resonated as we came nearer, then it began to pull away.

"Wait!" I shouted, but the car continued moving forward.

He wouldn't just leave us, would he?

Caitlyn whizzed past me and within moments stood parallel to the moving vehicle.

"You wanna stop?" she demanded, as the red taillights shone brighter in the darkness.

From beside the road where I was standing rustling sounds erupted that sent bitter chills up my spine, and then I saw it; a shadow as it rustled its way out of the bushes and shuffled towards me. The red brake lights shone back onto me and I saw Splint stumbling my way.

"That, that son of a bitch took my keys…" Splint said, as I caught him. His bare right arm was covered in blood. and I noticed that there were several bite marks along his flesh.

"Hey, man I got ya." I turned with him in tow.

"There were two of them…" Splint was out of it as he slurred.

"Okay man. Come on, let's get out of here," I added.

"The, the girl; she's out there somewhere."

Splint tried to break away from me and head back. Luckily he was too weak so I pulled him back onto our path towards the car.

Up ahead Caitlyn stepped back and pulled out her trusty stun gun. A small spark lit up as she tested the device and she opened the driver's door.

"He's a vamp, Cait," Splint tried to say and made an attempt to walk forward. He was still cradling the bat which was smeared in blood.

I grasped it and managed to wrestle the thing off him.

"I got this man," he said, but it was clear that he didn't have this at all.

Abruptly from the Mustang driver's seat, a set of feet viciously kicked out sending Caitlyn reeling and stumbling backwards.

I let go of Splint and he fell to the floor in a daze.

'He'll be okay for a few moments,' I told myself and headed towards the car.

In that short time the driver had already got out and begun to stalk Caitlyn. He growled softly and then moved in.

The main difference between an amp and a vamp seemed to be their superior speed and strength. This guy had quickly closed in and managed to twist Caitlyn's arm behind her back making the stun gun useless. She gasped out in pain and shouted,

"You're so gonna pay for that..." he wrenched her arm further back in reply, making her struggle more.

"Yeah, we'll see about that," the vamp grunted, and I immediately recognised his voice from the couple behind the house.

As much as I wanted to hold back, I couldn't.

"Hey. You're Greg, right?" I shouted, and promptly engaged him with the pointed baseball bat primed.

"This your boyfriend?" The vamp sneered at Caitlyn, and broke his grip. He turned to face me.

I didn't know what to do other than continue to charge.

A primeval glare scanned me as I closed in, and I braced for impact gripping the bat tightly.

Caitlyn watched me advance and rolled away defensively. I closed my eyes as the sharpened wood made contact with the Vampire's upper chest. He grabbed the bat with both hands, intending to fling it away but they slipped on the blood. My momentum pushed him back and into the Mustang. There was a loud thud followed by the pop of bone.

I cringed as the bat broke through his chest cavity and into what must have been the heart. Panicked, I let go and reeled back to see the man exhale into a high-pitched screech. From where the bat was imbedded came a bright red flash followed by a mass of orange which crept over the vampire. His body started to burn up as he transitioned from flesh into dust. An ash-like outline remained where he stood before dripping into a pile on the woodland floor.

"Holy shit," I said, as the bat fell on top of the smoking pile of ashes.

With two wide eyes I stood looking at it for a moment, then watched the rising smoke through the red brake lights.

Did I just slay a vampire?

From behind came Caitlyn, dragging Splint towards the car.

"Let's get out of here," she said, lowering and grasping the bat.

"Guess this is yours now, Blake," she added, handing it to me.

"Yeah, man. You earned it," Splint mumbled.

We loaded him into the back of the Mustang and got in ourselves. Caitlyn stepped on the gas and we roared out of there.

"Is Splint gonna be okay?" I asked, breaking the lengthy silence over the Mustang's roar.

"He's just taken a beating. He'll live," Caitlyn said, without emotion. She turned the wheel as we came back onto the road.

I looked back at him as he lay along the back seats, motionless.

"What about the blood? He's lost a lot of it."

"He's just been cut. It may look like a lot, but it isn't; I can smell it in him. He'll live." Caitlyn remarked while forcefully changing gears.

I got a vibe that she was off with me, so again I tried to test her mood out by talking,

"Crazy night, huh?"

"Yep."

She was definitely off with me, maybe it was about the diary.

"Look. I... uh... about my diary."

"Yeah, I didn't read it. I wanted to, but then there were three amps in my apartment so I couldn't. Sorry," she said plainly.

I sat in silence for some moments, until she spoke again,

"I wanted to find out something about you, Blake. We didn't really get to talk that much about you last night. You just seemed to be asking me all about being a vampire. I wanted to know something about you," she said, and shot a curious smile my way.

"What would you like to know?"

She smiled and turned to me again.

"A loud Mustang isn't the best place for a conversation. There's a lot to talk about, and I mean a lot," she said, as we came back into civilisation. The soft glow of streetlight shone across her striking face.

"I'm willing to stay up late and talk. I did just slay a vampire, so I guess I'm in," I said.

"I guess you are."

From behind came a groan, followed by Splint murmuring, "Where's the party guys?"

"Party is over Splint. We're heading back now," Caitlyn said, looking in the rear-view mirror.

"He's in trouble. You? Not so much because you're new around here. Splint knows better than to head into the forest like that," she added.

Splint groaned again before lurching back to an upright seated position,

"We thought you were in trouble Cait..."

"You know the signal, Splint. We have been through it a thousand times," Caitlyn argued as she turned the Mustang into Main Street.

It was the book. She'd left it out as some signal, but obviously not the signal we had thought.

"But the book, man?" Splint protested.

"Yes, the book told you where I was going, but we don't use the bookshelf to indicate I'm in trouble though, do we?" Caitlyn asked, as if Splint should know.

"I don't know, man. You were gone so we got worried," Splint said, throwing himself back down like a child having a tantrum.

"What did the book mean?" I asked, and Caitlyn looked my way.

"That I had gone into the forest; willingly and without a struggle. Alexis wanted to discuss terms. If he wanted me dead, I would have fought them off. If they had tried to take me without my consent, then I would have left a sign. What's that sign, Splint?" she asked, looking in the rear-view mirror again towards Splint.

The pack of cards," he said, sarcastically.

"Exactly. We have a system Blake, and I know you broke it to save me, and thanks but I had it covered," Caitlyn said.

We were back. The Mustang pulled into the garage and Caitlyn turned the keys out. She exhaled for a moment as we sat in darkness.

"What's the deal with Angus?" I asked, breaking another lengthy silence.

"He turns people into amps for Alexis as far as I know. There's more to it than that, some kind of blackmail between him and Alexis. Come on, we should talk more at my place," Caitlyn said, and opened the car door.

We shuffled the half-awake Splint downstairs and towards Caitlyn's front door. She stopped us suddenly before going in.

"Someone else is here."

Splint came to life and walked between us. He opened the door and went in,

"Yeah. About that…" he said as we followed, "it's okay . She's out cold." Splint added.

Pam lay back on the sofa intermittently snoring loudly as she slept.

"What is she doing in my apartment, Splint?" Caitlyn asked, heading over to the kitchen area.

I sat in the armchair watching as Splint inspected his various bites and scratches.

"There were two of them and they got me good; some blonde bitch and that guy," he said.

"Splint? What is she doing here?" Caitlyn asked again.

"Uh, yeah. She came to the bar tonight. Got wasted and wouldn't leave." Splint limped over to the kitchen area.

From a drawer Caitlyn pulled out a small first aid kit and threw it to him.

"Here patch yourself up. Seeing as you're in a vampire's apartment who's been clean for years, you should make an effort to get rid of the excess blood. And don't make a mess," she said, and strode to the fridge.

"Thanks," Splint said half-heartedly. He perched on the edge of the sofa that Pam was spread out on.

"I should probably give you guys the full story." Caitlyn approached with a large bottle that appeared to contain a watery milk type substance.

She took a sip and jumped up onto the kitchen counter facing us.

Part Two: Cait's Story

9

I took another swig of Rebecca's potion and cleared my throat. This thick gloopy shit was one of the many chemicals that kept me near enough to human. That's my sister by the way, in case you were wondering. To get my blood fix most of the stuff I take is either a pill or a potion, and sometimes just to keep it interesting, both. She does that medical mumbo jumbo for me, while I kick ass, but it wasn't always that way.

Here's the part of the story where you read about my deal. Caitlyn the 'friendly' vampire, you could say. Truth is sides were chosen over time and stuff happened, but never had I got to the point where I could tell anyone my story, I guess that time has finally caught up with me.

I mean sure, Rebecca and I, we've run with the crews before; slaying anything remotely vampire-like that came into town. But before that, we were the opposite kind of a team; killing people in dark cobbled streets, taking their blood in the night. We were straight up bad guys, but that was then and this is now.

What's my take on vampirism? It's a disease and it changes your agenda in life; getting that next blood meal sits pretty high on the agenda.

I looked across to see Splint. I could see that he had begun to bandage the many slashes and bites he'd got out at the house. Although he knew some stuff, I chose not to share my past with him as much as he didn't share his with me.

There is a mutual understanding; we'll run together and kick any ass that comes into the bar. Our relationship, if you can call it that is based on mutual violence. His end of the bargain is to create an environment that I need; the bar upstairs. where I can pipeline myself into the social deal and take out anyone connected with Alexis.

This all stems from the amps that began appearing in town; people were getting attacked at night by young adults behaving wildly and out of control. Of course the press and the authorities blamed drugs and booze, or both, it's well known that throughout the generations there has always been a blame society, not accepting reality and finding an escape, that's humanity's real coping mechanism.

Splint loyal to the end, he's both crazy and stupid, the guy can only fight with weapons as he never really grasped defence. Maybe that's why he was so tough, because he was used to the beatings. In the last few years he's unconditionally helped me through a lot of stuff; he's one of the good guys.

I glanced over to Blake, his long hair and curious features. A face last night I just wanted to kiss. Right now, that could have been all it was or even just a casual hook-up. Either way I would probably do something to mess it up. The main thing that intrigued me the most about him was his scent. I can tell a lot about someone by their scent, but his was a familiar and yet distant one. Hence the mysterious demeanour, I like it and that's all this is right now.

He had been through the paces in the last night or so, and still he's here. Perhaps there was a real man underneath that scent, or maybe that was what I'd always craved. Even in my previous mortal life, there was simply no one. Okay, one and we'll get to him eventually.

The weird girl who worked across the street bothered me. Right now she was lying on my couch snoring away, obviously not a drinker. An introduction would have been nice, Splint? If you get my drift.

They're waiting, so I guess I better tell my piece. This is something I've lived through many times in my dreams or nightmares. Many conversations will get paraphrased, just deal with it; this is a story within a story after all.

The question is how far do I go back? Maybe around two hundred years, after all that's when my arrival to the Heath came about.

"I'll take you back," I said, getting their attention. Blake was already focused with his curious gaze directed towards me.

"Before I became what I am today." I began.

"We lived in what you would call privileged surroundings.

By the time I became a teenager my mother had passed on. She'd endured a long illness which eventually won out. After losing one parent I grew much closer to Rebecca, we had that inseparable siblings bond.

Neither of us showed any interest in getting married, no matter how many suitors our father offered our way. Believe me there were a few, and they all tried various levels of games to find our affections, and over time there were a lot of shitty set-ups. All the time Rebecca and I were in a daze or thinking about something else, we never really wanted to be there at the time. We would go to all of these Balls and Opera evenings; high society loomed ahead of us, but it wasn't our scene."

"Already this is like some lesbian Cinderella," Splint said, interrupting.

"You wish. As I was saying," giving Splint a look of disdain.

"Our father, we'll call him old man Turner in this story. Everyone else did, just not to his face. He owned land, farms, a mining business and practically the entire town that our big house overlooked. This was all in the magical kingdom, Splint, or what is known as the United Kingdom.

Rumours began to spread that the two brunette daughters of old man Turner's Manor had something wrong with them. Even today you see a girl in her mid-twenties who's single and people talk. All kinds of crazy stuff about us started to come out, things like we practised demonic rituals or even witchcraft."

"Did you? Practice witchcraft?" Blake said this time .

"We'll get to that," I said, and continued with the story. "Back then, everyone was naïve to that stuff, people in numbers will believe anything when you throw a little irrational thought their way. Mass hysteria was the fashion. I'm gonna paraphrase some of the talk, you weren't there back then, and I can't remember the way we used to speak," I said.

"Paraphrasing works for me," Blake said, and I continued.

"Old man Turner decides one day that we were gonna up sticks and move across the seas to the new world. We were to meet with his brother who was already out there, a man who had been mysterious and distant to us our whole lives. He had travelled well and corresponded with old man Turner often, and soon enough we had begun our own travels.

There was no jumping on to a plane back then. First we had to cross the sea and then travel up through American country. Finally, we eventually smelt the pine that made up the Darke Forest.

This place was different back then, the town itself hadn't really been built. Where we sit now is the new town, back then it was just plain farmers' fields in the valley.

Day one in that forest signalled things to come, and so my first encounter with the place happened.

I sat alongside Rebecca in our best dresses, with old man Turner opposite, looking smart and regal; all of us bouncing around in the coach riding on a track road without modern suspension. Out front the Coachman led our two horses forward through what seemed like an eternity of trees.

'This forest goes on forever,' Rebecca had said, looking out of her side of the coach.

'Yes, dear. Get used to the trees for they are your new home. Soon enough we will arrive. I know it has been a long and enduring journey,' old man Turner said, apologetically to us both.

'I have quite enjoyed our tour across the new world. So much to see and experience,' I'd said.

From the front came a loud neighing, the horses had both seemed unsettled throughout the journey along this Forest Road. The Coachman repeated his command for them to calm,

'Easy,' he shouted, as the coach shuddered.

The horses' ears twitched in alarm as they neighed louder.

I looked out of the window to see if I could get a glance at what disturbed them, there was nothing but afternoon forest. As I pulled my head back into the coach everything suddenly jolted up and down. My head painfully struck the door as we were thrown to one side.

Horses screaming in fear and struggling filled our ears as the Coachman yelled in panic. The wheels continued to spin as we chaotically left the road and headed down the side of a bank, still the horses cried out. Just as it looked like we were about to crash, I could have sworn I heard another cry, not that different from a horse, but this sound was a higher pitched screech.

The last thing I remember was the cart being thrown to one side with our luggage flying all around. I blacked out.

Sometime later I woke in a daze with a throbbing pain in my head; everything from the neck up seemed to ache. I appeared to be sitting against a large tree with no recollection of how I'd got there. All I could see were trees all around.

'Thank God, you are awake. Can you walk?' Rebecca asked, as she placed a hand on my shoulder.

I winced in pain as she helped me up.

'Are you hurt Sister?' she'd asked.

'Yes, but don't tell Father. The poor Coachman might not get a single coin if we complain,' I said, gathering myself.

'Agreed. How on earth did you manage to get all the way over here?'

We slowly walked towards the crash site and I too realised it was some distance away.

'I'm not sure. I did take a blow to my head quite hard,' I said. I tried not to think whether something or someone could have dragged me.

'There's something strange about this forest. It must have disturbed the horses. Come on Caitlyn, Father is gathering our luggage.'

I followed her back to the scene. The scruffy Coachman took a lecture from old man Turner as they both gathered up our belongings.

'There you are. Where have you been?' he asked, taking both of my hands.

'I was just here,' I said.

Then I turned back, not because I chose to but because something drew me back, an invisible force of some kind. It pulled my feet to return.

Only Rebecca calling me back forced me not to return. That was the first time I felt something in that forest.

'I would very much like to go,' I said to everyone.

'I'm afraid you lasses are on your feet from here. Especially as both me horses have gone walkabouts,' the Coachman had said.

'It ain't far, and I can lug some of your bits. This way.' The Irishman led the way and back up onto the road.

Onward we went with Rebecca arguing with the Coachman, and then old man Turner chiming in where he could. I hung back and continued to feel haunted by something or someone. It was pure luck we had arrived in the daytime, although the sun was blocked out by thick clouds hovering above the canopy of trees.

We walked along the Forest Road for what seemed like hours. It probably felt longer than it was, but considering I was wearing the whole full skirts and corset get up, you can see why. Not forgetting there was the third degree whiplash.

All around, the place seemed real ominous. No breeze, no birds chirping, nothing. Just huge pine trees spread around like still giants in all directions. If it wasn't for the road you could easily become disoriented and be claimed by the forest, or whatever else lurked nearby, because something was lurking, even back then I could feel it.

The deeper we trudged the more uneasy I felt about something watching or following us. Being a girl who had spent much time in her head it took several calls from old man Turner to awaken me from my daze.

"Caitlyn?" he asked, as Rebecca and the Coachman seemed to join him in staring right through me.

"You dropped your scarf," Rebecca said, dramatically rolling her eyes and they continued forward as I turned back.

As I lowered myself down, the bushes rustled nearby. Not just a few leaves rustling, but the whole bush shaking like somebody prowled inside, waiting and watching me. Quickly I grabbed the silk scarf and scurried back to my group."

"Is this gonna get good at any point?" Splint interrupted again.

"Splint, you must endure the whole fruit to appreciate it fully," I replied, in the same manner of the time, before resuming.

'There's something following us I'm sure,' " I warned our little group.

'Probably one of the farm kiddies looking to scavenge for scraps,' the Coachman said dismissively.

'I'm sure there are no prowlers out here, Caitlyn. Ah look, we are nearly here.' Old man Turner pointed to a small plume of smoke on the horizon.

Soon we came across a small village that stood overlooking a large brick built Manor house.

That house.

'Darke Village' was carved into a tree trunk as it lay by the track. A series of cottages and huts stood in an arrangement around what looked like a farm community, there was even a small church. For the first time in that whole journey I smiled.

There were men working on the various crops in the central garden whilst children scurried around, all with their mothers calling to them never to be far away.

One kid dashed our way and offered to help lighten our load.

'You must be the Lord's brother, ain't ya?' the scruffy looking boy raised his dirty cap to us.

'Lord? What has my brother been saying?' 'old man Turner said, not surprised by our Uncle's antics.

'Lord?' Rebecca asked.

'I suppose you can be who you like in the new world. Now come on, the Manor is this way,' the Coachman said, leading us through the pleasant little village.

Everyone we saw either nodded or waved our way, and a group of young children presented themselves as we paraded by.

'It's a charming place, Father,' Rebecca said.

The house as you know it now, all covered in off-green and whitewash wooden slats, also looked a little different back then. We walked around the front to see brand new red brick with two white pillars standing sentry to a large white wooden door. All the windows were neatly presented with clean window frames; there was immaculate glass and even boxed plants. It looked exactly what it was called, a Manor.

'Darke Manor,' Rebecca said, reading the engraving above the door.

'Young ladies, welcome to your new home. Now where is your Uncle, I mean Lord?

Old man Turner lowered his large decorative trunk and winced at the ache in his back.

'Father, your back?' I said hoping to comfort him.

'I am fine Caitlyn. It has been a long journey and my bones aren't what they used to be, especially with my gout.'

From the front door came movement and to our complete shock came a man not of our colour; back then you know, you had to appreciate we had never seen somebody from Africa, and then out stepped Alexis. In those days he went by the name of,

'Alexander, pleased to meet you and your acquaintances. I run the house staff here at Darke Manor, and you Sir, must be the Lord's brother,' he eloquently remarked and took a half-bow.

Rebecca giggled as I stood transfixed, probably by the sight of how decent he seemed. I watched, totally entranced by his voice as Father extended a hand and they shook.

'Pleased to meet you, Alexander. I am Reginald Turner. These are my daughters Rebecca and Caitlyn Turner.'

We both curtsied to him bowing our heads, as women did back then."

"Wait a minute," Splint intruded once again. "Your second name is Turner? Huh," he said and shrugged.

'Pleasure to meet you both ladies. Now please do come in...'

'There's just the matter of two horse's I am owed,' the Coachman said, stepping in front of us.

Just as confrontation loomed, Alexis smoothly moved in.

'Please, do follow the path back to the village and see our resident stableman. He will set you up with suitable replacements. Tell him Alexander sent you. Good day Sir,' he said in such a way that seemed dismissive and decisive at the same time.

'Top man. I'll saddle up and bring the rest of your luggage by sundown,' the Coachman said, heading off.

'Please, ladies first,' Alexis said, guiding us into the warm and homely Manor house.

The hallway hasn't changed in all that time, except the wood was freshly varnished then and clean. Soft carpeted rugs lay on every floor surface and the smell of rosemary filled the air, everything about it had that new feeling.

We were home.

'It's perfect,' Rebecca breathed, taking my hands.

Old man Turner followed us in and chuckled to himself.

'Edward has done well. Where is the old devil then? I mean lord?' he chuckled, as Alexander began to gather our things inside.

He stood up straight and looked at us all with a stern face.

'I'm afraid Mr Turner, ladies. It is not good news.'

'What is it?'

'I strongly recommend that you take a seat Mr Turner,' Alexander said, leading us to the right and through a large open doorway where we came into the lounge. Plush seating sat arranged around a wooden coffee table.

Today, that's where those cells are.

We quickly took our seats and waited to hear the fate of our Uncle.

'I am afraid Lord Turner is missing.'

* 10 *

Old man Turner shot up and charged for Alexander,

'You're telling me we have travelled across the world to find out Edward is gone!'

As I was nearest, I leapt up and stood between them.

'He has done nothing to deserve your aggression, Father,' I said and found a strength I never knew I had.

'Preposterous.!' he barked. 'Once a slave always a slave. I suppose you murdered your last Master as well?' he demanded, and then even Rebecca stood up.

'Please, Mr Turner, if you will just allow me to explain?'

Alexander stepped away calmly. Never once did he lose his cool or his strong facial expression.

'The farms in the valley, they haven't produced a good crop in many seasons. Your brother left on an expedition with two men from the village, they were in search of land that could be mined. On higher land that is and they had begun mining nearby, but to no avail. That is why he asked you here for help, but since then the expedition hasn't returned. They set off as you started your travels here,' he explained.

Father's tense shoulders slowly loosened, but then they soon tightened again,

'Why aren't they out there searching for him?'

'Sir, If you would perhaps join me in his study we can talk about this in some detail. Your daughters don't need to hear the details...'

'Nonsense man, these are grown women. They deserve to hear. Now be out with it.' Old man Turner got close to throttling distance, and again Alexander stood tall and proud with no fear, then he glanced at Rebecca and me and he shifted uneasily.

'These people won't venture any further into the forest; especially the unexplored lands. There are all kinds of stories about these woods, Sir. Some say a bear might have killed them; others think a tribe of natives. I have even heard talk of a dragon and a mystery woman riding on horseback in the dead of night. Then there is a small group that think there is a curse. You must appreciate these are superstitious folk.'

'Well? What do you think?' Rebecca asked.

She gently took old man Turner's hand and pulled him away.

'There is something within those trees that isn't normal. Many, many people have fallen off the path and never returned. You must never go out there alone, and you must never be tempted by it,' Alexander said.

So, there was something out there drawing me to it. At the time I didn't know what it was, but Alexander knew it was there and that made us all uneasy.

'We can discuss this in length Mr Turner, but right now I understand you have had a long journey. All of your rooms have been prepared for you and I can have the kitchen workers prepare you a meal if you wish,' Alexander said, indicating for us to follow him.

Again old man Turner needed persuasion,

'Discuss what at length, Sir?' he asked.

'Well there is much happening at the moment. We are to open another mine not far from here and then we are looking into building a real township…'

'Who's we?'

'You and the Lord of course. He spoke quite highly of you. There are plans in place to begin building the township next year, after the winter has passed. He told me of your planning expertise,' Alexander explained.

'Very well. I must beg your forgiveness for my hostility, it has been a long journey, and now my brother is missing it has become all the more stressful,' Turner explained.

'It is quite alright. Let me be the first to welcome you and your daughters to the Manor.'

After a rocky arrival things began to simmer down into somewhat of a normality for us out in the forest Manor house. The proposed chalk mine plans went ahead and it served the local village well for work and trade.

Rebecca and I, the Turner Sisters, soon became friendly with the villagers especially since the mine was providing work. People had jobs which attracted new settlers to the now growing village. They looked at us as a level of royalty, and of course we were gonna lap that up.

Months passed and we all put our missing Uncle to the back of our minds.

Alexander became good friends with all of us. He had escaped the slave trade from the South and then met Lord Turner on his travels. They had become friends, or 'equivalent' as the Lord would say. Alexander had agreed to be the head servant of the Manor so no one would suspect he was a runaway slave. Slowly, and over time, even old man Turner saw this too, and they also became friends. Even though his anger simmered over sometimes, Alexander had been through much more adversity as a boy and had remained a stable aid.

The whole fear of what could be lurking in the forest eventually died down and became a thing of the past. Too many people around gave the place a buzz, a feeling that we weren't alone amongst the trees, and so it slowly fizzled away. Whatever lurked out there, no longer felt like a threat. And yeah there were still the stories.

This could have been a happy ending, the village would eventually have transitioned and moved into a newly built town. The population would grow and the mine would fund it all. That isn't how it went. Sometimes I wish it had.

Around six months after arriving at the forest, one evening after dark something woke me. From above my bedroom came a dull moaning followed by the creaking of floorboards; somebody was up there. Did we even have an attic? I was about to find out.

Sluggishly I got out of bed, nightdress and all, and with me I took a small trusty lamp that I left burning every night, this was the middle of the woods after all. Creeping across the carpet barefoot, I slowly opened my bedroom door. Directly in front of me was the soft glow of an orange light coming from above and with it I could see a wooden ladder in the middle of the hallway stretching through a square opening above. Guess we did have an attic.

A soft giggle wafted down, followed by the sound of what seemed to be chanting.

I had to find out what was going on. Silently, I crept towards the ladder and gently stepped over every creaking floor board possible. Leaving the lamp on the ground, I wrapped my hands around the rough wood as I climbed up.

The dull chanting of voices then became apparent,

'I use the earth; I use the earth.

To power growth of life, within my strife.'

Again came the giggling and I recognised it as Rebecca's, what was she doing?

Somehow, I got up into the attic without detection and managed to hide behind a wooden crate. Taking a peak, I could see she sat within a circle of flowers, my sister. Candles were lit all around her and she had both her hands held out. She chanted,

'I use the earth; I use the earth.

To power growth of life, within my strife.'

In front of Rebecca stood a china vase, and from inside it grew a single red rose. The flower began to move and grow upwards. Soon enough various offshoots of the vine-like plant began to multiply.

I watched open mouthed as this growing plant morphed into the shape of a hand. Rebecca slowly took hold of it.

Trying to get a better look, I nudged the crate which concealed me.

'Who's there?' Rebecca demonically jibed; I had disturbed her. The candle lights flickered as if a wind had blown my way. The growing vines rapidly receded and all that now stood was a solitary red rose. As I spoke the indoor gust calmed.

'Sister, it's me.'

'Caitlyn?' she whispered, mischievously.

'What are you doing up here?' I asked, slowly creeping her way.

She waved excitedly for me to join her.

'You must see this. Come. Sit.'

'I saw it. The rose, you made it grow?' she nodded slowly,

'Do you remember when we were young, I said we would talk to Mother again? Well here she is,' Rebecca said, bowing her head.

I sat in the circle surrounded by flowers as she began to chant. The rose swayed once again, and began to spawn several finger-like tendrils that coursed towards me. A plant shaped hand opened.

'She's here,' Rebecca said, looking up at me proudly.

'What do you mean?' I asked.

'She wants you to take her hand.'

I held out my hand and the vines interlocked with my fingers. Her grip instantly took me away to my childhood, where my mother held my hand. I became breathless for a moment before my sister comforted me.

'Do not fear, Sister. This is what she would have wanted, for our mother's craft was of life itself. Before she left us, she gave me this.'

Rebecca reached out of the circle and took hold of a book. It seemed to be made from some kind of old leather and on the front in gilded writing read 'Wych Kraft'.

Alarm bells began to ring in my head. Back then people hung or burnt witches if they found out about them.

'Sister, you know how superstitious the village folk are around here. If they were to see this, we would be… , we would be…'

'Young Caitlyn, they will never know, I will make sure of it,' Rebecca said, taking my hands. 'Our secret is safe here.'

Back in the present, Splint sat forward and cleared his throat loudly, I spoke before he could.

"Yes, we were witches or what was known as Life witches. Rebecca had already grasped many of the incantations and charms from the books she had read. I just kind of assisted. She would claim that I had some energy she could use. A gift she would feed her power from…"

"You were a familiar?" a timid voice asked. Not from Blake, or Splint, but the Korean girl who worked across the street.

She was awake and sat up. Her eyes glanced towards me as she yawned.

"Welcome back to the party, Pam," Splint said.

"Splint, what happened to you?" she said getting off the couch.

"I'm good. Please..." he put his hand up as she tried to get close to him.

"Can we... uh, continue with the main narrative?" Blake said, as Splint and Pam exchanged hushed words in each other's ears.

"I guess you can stay," I said to Pam, finally getting her attention. "Sit down." I pointed for her to go back to the couch.

"I know all about this witchcraft stuff. You were a familiar to a real witch?" Pam asked, as she patted the couch for Splint to join her.

"Rebecca called it the life spirit of familiar. I was one with nature and spirit, nature and life being our craft; holder of the energy, keeper of feelings. Even today people think broomsticks, cauldrons and eyes of newt when it comes to witches , that they are just evil old women putting curses on folks, living as outcasts by their own people. We were the complete opposite and so was the craft we practiced."

"There are other crafts?" Blake asked.

"There are three," Pam said, as I nodded to her. I then took over from her and explained,

"Rebecca practices as a Life witch, or today we call it Earth witch; potions made from plants and powers to give aid, all the good stuff to do with the craft. Then you got a Death witch; dark, depressing and powers for everything bad. Finally you got a Fire witch, never met one so I wouldn't know, although they are the most badass of the bunch."

"Fire witches are legendary and also rare. They hold the greatest and darkest of powers," Pam added.

"Back to the story, the people of Darke Village pretty much adored us, even though they would never know what we did up in that attic. We chanted good luck charms or even blessings for those who had found themselves on hard times. and when a child became sick, we worked our ways to help them. We would say that we prayed for them, but we did more than just that.

Even the farmers' crops returned and the soil became fertile again. Still nobody knew what we did.

Alexander would join me in the afternoons as I ventured out into the Manor garden which is now the old cemetery. We would link arms and he insisted on carrying the basket in which I'd put the many flowers and plants, unknowingly to him that they were to be used for our circle up in the attic.

'Tell me, Miss Caitlyn. Excuse me for being so forward, but has there ever been anyone in your heart?' he'd asked as I stopped.

'I apologise, that was too forward of me...'

'Please don't apologise, Alexander, and no, before there were many suitors, but no love.'

'Ah, I understand. Love is something that cannot flow like a business arrangement. It is to grow out of something more than that,' he said lowering himself to pick out a single flower.

'For you.'

'A true gentleman. Do you speak of love from experience?' I asked.

'Oh no, Miss Caitlyn. The only woman who has had my heart is my mother. He bowed his head for a moment and then I picked him a flower.

'For you, kind Sir, for always escorting me out here.'

He nodded to me before placing the flower in his breast pocket.

'And what occasion should I wear such a beautiful flower?' he asked, looking me in the eyes.

For a moment I thought we were going to kiss, but both of us knew my father would not approve, and neither would the village; it was the classic forbidden romance story.

'The occasion... for flowers? There never needs to be an occasion,' I'd smiled.

'Quite right, Miss Caitlyn.'

'I would like to ask you a personal question if I may, Alexander?'

'Of course.'

'My father can be an overbearing angry beast sometimes. How do you manage him?' I asked, and he looked deeply into my eyes. For the first time I saw what was really there; Alexander had seen and been through some real horror.

'I wish not to upset you Miss Caitlyn, or even try to mentally revisit a place from the time before, but there was a man, a vile, loud and violent beast. I escaped this horrible man's clutches to be here, some weren't so lucky. Those I loved were tormented and tortured until death claimed them, giving this man victory. My memory of this vile man haunts me forever and when anyone brings their anger towards me I think of him, it sets my perspective,' he explained, not once showing any emotion in his words.

'You are a man of peaceful tranquillity,' I comforted as we linked arms again, then frighteningly a loud cry came from the village.

'What is it?' I asked.

'It could be danger, Miss Caitlyn. Return inside and I shall investigate.'

* 11 *

"As Alexander rushed me back to the house, old man Turner emerged from the door,

'Did you hear that infernal scream, Alexander?' he asked.

'Yes, Sir.'

'It came from the village. Come, a crowd has gathered; Caitlyn you are to stay here with your sister.'

Of course, I was a good girl on the surface and followed the old man's instructions. Into the house I went to see Rebecca standing at the top of the stairs.

'Come Sister, something is happening in the village.'

I ran to her and we headed to my bedroom as the windows looked out onto the village. We could see the old man hobbling next to Alexander as they headed into a crowd of people.

'Can you see anything?' Rebecca asked from the other side of my bed.

'I see a man; he looks scruffy and dirty. That is all,' I said.

'Come, Sister. We must have a closer look.' Rebecca shot me that mischievous face, like the first time she'd first shown me her powers of witchcraft.

'But, we were told to stay here...'

'Have you forgotten who we really are? The witches of the Darke Forest. Now come on, it's probably one of our charms anyway,' she said, leading me back downstairs.

We could see quite a crowd had gathered around the man, he looked rough and beaten and dried blood had stained his partially torn jacket. The old man ordered everyone to give him some space.

'This view will have to do for now,' Rebecca sighed, as we stood behind the villagers.

'Tell me good Sir, have you seen or heard of anyone else from the expedition? Enquired the old man as he and Alexander attempted to help him. The woman next to him must have been his wife and she somewhat unwillingly let go of him.

'Not for some time I'm afraid. We were split up at night. Something disturbed our camp...'

'Do not to concern yourself, you must be exhausted and hungry. It has been months.' Old man Turner stepped in quickly and played down what the man had said, smiling to his audience. Village politician that he was, it stopped any cause for panic.

'Alexander, see that this man is brought to the Manor to be fed and bathed. What do they call you, Sir?'

'Smith, my name is Thomas Smith,' the rough looking man said.

'Mr Smith, when you have rested and are decent we shall discuss your experiences in the forest. Sir, your family will join us for supper.' Turner faced and said to his villagers, 'we must all be thankful that he is alive and well.'

'Where could this man have been?' Rebecca asked me, as we headed back to our Manor.

There was something about the guy that seemed weird and shifty to me. The way his eyes glanced at everyone in a vacant, glazed way, almost as if he had no care for them, he clearly had something else on his mind.

'Inside my feelings are bad, Sister,' I said.

I looked up at the Manor, firstly to my windows and then above to the circular side attic window. Through the glass I was certain something moved, for a moment I swear, I could see a pale face. A man had stared down at us.

I stopped.

'What is it?' Rebecca asked.

'There's a...' Looking again he had disappeared.

'Never mind, Sister. It was just a bad feeling.'

That evening I decided to stay in my bedroom. The feelings I'd had earlier continued to stir inside me, their nauseating effect made worse by the jolly voices coming from downstairs. This man Smith and his family were down there, being entertained and fed by the old man and my sister. I couldn't face them, especially him and this weird aura he carried.

Above me I heard creaking. Maybe I had seen something earlier; perhaps a prowler or intruder had stalked me up into the attic, the very place where we practised our spells and incantations. If it was a villager, they would blow the whistle on us and that would mean only one thing, a rope around our necks.

I decided to investigate the creaking as everyone else, I presumed, was downstairs. Upon opening my door, I found a figure standing immediately in front of me. At first I didn't recognise him without the dirt from his time in the trees, but this was Thomas Smith. I stood on the receiving end of his glazed eyes as they stared into my soul.

'Excuse me, Miss Turner, but I thought I would pay you a visit. Seeing as you were absent from the proceedings downstairs,' he said, not taking an eye off me.

'I am not feeling well at present, I'm afraid Mr Smith. I must apologise for not attending.' I'd told him my piece, and now wanted the creep to back off.

He stood firm and then slowly began to push at my door. To my surprise, he forced his way into my bedroom.

'Mr Smith?' I demanded reeling back as he marched my way. His bony hand wrapped itself around my neck.

'What is your sister? Tell me,' he demanded in a tone that could only be described as demonic. 'Her mind won't allow me in,' he added.

To begin with I wasn't sure of what he'd meant; I put all my efforts into trying to breathe.

With his free hand Smith slowly spread his fingers and placed them on my face; what was this guy doing?

'Let's see if you will turn,' he said as the door behind burst open.

Rebecca stood there and realised what was happening. She lowered herself into a defensive stance before quickly holding her arm out; she flicked her hand towards us,

'Release,' she shouted as a force broke Smith and his confining neck grip away from me. He stumbled back as the powerful witch my sister had become approached.

He steadied his footing.

'You are witches. Both of you. What has this village become in my absence?' Smith shouted, causing me to panic, but not Rebecca.

'Any more words and you will lose that tongue without me or my sister lifting a finger,' she said standing firm.

Alexander burst into the bedroom with old man Turner following.

'I beg your pardon, Mr Smith, but may I ask what you are doing in Miss Caitlyn's bedroom?'

'Never mind that Alexander, why is Mr Smith bleeding?' The old man pointed to Smith's hand. I must have scratched it in the struggle, or maybe Rebecca did it.

'Your daughters are witches Sir; I am certain of it. I merely came to give my regards and best to your daughter and I get repaid with this,' Smith said, before storming towards the door.

'These are bold accusations, Sir. Do you wish to elaborate further?' The old man demanded.

"Oh, I will. Soon," Smith barked, as he headed towards the stairs.

The rest of that evening was spent with old man Turner interrogating the shit out of me and Rebecca. We denied the accusation and even had the proof that Smith had put his hands on me, but that wouldn't stop him from influencing the other villagers, or doing to them what he had planned to do to me. Something had infected him and it wasn't vampirism.

Soon Smith's poison spread towards other villagers. People looked at us differently, not because they thought we were witches, but because something had taken hold of their minds.

Whatever fate Thomas Smith had met out there in those woods, it was now in the Darke Village. He spoke of our missing Uncle in only a few words saying their camp had been disturbed and everyone had split up from each other; his whereabouts unknown.

It was a few nights after the Smith incident when the creaking sound of floorboards returned from upstairs.

Instead of just a lantern, I used several candles to keep my bedroom well-lit at night. In a half sleeping state I realised that suddenly all the flames surrounding me had been killed in one swoop. My bedroom had been plunged into complete darkness. I could feel the presence of eyes upon me and as I sat up I saw a shadow standing at my door.

Slowly I lay back as an irresistible force come over me. I remembered having had that same feeling of being drawn away before, but this time the feeling felt stronger than ever; instead of urging me to go towards the shadow I couldn't move. The power emanating from this being overwhelmed me and left me staring in wonder as it floated forwards . I couldn't force any words to come out, just as I couldn't resist as its cold hand touched my shoulder.

With a firm and strong grip I was pushed back down into the pillow. Its other hand turned my head to the side as this presumed man came closer to me. I felt his oddly cold breath on my flesh, and then he whispered softly,

'Dear Niece, I have returned home. Now I must cleanse your soul and stop you from becoming a creature of the demon. Like me you will join the people of the night instead. I was saved by a beautiful entity. This village has fallen victim by the curse of this forest. We must destroy it. Burn it with fire.'

"Uncle?" I whimpered.

'Yes, dear Caitlyn. How beautiful you have become, now you must sleep. Then from tomorrow immortality will rule your soul.'

He forcefully held me down onto the bed. and I didn't struggle against him. His lips touched my bare neck and then sharp teeth followed, I felt them puncture me and then a warm trickle of blood; there was no pain, only a pure dizzy type of pleasure. As the blood left my veins something else coursed through me, a power like nothing I had ever felt before.

Moments later, he pulled away.

'When you awaken you will be an ageless immortal beauty of the night. In sacrifice for this power you must never face the light of sun again. In the Darke Forest an easy task at most times. Now sleep.' The dreamy voice carried me away into a deep and tormented sleep.

Vivid dreams came of my father suffering and the village being consumed by something I couldn't quite see. A loud and piercing screech remained as a constant theme. I thought at first it could be a horse, but even they didn't make a screech that high. I saw the coach that had brought us here and the Irishman trying to tame his wild bucking horses as they fell. After a flash the next image was of him lying in the road in a pool of blood, with his horse claimed by the same fate.

I watched as Thomas Smith and his bony hand clasped itself over the face of old man Turner. I screamed for it to stop as I stood with Rebecca, but nothing could be done.

Lastly, I saw Alexander. He disapproved of me and my sister's ways, now revealed to the whole village, people stood and looked at us with the same disapproval; in unison they all as one put a hand over their faces .

As quickly as the deep sleep came, it went again and I was faced with a hangover from hell. The light knocking on my door seemed deafening now with my newly acquired heightened senses.

'Miss Caitlyn, are you decent?' Alexander asked, as I lay in a daze. From between the seams of my thick curtains was the dull light of daytime.

You must never face the light of sun again.

'Miss Turner?' he asked again, and this time the knocking wasn't as loud.

'I am under the weather today, Alexander, and wish to rest,' I said with a croaky sore throat.

'Very well, Miss. I will arrange to have breakfast brought up to your room. Is there anything else you require?'

'No thank you, Alexander.'

'I will leave you in peace, but your sister seems to be under the weather also today. Good day, Miss.'

So, he had got to her also.

To begin with the sunlight theory was something I thought might be bull. So just to make sure, I got up and drunkenly moved towards the nearest curtains. Being careful to stay out of the sun's path I peeled away the curtains and a powerful beam of light burst through.

Typically, the first day of me being a vampire was the brightest day on record.

I lifted my night dress to expose my bare skin. With my toes pointed I slowly moved them into the sunlight."

"Did you fry?" Splint asked, enthralled. In reply I unzipped my right boot and threw it down.

I pulled off my sock to reveal a heavily scarred foot.

"Shit," Blake muttered.

"The small fire that my foot had become, I put out with a fresh vase full of flowers nearby. I contemplated calling for help, but didn't. The rest of the day I spent asleep. In this time my body began to transform away from the ideal figure of the seventeenth century girl to this more athletic cut."

"I had the feeling Alexis had turned you into a vampire. It was your Uncle then?" Blake asked.

"Yeah, he turned me and Rebecca. As the sun went down we both emerged from our rooms and compared neck scars and bicep muscles. The third degree burn on my foot fully healed and just scarred. We both had this overwhelming amount of energy, it felt exciting to us. Most of our nights were already spent up in the attic, now we could do that and more. Our only obstacle was the villagers; the people that Thomas Smith had got to first.

As I tied a scarf around Rebecca's neck scar, we were both summoned by Alexander. He came to us flustered and out of joint,

'Ladies, your father wishes to speak to you in a somewhat urgent manner,' he told us, and so I approached him to see what was the trouble.

He quickly reeled back from me in an almost fear-like reaction.

'Please,' he said, putting both hands up as if to surrender.

'Follow me to his study, please.'

So, we did as ordered. Down the stairs we went and along the ground floor corridor, all the time our friend appearing on edge and full of tension.

'I would quite like to pick some more flowers after speaking with father, if you would care to join me?' I suggested to him.

'I'm afraid not, Miss. There is an important meeting tonight with the villagers. We are expanding the south mine you see,' he said, with an excuse. He then wrapped on the door and into old man Turner's study we went.

Alexander nodded and left the room but I found I could smell him just behind the door listening in.

We stood at his desk like two school kids in trouble, then I noticed the book; the witchcraft book! Turner spoke as he looked down at it and made no eye contact at all.

'Can either of you explain this? he pushed the book towards us.

'Mr Smith did indeed make a very lewd and wild accusation towards you both, did he not? Now I find you to have this in the Manor.' He stood up and held up a shaking hand to stop either of us from protesting.

'Your mother used to read such things and it was responsible for her fate in the end. Have you never listened to what I have said? You both should know meddling with anything like this is just plain witchcraft. My own two daughters, committing such foul acts...'

'We intended to cause no harm Father. Our charms are –'

'A blasphemous curse. You are both cursing this village with these 'charms'. I am not as religious as some of the village folk, but If they were to find out their Lord's daughters were witches; you would be lynched.'

I stood wanting to cry out, but something inside me stopped that. There was a new feeling coursing through me that didn't allow any remorse for the old man's disappointment; being a vampire now meant we didn't give a rat's ass about what anybody else thought.

Later, I would go on to call this effect the Asshole Gene. Once sired as a vampire the old personality is quickly overshadowed by nothing but a demon that will do anything to get their blood meal, even to the point of stepping over your family to do so.

'It is what Mother would have wanted,' Rebecca said.

'The village workers will meet this evening here in this very house. Rumours are already spreading about demons surrounding us here. Are you responsible for this?' he demanded, as Rebecca attempted to protest.

'I thought you were supposed to be our father,' I shouted, realising this was the first time I had defied him.

'What did you, say?' he shouted, and couldn't get around that table quick enough.

He grasped my arm and pulled me hard as if to get my attention; I could sense a backhander coming my way.

'No. Stop.' I said through gritted teeth, as he raised his hand.

To his surprise, Rebecca abruptly stepped in and pushed the old man back. She moved in and gripped him by the scruff, her angry strength lifting him clear off the ground by a few inches. Instantly, as her face morphed he became terrified. I looked on, pleased to see the old man squirm in our power.

'My dear daughter, please stop. I am an old man. We are family. What has become of you?'

'We are superior now,' Rebecca said.

We had both discovered our true power. This little mortal man was no longer a threat, and now he knew it."

"Damn. That's badass. I'm scared as shit of my old man," Splint said, offering his usual opinion of the story.

"Rebecca bargained with him to leave us be for now. We didn't mean any trouble or harm. Let us practice our charms in peace and we would leave him in peace.

'The villagers are beginning to suspect that you two are both up to such activities that would involve witchcraft. They will see you as a curse...'

'We are but a blessing,' Rebecca interrupted him, and he bowed his head in defeat.

She walked to his side of the desk and took the book back.

Before we left, he asked us one last question.

'That Coachman, the Irish man who brought us and many others here. This morning he was found dead, shredded from the head down. Did you have any involvement with this?' His concerned eyes bored into mine, seeking an answer.

Then I remembered him in my dream.

Alexander burst into the office.

'Lord Turner, I am afraid there is some bad news.'

'What is it, Alexander?' the old man asked trying to appear normal and not defeated.

'Another Coachman has been found dead on the main Forest Road. Mr Smith has just discovered him now,' Alexis showed Smith in. He glared straight at us.

Again, my gut feeling didn't feel right around him.

'Mr Smith, what did you see, Sir?'

'He was, all torn up, Sir. Cut up and bloody. Like an animal had attacked him Sir,' Smith said. I noticed his nostrils flare as we came past. He could smell us.

Rebecca urged us to go, but I continued to listen whilst walking away. My eye caught Alexander's and he closed the door on us, and maybe their fate too, because that was when things started to get real weird around the village."

* 12 *

"I discovered the cellar by pure chance. As the asshole Smith led his two newest recruits out of the study, I just happened to be standing at the top of the stairs when their voices carried up to me over the balcony.

'It is time for the village meeting, Sirs. You may be surprised by where it is,' Smith said.

But nobody headed for the front door; he led them under the staircase. His fist knocked on the wood panelling three times and directly next to our family portrait a door appeared, I gasped in surprise and began to creep closer for a better view.

'After you both,' Smith said, as he held this mystery door open.

Old man Turner and Alexander headed into the cupboard with their new 'friend' behind them.

I rushed back down the stairs and onto the hallway carpet. With one outstretched hand, I caught the door before it closed. Voices echoed from the darkness and whispered of the mystery that lay below.

What was I doing? Maybe at that point I should have got Rebecca and just run. Get out of this goddam village and away from those creeps forever, but these villagers were meeting under our house, how long had this gone been going on for?

I almost let go of the door and ran, until I grew some balls and decided, screw it. Into the unknown darkness I went, down the wooden steps.

Voices reverberated from further down as a soft glow of candlelight flickered against the stony cave walls. Instantly the place felt church-like, with the echo of a large space. The steps ended as I faced yet more flickering light and then what came next seemed impossible.

Back then, candles were placed all around the huge cave that sat under the foundation of Darke Manor. The actual wooden cellar was just a small area with the lower circular cave surrounding it, kinda like a stage.

I didn't have the balls to go anywhere further than the opening of this stage. So, I stayed out of view whilst some ritual took place in front of me.

Smith had put on a dark hooded robe and I noticed Alexander helping old man Turner dress into one also. Another cloaked figure handed Smith a candle and he faced his surrounding audience. What must have been most of the village stood around them, all in cloaks, and some with candles.

'Our congregation is near completion,' Smith projected to his audience, the sound echoing all around. He continued,

'The ascension shall begin soon and there will come the purge. May we welcome our new brethren.'

The village replied in unison,

'May we welcome our new brethren,' they intoned creepily, and then they all uttered something else which still creeps me out to this day. Somehow, they must have noticed me; maybe I had stepped on a creaky timber because in complete unison, including old man Turner and Alexander, they all faced to me,

'If I can see you, they can see you.'

Holy shit! I have never run upstairs faster. Out of the cellar and up the Manor staircase, calling to my sister in complete panic and fear. Although the asshole gene kept me feeling mostly fearless, this had spooked me big time.

'Whatever is it, Sister?' Rebecca asked, with an attempt to calm me.

'We must leave, now. They have got Alexander and Father. Please let us run...'

Wait, Sister, what is this about? she asked, trying to translate my irrational words.

'They were all downstairs in the cellar under the house. Wearing capes and hoods...'

'Capes and hoods?' Rebecca questioned, as she looked down and past me.

I nodded and turned. Alexander and Smith stood staring at us from either side of old man Turner.

'Burn the witches with fire!' Smith shouted, and with Alexander he sprinted up to us.

Rebecca took lead and with her witchcraft book clutched in one hand she impressively somersaulted off the upstairs landing and down onto the hallway floor.

'I won't be forced to hurt my own kin,' she said, as her face morphed.

Smith snatched at me as I flipped off the stairs and used my vampire agility to full advantage. Landing softly, I witnessed Rebecca be as gentle as she could in pushing our father out of the way.

'Now we are to run,' she said, grasping my hand.

Out of the door we went ready to stride away but a mass of black cloaks faced us. From all directions, they surrounded us as we stepped out into the evening darkness. We were trapped.

Smith charged himself at us.

'We will burn the witches; they will be our offering.' The crowd of cloaks cheered in agreement.

'There will be gunpowder and firewater, it is already in the village!' someone shouted to more agreement.

'Blow the witches up!' another shouted.

These angry mob bastards were serious.

'Father, Alexander?' Rebecca pleaded with them, but they both stared back at us with a vacant look on their faces.

'You shall be the offering,' Alexis said.

'If I can see you, they can see you,' old man Turner added blankly.

They both just watched as the crowd mobbed us. We were kicked, pushed, groped and beaten several ways from Sunday. Whatever messed up ritual they had planned was gonna take place in the village centre and that's where we were dragged.

'This will not end badly for us,' Rebecca cried out as the mob pulled at our hair and dresses.

Some of the cloaks outside the group held lit torches and a chill ran down my spine as I saw large portion of gun powder had been thrown over a pile of fire wood. We both dug our heels in, but to no avail as the sheer amount of them pushed us further towards what would be a painful smoky grave.

'Bring up the firewater!' Smith shouted, as he cut his way through the crowd. He reached to Rebecca and pulled her to her feet before violently backhanding her.

'What have you to say, witch?' he growled.

She strongly refrained from showing any pain and instead laughed, before spitting blood in his face,

'Yes I am a witch.'

The mob grew angrier.

'But my sister and I are also immortal,' Rebecca shouted, as her faced morphed again into one of a vampire, and I felt mine follow.

Some people gasped whilst others grew angrier.

'Kill them now! Burn the witches!'

'They are demon witches!'

A group of men walked through the crowd, they carried the firewater; I could see our flammable death await us.

I grasped hold of Rebecca thinking this was the end. We were ready for the worst, but I wouldn't be here today if that was what had occurred.

Before they began to dose us in firewater we both caught sight of several shadows on the edge of the village. They seemed to watch us intensely before moving our way.

'And so your curse arrives,' Rebecca screamed, which she followed with a loud cackle in true witch form.

'These demons are your death!'

'Demons?' A villager cried out, as she turned to see the approaching figures.

Others followed to see these hunched shadows approaching from all angles; they weren't vampires, they weren't even humans. What they are, even to this day, we don't know. Some of them pounced from the thatched roofs as others seemed to emerge upwards from the ground, but all of them would be remembered for their piercing screech.

'What spell have you put on them now?' I asked, as the mob spread out in panic. Maybe Rebecca had summoned these things.

'No spell, Sister...'

'They are the true demons of this forest. Now come both of you,' a familiar and comforting voice said.

Our Uncle, Edward Turner stood tall between us, immaculately dressed and feverishly handsome.

'These creatures survive on the terror of man; they can also turn a man into one of their kind. Now come,' he said, and took our hands.

We were literally plucked from the brink, as Edward escorted us towards the Manor and out of the panicked crowd. As a young lady ran close by, he snatched at her.

'Sleep my dear, your use is for my gain,' Edward crooned hypnotically, and his face morphed. With a monstrous glare he sunk his teeth into her as she screamed. Blood flowed and spilt across her white dress as she quickly fainted.

He offered the young girl's exposed shoulder to Rebecca who then promptly sunk her teeth into the flesh of this woman.

I looked all around as people ran in terror; the creatures stalking them with their claws striking and swiping, fresh blood spilling everywhere. It wasn't long before various fires broke out; some of the thatched roofs caught up and an orange glow filled the night's sky.

'Some of these people will become them by the end of the night. Others might be fortunate enough that I may feast on their blood and so save their suffering. Fire will kill such an abomination,' Edward remarked picking up a flaming torch.

'I will not allow you to live through this purge. You are the offering!' Smith shouted, as he came striding through the crowd to face us.

His face seemed more goblin-like than before as he stared us down. I noticed his bare arm had begun to turn a strange grey and extended longer than normal; he was becoming one of these demons. This guy was transforming in front of our eyes.

'Smith, the Deserter. First you leave us for dead and then you fall to their ways. For that you must burn,' Edward replied, and charged at the half-man half-demon.

He drove the flaming torch into him and a mass of screeching filled our ears. The flames grew higher as the burning took hold.

'Nothing can save him,' Edward said.

'Other than the flames,' Rebecca said, grabbing a nearby torch.

We continued away from the village as the nearest cottage became a roaring blaze, and the crops in the middle burned with ferocity; a sheer sight of pan-demonic terror. No pun intended.

'Caitlyn, please.' The growly voice pleaded from behind.

I turned to see Alexander on his knees. His left arm had turned to grey with long claws dragging across the floor, they twitched every few moments.

'I don't want this, you must help me,' he pleaded. Large veins began to pop from his neck; this man was next.

Then I remembered our friendship and how once I had wanted him to have my heart; the kind gentleman who would accompany me out in the grounds of this Manor.

'Come Caitlyn, none of them can be saved,' Edward said, but I had already run back.

I lowered down to Alexander as he struggled to speak, my hand felt his warm flesh. With my heart yearning for his, my face morphed and I found myself open-mouthed around his neck.

'No Caitlyn. You cannot feed from the tarnished!' Edward shouted.

He came surging my way, but it was too late. I had gulped down Alexis' blood and he fell to the floor.

I growled at both Rebecca and Edward as they tried to lay their hands on me.

'What will become of him?' I asked through sharp teeth.

'He may yet survive, but will forever be disfigured, an abomination perhaps.' Edward said, taking hold of the dazed Alexander.

'Drag him away from here and he may yet live,' he added, as we took Alexander up towards the Manor.

'What is happening?' Rebecca asked, as the ground behind us began to shake and tremble.

I continued to drag Alexander up the hill but lost my footing with the force of the tremors, just as the whole of the village began to collapse.

The land slid away only a few yards from our feet. Houses lowered as the area somehow sunk and collapsed. Old man Turner called out to us. Somehow, he had got away without falling into the various holes where the village had once stood.

'Father,' I called to him, as I stood on the edge of chaos and destruction.

From below came a screech as a shadowy demon jumped out of the ground. It clocked old man Turner and began to stalk him. Two long clawed arms were stretched out and primed. In a flash move, Turner ducked and fell back onto the soft grass. A fortunate escape as the creature fell into the craggy abyss of what remained of the village.

'Father,' Rebecca cried, running to him. She took his hands and with ease pulled him to both feet.

Before he could speak, his breath was taken away. What followed next was a river of blood that flowed from his mouth.

Rebecca cried in terror and stepped back to see a long claw through our father's abdomen.

'Father,' I screamed, as Edward pulled me back.

'His life is claimed already. Dear brother, I am sorry I brought you to this fate,' he said with deep sorrow, as we watched our father get dragged into the unknown of below.

I ran to her and we embraced, both of us wounded by the loss of our last living parent and until that moment the only man in our lives. Our grief shrouded by his disapproval of our ways and the way we had acted towards him in those final days. We were never were we able to settle with those differences. He took that opportunity with him to his bloody grave.

'The leader emerges.' Edward pointed to a central area of the village that was still left intact.

The surrounding flames projected light onto a large shadow as it moved from the undergrowth.

None of us could get a good look as this thing roared; its vocal screech echoing throughout the mostly still and quiet forest. Its arrival was to be short lived as the oil and gunpowder destined for the witches of Darke Forest was now to serve a very different purpose.

After a final roar the thing headed forward until stopped by the flames as they made their timely connection and reached the gunpowder. There came a bright momentary flash, then a deep thudding explosion.

The dark sky was filled with an orange shimmering heat from the detonation, so hot it could be felt on our cheeks.

Only once more were we exposed to the loudest of roaring screeches before the flames consumed everything that had moved in that now wrecked village."

13

"So, uh… these demons. Would you care to elaborate further with them?" Splint asked, as expected. "We're getting a lot more questions than answers here, Cait."

"I'm sorry if my extended back story is an inconvenience to you, but I'm gonna tell it anyway. This place's future depends on it. We never found out what those things were. Between Alexander, my uncle and sister, their opinions differed. It seemed they were once human and came out mainly at night and since the village burned down, they've disappeared.

The legend of Darke Village simply became just that, an old myth that ended in flames and misfortune. The ruined village soon turned to undergrowth and looked more like a wild garden. Rumours kept people away from the deepest parts of the forest, and any brave soul who turned up at the Manor faced a choice of four hungry vampires. We were branded the 'Darke Four'.

Stories of the misfortunate spread throughout the township of Darke Heath, the town my own father had helped pioneer and plan with his vision of a Main Street with the Manor-like Town Hall right at its core.

One summer's night, I stood looking up at the pillars supporting the roof of Darke Heath Town Hall. With my arm linked around Alexander's, we had ventured there every so often and found ourselves in a tavern. Over our shoulders we would hear the townsfolk whisper about our presence, some of them knew who we were; less informed folk would suffer the consequences on a lonely drunken walk home. An easy meal for any vampire, and believe me there were a few by then.

Some would even join us back at the Manor and live with us. The forest and town were both rife with rumours of our existence. All it would take was the wrong person to die, and shit would really hit the fan. Well guess what, that happened.

After a night spent in one of the many watering holes back then, it came time for us to feed, it was why we were in town. We agreed that every time we would meet Rebecca and Edward outside the steps of the Town Hall.

From around the building came two shadows, a couple we thought, or my sister and uncle. From a distance and in the dark it wasn't clear. They laughed and joked whilst slowly coming our way. Alexander as always urged us on; his appetite for blood was the most powerful, especially after a drink or twelve.

'We shall wait for Rebecca and Uncle,' I said trying to influence him back.

The couple closed in, a girl no more than eighteen with a soft laugh and the purest of white skin. She held the hand of a boy no older than her and I could sense the love between them; neither noticed us in the shadows.

The boy's eyes first met mine but he hadn't seen Alexander yet.

'Evening Madam,' he said, tipping his hat.

The girl bobbed her head as I stepped out in front of them.

'Pardon me, Sir and Madam,' I said.

'She smells radiant,' Alexander breathed, bursting out of the shadows. He took hold of the girl and quickly exposed her neck.

'Alice,' the boy cried out in terror.

He moved to try and save her but I quickly intercepted and with my superior strength separated them and before the girl could scream Alexander had sunk his teeth into her and the blood flowed freely.

'No! Please, no...' but I did the same.

Back then we had no guilt or shame. We were animals that feasted on anyone in the night. This young couple with their whole life ahead of them; we took it all away in an instant. Neither of us was in a giving mood, so we fed from their shoulders as opposed to their necks. This way they would die from the low blood count in a matter of moments.

'There won't be much for Rebecca and your uncle, I am afraid,' Alexander said, dropping the limp girl onto the cobblestones.

'I am not sure they will be joining us.' And with that, after claiming another two victims we disappeared into the night.

Over time the Manor became run down, the windows dirtied and the paintwork faded. Vines began to grow up one side of the brickwork. Outside, the trees grew closer and made the place darker. You've heard the stories of haunted houses in the woods? Well this place wasn't far from it.

Inside it remained like before, but shrouded in darkness and burning candles. Curtains had to remain drawn and very little of the outside world got in. Meanwhile in my bedroom, all the windows were curtained off as I lay in flickering orange light while Alexander sat at the end of my bed. He started to get distant with everyone, especially as he now had the arm of a demon creature. He didn't see himself as a pure vampire. I could see past that and desperately wanted him to lie with me, but he never did.

'I am an abomination, Caitlyn. You must see that?' he asked.

'I see only the man who would accompany me to pick flowers and be there with me. A strong and decisive man who could tolerate something much worse than my father,' I replied, and slowly sat up, the blanket over my half-naked body. Still he didn't look my way.

'Your sister is a powerful witch. Perhaps she can rid me of this all together,' he said, looking at the floor.

'Perhaps, but maybe you should lay with me a while.' I threw it out there. He had no choice but to tell me how he felt. Neither of us knew, right then; we were about to pay for our last kills.

That couple from outside the town hall, well they turned out to be the just married Mayor's son and his wife. As I said every action...

As Alexander turned to me there came the crashing sound of an explosion.

The force knocked him off the bed and I cowered underneath a pillow as debris filled the room. A dresser tipped to the floor, as did an array of glass. From outside came the crack of gunfire and I saw a set of curtains blowing wildly, dancing in the newly arrived breeze.

I reached out to him and he came to me; my arms wrapped around him,

'Stay down,' Alexander said. Unwillingly I let him go and he stood up heading to the flapping curtains.

He looked out from what used to be a solid wall and window, there now stood a jagged outline of brick.

'It's an attack,' he muttered, looking out into the forest.

Outside came the neighing of horses and the commotion of men.

My door swiftly burst open and Edward stood there half-dressed.

'Dear Caitlyn, Alexander, are you hurt?'

'No, we are fine,' Alexander said, and handed me my nightdress.

'It would appear that we are under attack...'

The whole house rumbled as an explosion came from downstairs.

'The township of Darke Heath has descended upon us. We must flee before they descend upon our lives,' Edward commanded.

'Quickly dress yourself and follow me...' Again, another crashing vibration came. The whole house shook and Edward stumbled to the floor.

I shot out of bed and threw on the nightdress.

'Curse these mortal minions bearing weapons.' Edward stood and shook off the impact.

'Follow me. We shall take the secret route out of here,' he added, so we followed him to the stairs.

Down below Rebecca stood with two others.

'We must fight them all,' one of them said as his face morphed.

'Come, now.' Edward surged down the stairs and took hold of Rebecca's hand. In the other she clutched her prized book.

'We will not win this battle. I assure you...' Another explosion rattled through the house from behind my father's study. Then came the shouting.

'Our home... They are in our home! We must kill them all.' Rebecca demanded, as her two vampire friends followed her. She tried to break from Edward, but his grip remained firm.

'No, my dear Niece. We must run,' he ordered, and then the front door exploded.

'Yee haw! We got some live ones,' a southern accented man whooped, as several others in uniform stood on our threshold. I saw flames and several shadows descend upon the house.

Shouting came from outside, all directed at us.

'We are here to arrest 'the four'. Come quietly, our cannons are aimed and ready to fire. We will bring this building down and pluck you from the wreckage,' a stern voice bellowed.

'Come on,' Alexander urged. He grabbed a lit oil lamp and followed Edward who pulled Rebecca unwillingly towards the cellar door.

Her vampire friends flung themselves towards several of the men and a barrage of gunfire erupted our way just as I was the last to close the cellar door.

We faced the darkness with Edward leading us down the stairs.

Before you ask, they were civil war soldiers. They just happened to be passing through the town when the Mayor called for our lives.

As we stood in the cellar below our home, we could hear footsteps and muffled shouting from above. Every so often a gunshot could be heard or a loud earth shaking explosion would rock the house. The very foundations shook and dust rained down on us as the chaos above unfolded.

'This way. It is our only choice,' Edward said, leading us further into the darkness.

The wooden floor abruptly ended and we were standing on smooth rock. Deep in the cave we went, the darkness preventing us from seeing how big this place was, but we kept going.

'Stay close,' our uncle said, as the route slowly sloped upwards.

'What is this place?' Rebecca asked.

'There are many caves and tunnels underneath the trees. This one will lead us to higher ground...'

From behind came a loud crack; then came the voices. Lots of voices.

'We are no longer alone,' Alexander said.

In the far distance, we could see soldiers standing with lit torches, and others with rifles. They looked like toy soldiers on a dark stage, but we were still close enough to be seen.

'They have noticed us,' I said, pushing myself further forward and level with Edward.

A loud crack echoed from behind and the cave wall beside us sparked. They shot at us a few more times as we climbed up and into a small tunnel.

Alexander helped me up and followed, just as a trail of dust dropped down on us as and the ground above shook again.

'They'll destroy the house with a handful of cannons,' Edward said.

Continuing down the narrow cave we eventually came to a split. In the flickering light, we had two choices.

'Which is the way?' Alexander asked, as Edward turned to us.

'Left is a shorter route to ground level. Keep walking straight and you will find an old mine and quarry. Alexander and I will take the lamp and head right...'

Again, voices came from behind, they echoed loudly; armed soldiers were close by.

'We will create a diversion and meet you on the surface,' Alexander instructed, taking my hands.

'No please, just come with us...'

'Go. I will live to fight another day, or night in our case,' Alexander ushered us into the left-hand tunnel and we slowly walked into darkness.

'Just come with us,' Rebecca pleaded.

As we rounded a corner I turned back to see Alexander disappear as he dashed into his cave. I frowned as he just seemed to leave our uncle behind.

'This is bad, Sister,' I said out of breath, as we trudged away. Still Edward was in view as he taunted the soldiers.

'Catch me if you dare,' he shouted, and turned with a loud laugh.

A barrage of gunfire came his way and from above the ground shook violently. This time it was bad. I fell to the floor as did Rebecca, rocks began to fall on us and we crawled forward. The last thing I saw was Edward dashing into his cave as large rocks rained on him and the tunnel collapsed.

'Uncle?' I shouted for his life.

'We have to move,' Rebecca cried, as she pulled me to my feet.

We were in complete darkness in the damp cave. It panicked me and I began to feel short of breath and about to have a damn panic attack. That was until Rebecca spoke again,

'Give us the light from the ground, let us see all around.' From her hand came a sparkling glow that filled the cave with a magical illumination.

We had light and slowly it led us forward. We went for some distance slowly climbing to the surface.

My bare feet stepped along the cold smooth stone. Up ahead we could see more light, but surely it wasn't morning already? Not a chance. As we climbed to the forest surface our fate had finally caught up with us. A large circle of men stood waiting, some with rifles others with lit torches. They all faced us, all of them in uniform.

'That's them; witches, the pair of them,' a voice said. The circle parted as two men came forwards towards us: one of them Alexander.

'You are sure, Sir?' another man asked, he too was in uniform; probably of higher ranking.

'And you say there is no four?' he asked.

Alexander nodded.

'They have kept me in their Manor for many years. Their uncle is somewhere below in the cave. Witches, all three of them.' He didn't even look us in the eye as he spoke. Somehow this soldier had decided to believe him. Inside my heart died, I mean it hadn't had a beat since I was sired, but you get the point. He double crossed us to survive; son of a bitch.

He must have run ahead and got to the surface before us. From thereon he lied and the lies kept coming.

'You heard the man. He's down in the cave. Go!' The man ordered his soldiers to move and a group of them headed down into the cave.

'As for you two, on behalf of the Darke Heath Sheriff and Town Hall you are under arrest for the murder of Gilbert Hudson and Alice Hudson. You will face trial at the Darke Heath Court of Justice. Take them away."

Bags were thrown over our heads and we were dragged from the forest. They never found Edward's body. To this day, he remains entombed in earth and rock."

* 14 *

"Everything seemed distant and blurry for a while. Man, this was a hangover from hell. The bag they had thrown over my head was now drenched in a layer of sweat, not blood, I hoped. Talking came from nearby and my ears tuned in.

'I consider myself a man of rational thinking,' a voice with a rough-cut English accent said. It stirred me, as I came to.

Trying to move I realised both of my arms were chained. Bright light blinded me as the bag was lifted from my head. To begin with it was difficult for my eyes to adjust; all I could see out in front were bars. To my right and separated by more bars was my sister.

'We can come to some level of agreement, I am sure,' the voice spoke again, and a tall wide shadow appeared. He stepped forward to my cell door and revealed himself.

The man stood tidily dressed and well kept. There was a range of scratch-like scars strewn across his stern and slightly conflicted face.

'You were responsible for my son's death no?' he asked me. I felt his eyes piercing me as I looked to the floor. A floor covered in ash.

'Yes,' I said croakily and nodded.

'And what are you going to do about it?' Rebecca demanded.

The Mayor's anger sizzled in the air. He exhaled loudly and stepped back.

'First, I must convince you both that there will be repercussions, as you kneel on the ashes of your former brethren. Yes, I have met your kind before, many times. This is Darke Heath, after all; the place where all the rumours are true. I have travelled to many lands and seen many an abomination of something once known as man or woman...'

'What's your point?' Rebecca asked, again stirring the Mayor.

'You were both once respectable ladies. Then you fell to an illness, a disease. Now, I could just open these curtains behind you and that would be it, but what you have taken from me is personal; just a young boy, in love with mere slip of a girl, their whole lives ahead of them. You will both pay for that with time itself.'

The Mayor turned and headed away.

'What's that supposed to mean?' I asked Rebecca.

'He plans to kill us, Sister. We must escape,' she said, as I heard her trying to pull apart her shackles. Perhaps she could use one of her incantations or spells to break us free.

From outside of our cells came the sounds of struggling. The Mayor soon returned with a group of people dragging a figure along the floor. He was dressed in rags and looked as if he had been beaten to within an inch of his life. A bag covered this prisoner's head, but we could see he had faced torture of some kind.

'Please, just kill me.' The muffled voice of the defeated prisoner pleaded.

'He begs for mercy now. If only he'd shown compassion for the children he slaughtered,' the Mayor sneered, taking hold of the concealing bag. He pulled it off to reveal the pale beaten face of someone who'd once resembled a vampire.

Maybe Rebecca or I had recognised him from when we'd sunk our teeth into his neck, neither of us could be sure.

'One of your kind, yes? Whether you know him or not, we like to associate you types with each other,' the Mayor said, and he nodded to one of his men.

The sound of rusty, creaking metal filled our ears as my cell door opened. I was yanked to my feet and out of the cell. The Mayor used his large frame to push me back to my knees, and then held me down as two others dragged their bloody and beaten captive into my cell. The door clanged shut.

'You can call me Hudson, and for now our operation here is small,' our host advised, as we watched the prisoner barely able to kneel.

'But you both can be of benefit to this town: by ridding it of your kind.' Hudson clicked his fingers as the two guards took position either side of the cell door.

They started to pull in unison on a length of rope.

A drape slid open behind the cell to reveal a window where a powerful beam of sunlight shone directly down onto the prisoner. He writhed in pain as the burning sun consumed his skin, turning steam to smoke as he burst into flames and howled in pain. Small infernos began to ignite all over every part of his bare skin. His flesh turned to molten flame as he lived a death of unimaginable pain.

We could all smell his flesh cooking from the quick burning. This vampire had been incinerated in mere moments and now all that remained was a pile of ashes.

I looked on in terror, Rebecca even more so as she was kneeling much closer to the unfortunate.

'Now that I have both of your attention, let me tell you this is how your life will end, if you so choose. Or you can discuss further terms with me. That is, to take up residency here in Darke Heath and rid us of the infestation of certain night people.' At that moment, Hudson turned to his group, and there standing behind them was another figure. I could make out it as a girl or woman, and that she wore native American colours with a large hood covering her face. Clutched to her chest was a large brown leather-bound book.

'Our following could benefit with more like you two. I shall give you a day to think about the choices you make. If no, then the sun's power awaits you.'

In a few movements, the drape had covered the burning sun again and I was pulled up. They threw me back into the cell and my toes curled into the warm ashes. The cell door clanged shut again and we were left to our own thoughts.

Even with the asshole vampire gene, I felt fear, this was our lives after all.

'Perhaps we should accept his terms, Sister,' Rebecca considered.

'We did this to the Heath. The Darke Forest witches, that is what we are; killing and slaughtering the innocent came after that.'

Her words were spoken with a rationale unheard of in a vampire before, maybe for the first ever, but I reckoned something inside my sister was trying desperately to break out. The witch within her fought to rid herself of vampirism.

'What will become of Alexander? And our Uncle? He could have lived...'

'It's time you saw life as I do, Sister. Alexander betrayed us for his own survival. Whatever becomes of his fate now is no longer our concern,' Rebecca said decisively. But my heart spoke another language, one of forbidden and complicated love.

Even though Alexander had sacrificed us, I still foolishly felt for him.

'I can see the conflict in your eyes, Sister. Love is but a distracting subject even with our condition. We hardly have a choice. We either die in a cellar or live to one day see the sun again, without it burning our skin' Rebecca explained.

'How so?'

'Of course, we agree to the grand Mayor's ideas and terms. There are many people of the night who this town can do without. Admittedly, we are liable for their existence. We are also witches, there has to be a way, to cure us of this disease as he said.'

And there it was; Rebecca's first mention of curing herself and me. The vampire inside me begged to differ and would simply play along for now, at least until an opportunity came to leave the town and return to our Manor, with or without Rebecca if need be; love ruled my head, even though the insides of me were rotten to the core.

'Alexander is nothing but half a man. You, Sister, can do so much better,' Rebecca added, but deep down my decision had already been made.

We agreed with Mayor Hudson to begin ridding Dark Heath of vampires. The Slayer Sisters, as some people knew us by, we had minimal contact with anyone who represented the Mayor but did our job anonymously; following the creatures that would prey on the innocent, with a varnished stake in hand ready to drive it through their black shrivelled hearts.

Rebecca would use spells and incantations to our advantage, just as I preferred to use my fists and physical strength. We got good at physical confrontation, real good. The best two fighters in town were girls and although we dressed as men, in our riding boots and trousers, people knew we were women of power.

Some years passed and in all that time my yearning to see Alexander never left me. Eventually I had to act on it and in a move of pure impulse, I left a note for Rebecca and took my leave. I expressed my sisterly love for her and hoped maybe in this life or the next we could be together again.

Into the trees I went, wearing my slaying gear with its tight-fitted jacket for ease of movement, making sure to keep my hair hidden underneath a cap, I could easily have been mistaken as a young man. With me I carried my trusty wooden stake, just in case I needed it.

As the sun went down I moved through the trees, along a well-cut road that was once a dirt track. My feet crunched on cold stone as the old Manor grounds appeared on the horizon, somehow different to how it had once looked.

The entrance had been cut short by brick and metal bars that ran around the place and from behind the fence I could see where Alexander and I once picked flowers; now it had been turned into a cemetery. Light further up must have been the main house, as trees and foliage blocked any view of it.

My breath was taken away as to what had become of my old home. What was it now? My feet urged me to move quicker towards the place, and then I saw it.

Written on a stone plaque beside two large metal gates were the words 'Darke Forest Manor Asylum'.

'An asylum?' I murmured in panic. What had become of my home?

My hands took hold of the thick barred gates and I tried to get a view of the house.

'Are you lost, Sir?' a voice enquired from behind, and I quickly turned to face a figure in a brown cloak.

'Oh. Pardon me, Madam,' the man said as his eyes met mine.

'Caitlyn. My dear Caitlyn.' It was Alexander and he pulled his hood away.

'I have returned Alexander. For you,' I said, almost in tears and reached out to him.

We embraced for the first time in so many years; I was such a sucker.

'There is so much to explain, my dear,' he said, but I didn't let go.

'No need. I am here now,' I said.

'Why are you sad?' he asked, you are home now where Doctor Alexis Turner can treat you.' He broke away from me, and stepped back.

'Doctor? What?' I asked, realising I was now surrounded. Several cloaked figures had appeared from nowhere.

'Alexander, please,' I begged, as they closed in. He stared back at me vacantly, like when those creatures had infected him.

'Our latest patient must receive the best of care. Take her to the Manor,' Alexis ordered, as I was grabbed and pulled.

Out of the pan and into the fire I went, that bastard had got me. So, I had returned to the partially rebuilt Manor asylum where white slats of wood covered the outside walls and many of the windows were barred. This is back when any type of psychological medicine was damn near primitive and this place was run by some dissolute vampires who called themselves doctors.

I faced the same treatment as every other torture admission would. Every day like clockwork 'Doctor' Alexis would have me dragged down to his torture chamber, which had once been the cellar. Some days he would let his minions stay and watch, other days he would ask them to leave, and then do things to me I will not speak of.

'I thought witches were stronger than this,' he would say after rounds of physical and mental abuse. Another stinging slap smacked across my face and then in an instant he would lock lips with mine and passionately kiss me.

'Why don't you just kill me?'

'Death is too easy. For every one of us your sister kills, I shall make you pay for it physically. It's the circle of life.'

'Truthfully, I don't know what I want from you Caitlyn. What I do want in life is to find a cure for my obvious disfigurement. Torturing you has become my release,' he said to me as I lay on the chair, shackled and beaten.

The son of a bitch kept me there barely alive for I don't know how long, I never counted but he left his mark and now even though most of the scars have gone, on the inside, all I want to do is end him.

Many years had passed, when finally my prayers got answered, she came during broad daylight and strolled into the grounds and through the front door. Her shout piercing through the Manor. As I lay back on Alexis's torture chair, even we could hear her wrath from down there. The ground shook as she shouted for me.

Rebecca had become more powerful than ever. Vampires would pounce and with a flick of her wrist they would be on fire instantly. She wasn't a Fire witch, but she had learned the ways of harnessing great power.

'We have a visitor, Doctor,' one of Alexis's minions said. 'She is here for Caitlyn,' he added.

'I see,' Alexis said.

'Have Caitlyn cleaned and brought upstairs to join us.' Alexis rushed upstairs and after a rough once over 'clean up' I was taken to the surface.

'These are not tricks!' Rebecca threatened. Her foot stamped onto the Manor's floor and a shockwave rattled throughout.

I stumbled towards her as they dragged me to kneel beside Alexis.

'This is a reunion of sorts,' he said, as my sister glared at him. Her eyes never moved once.

'Who is this shell of a woman you present me with?' Rebecca asked. She appeared in a powerful beam of sunlight as the front door stood open. None of the surrounding vampires could get close, including their sick leader.

'Sister,' I croaked with a dry throat, she must not have recognised me in my frail condition. Only so often was I ever given any scraps of blood to nourish myself. 'It is me, Caitlyn.' I used all my remaining strength to carry my broken body to her feet.

She lowered herself, her caring face scanned me over.

'What have you done to her?'

'I let her exist. Barely, but she's still in there somewhere,' Alexis said, with that irritating arrogant voice.

'This is an intervention,' Rebecca said, slowly standing. She fixated her gaze back on to Alexis.

'The town of Darke Heath is concerned about the people going missing every year. It is time to stop,' she commanded. From her jacket pocket she took out a varnished and sharpened wooden stake.

'I am taking my sister back now. You interfere; you all burn.' Rebecca held out a hand for me to grasp.

'We are all friends here, no?' Alexis asked, trying to seek comfort in the hostile situation.

'It interests me very much to see what trick you have conjured up to stand in pure sunlight. You are a witch after all,' he added.

'This is no trick.' Rebecca quickly threw off her long duster type coat. Her bare arms passed over glistening sunlight.

The sun's warmth. Something I had craved for so long. My vampiric urges to stay in the dark slowly faded as I looked up at her.

'No I will not allow this,' Alexis shouted. His face morphed and quickly he grabbed me.

Growling came from the shadows in all directions, even more so as Rebecca walked further into the house and reached out to me.

'You have no say in this matter. Step away.' Rebecca commanded.

I could barely stand, but there I stood between them; my life being contended. The conflict in my mind stopped me from moving, torture or family.

"Did you really consider staying?" Blake asked me in a semi-defensive tone.

"It's complicated," I said, not sure how to answer. Even now my heart sometimes aches when I think of what Alexis and I could have been. Of course, I didn't tell the others that. This was classic Stockholm Syndrome after all.

A woman's heart can have secrets. A vampire's heart can hold dark wonders and deep mystery.

"Rebecca reeled back from me and stood ready to fight. She continued to hold the stake, and prepared to swipe at anyone from the shadows.

'You don't want to fight me. Any of you,' she growled, moving into a defensive stance. 'Caitlyn, you must come with me. Leave this all behind…'

'Shut your dirty witch whore mouth!' Alexis cried, and charged.

I was knocked down to the floor, as I saw feet and legs move all around me. Rebecca swiped and lunged with the stake into an approaching attacker's chest. Quickly he turned to dust as she caught the stake mid-air. The others stood off as the dust piled up.

" 'Come on,' " she cried, said pulling me to my feet.

'No, I won't allow it.' Alexis bellowed and charged again.

Rebecca held out the stake aimed at his chest. I pushed her arm away and they both stumbled backwards towards the doorway with Alexis on top. As they landed Rebecca flipped him over and through the door.

Sunlight drenched over his exposed skin and he began to smoke. In a panic, he grabbed Rebecca's duster jacket and used it to shield himself from the sunlight. He let out a pained groan before leaping back towards the doorway where Rebecca stood.

'Get back,' she said, to other vampires who began to creep her way.

'Otherwise the Doctor checks out of this asylum permanently.'

They did as they were told, as their leader continued to smoke underneath the thin coat he'd used for cover.

'Please, let me shelter from the burning,' he whimpered.

Rebecca stood aside and Alexis charged into the shadowy house. Some of his vampire companions met him and they huddled around to see if he was harmed.

As I weakly approached Rebecca, she threw something their way, and after the sound of smashing glass, a green gas began to fill the air. The vampires wildly dispersed as the smell of garlic entered our nostrils. Before I could do much else something dark and thick was thrown over me.

'Sleep Sister. For this will all be over soon.'

The last thing I remember hearing is Alexis,

'You will both pay for this!'

Darkness.

* 15 *

The life of a vampire is pretty much waking up after a long sleep and not knowing where you are. Again, I came to with both of my arms bound, lashed together along with my two legs. A musky odour hit me and the place felt cold, the light continued to elude me as I found myself blindfolded.

Rebecca loosened the rag that had concealed my vision and I found myself in the middle of a large circle made from loose plants and flowers.

Candles were on every surface and in the flickering light I realised I could see that the floor was painted with a huge black pentagram star; a star of which I sat in the centre of.

'I am one with the earth and sky. Give me the strength to free this soul. Let the spirits grant me access freely and let no demons see me easily,' Rebecca chanted passionately. She was knelt opposite me, inside a circle of salt.

My throat was dry and inside I felt weak. Blood was what I craved and at that point I didn't know how long I had been out.

As I began to speak my sister stood up. She came into the candlelight wearing a lab coat and glasses.

'I ask for this one's mortal coil and with it bring her soul. Take away this demonic vampire and bury it in a hole,' she said, and the ground softly rumbled.

The wooden chair I sat on began to vibrate and inside my chest began to burn. A cold sweat broke out from my forehead and I looked down to see a glow through my damn clothes. As I began to moan . Rebecca spoke,

'Do not fear it, Sister. Embrace the soul that is coming back to you. Let it bind to your heart and I will finally have back the sister I once knew,' she intoned, as the vibrations grew stronger and the burning continued. Light from inside me got hotter and brighter.

A storm began in the room; Rebecca's and my hair blew around in the vortex that surrounded us just as strange dark clouds gathered, illuminated by a flash of lightning. Abruptly she lowered and fled the circle of salt, another flash and the candles surrounding the pentagrammed room began to float.

'What is happening?' I asked, as the chair began to rise up with me on it.

Something felt like it was attacking me, not physically but internally, in defence I morphed and growled through sharp teeth.

'Do not fight it, Sister. Be one with your soul,' Rebecca shouted through the howling storm that engulfed me.

The pentagram at my feet began to project outwards and then raised up with me. In front of our

205

eyes the dark lines that made it began to screw together. The 'gram turned into a bony hand which opened up. The palm tried its best to close on me, fingers clenching as everything shook.

'Fight it, Sister. Become human again. Let your soul out of the world below.'

The hand continued to pulsate with me in its grasp and I resisted the urge to be a vampire, quickly shutting it off. My face returned to normal and every muscle in my body tensed.

A loud deep groan came from below as the hand rapidly aged and shrunk. With a flash, it smashed into a thousand glowing pieces before disappearing. My strength remained as I pulled my hands free and snapped the chair. My legs pulled the rope apart that bound them.

I stood at least a few feet in the air as this whirlwind storm continued. Inside me the glowing reached its burning maximum and for the first time in over a hundred years a beating within me began. In my ears the sound was deafening.

'It's beating. My heart,' I shouted emotionally, as a crushing feeling overcame me. The room contracted again as my eyes widened, and the storm around me stopped. All the candles blew out as I clutched my chest and now beating heart.

My feet slammed to the floor and down I went. The pain continuing as my lungs gasped for air; a crushing sensation swallowed me whole. Spots and stars began to appear in my eyes.

I fell back looking up at the wooden ceiling. This must have been a basement once, with its high smaller windows; the place where I now live.

Rebecca rushed towards me and in her hand was a syringe. She was holding it like a wooden stake and raised it up high.

'Don't fade away now, Sister,' she shouted, whilst driving the syringe into my chest.

A surge of energy came with the beating from inside my rib cage. The spots and stars disappeared as my breathing became easier again. Quickly I sat up.

'Lay back and rest, Sister; let your body rediscover its most important systems,' Rebecca commanded, and slowly pushed me back down to the floor.

'We will begin treatment when you awake again.'

Darkness, once more.

For the first time in a very long time, I dreamed; vivid visions of my life before back in England, my childhood friends and family. The beautiful image of our mother before she passed away with her hand holding mine. There were the grassy fields and sunny skies, I could even smell the Summer. Something inside me had returned along with the heartbeat, my soul was getting used to the body it had once belonged to.

My eyes widened, as I realised I was again awake. One of my arms was held up above my head and I couldn't pull it away from the metal bed frame. It had been chained as I lay sleeping under the sheets in a hospital style gown. The other arm was tethered to some kind of tubing and milk-type liquid was forcing its way through my veins.

Of course, I whimpered in slight panic and disorientation. Where the hell was I? Directly in front of me stood an archway."

I pointed to the bedroom of the basement apartment we sat in, and Blake glanced over to it.

"That archway to be precise, you can see the bed has been updated since back then, because the other one from before had been lifted from the Darke Heath General where Rebecca still works today.

"From behind curtains stretched across the arch came my sister. She wore a pure white lab coat and a colourful flowery dress underneath."

"Damn hippy," Splint said, as I tutted like an angry teacher for being interrupted.

"She looked happy to see me awake.

'How are you feeling?' she asked, and slowly perched on to the end of my bed.

'I... don't know. Strange I guess.'

'You will for some time. Your vitals are fine currently: BP and breathing are normal for a woman in her mid-twenties, which is what I am treating you as,' she said, gradually standing and coming closer.

'Treating me for what?' I asked.

'It's quite simple really. In my travels, I have managed to merge my old craft, you know all too well about that, with let's say - modern medicine. Caitlyn, you are well on your way to being fully cured of vampirism, much like me, then we can both feel the sun again,' " she said proudly and tapped the glass IV bottle full of milky fluid.

'Without overwhelming you, let's just say I have been busy looking at ridding this 'disease' from myself successfully, and now hopefully you. That is if you don't object to moving forward with the next stage.'

'Next stage?'

'The complete cure of vampirism begins to take hold. You experience the full side effects of humanism, including ageing, full use of internal organs and no longer a craving to feed from living blood cells. I urge you to join me, Caitlyn . Together we can help others and rid this place of the bad, like Alexis.'

She had it all planned. Cure me and take everyone else down, or cure the ones she wanted. That's why I had been chained to the bed, because she knew to begin with I wouldn't like it.

'No.'

'Quite right,' Rebecca said, without changing her upbeat tone. She turned and began to pull the curtain in front to one side.

'I have spent many years putting together an arsenal of weaponry and charms. You can see them here.' She headed to the large book shelf and reaching in she took out two books from between a divide; they were concealing door handles.

With a clunk the bookcase pulled forward, and inside was a large cupboard area filled with all kinds of weaponry; there was swords, axes and plenty of varnished stakes.

'This is what you face as a vampire in Darke Heath currently. They are the scourge of our society and deserve nothing more than what awaits them; their certain death. This isn't a threat to you, but to those you have chosen to associate yourself with.'

Rebecca meant business, I knew . I had to say my piece. Groggily I sat up.

'Careful. You will be weaker than...'

With all my strength, I pulled on the bed frame and the chain snapped.

'Look,' I said.

I yanked out the tube from my forearm. Something made me smell the gloop that came from the glass bottle. It smelled kind of good, like fresh blood.

'Firstly, there's no need for you to grab any of that. We are sisters. I'm not gonna hurt you.' I said, 'this stuff smells alright,' I told her, unhooking the bottle.

'It's a chemical compound solution. Imitation blood...'

'Not bad,' I added, after taking a large swig.

'You're saying I have to be cured to help out around here? Can't I just stay on this shit as a vampire and help out? After all I am a hell of a lot stronger like this.' I said, coming closer to my Sister who clearly seemed disturbed by my approach.

'Come on Rebecca, work with me here. Couldn't I just be as human as possible, but without actually being fully cured?'

She slowly nodded before walking into the large cupboard and came out with a full test tube rack. A range of coloured liquids filled the glasses.

'This is the cure. Take these and it's over Sister, please.' Rebecca reached out to me with one hand and took mine.

'Just think what your life could be? It's the twentieth century and the world is a much smaller place now. Go out there, see the sun, date somebody and get married, fall in love, have kids...'

'There is no one for me, Sister. My heart has been vacant all this time,' I argued.

'So has mine, Sister...'

'Well then, why cure yourself if you have got no one to share it with?'

She dropped her arm and stepped away.

" 'I'm sorry Sister. That was out of line,' " I mumbled, apologetically. said.

'Maybe you are right. Perhaps I should have waited for the right person before breaking my immortality.' Rebecca conceded.

'Why don't we put that aside and work together as sisters in taking out that half-demon asshole that is Alexis,' I said, fuelling the fire that lay beneath us.

'All he ever did was ignore my feelings and in the end he trod all over my heart,' I added.

'You truly are a woman scorned,' Rebecca said.

'Then together this could work. You will no longer need to suck the blood of any creature. I can medicate those symptom of yours. Then you will use the other symptoms, like your strength to slay these bastard vampires,' Rebecca said.

'Together.' I nodded, and that was the day this all started.

Rumours in the past had haunted Darke Heath about not going out at night or going anywhere near the forest, and now the two of us were putting that to bed. Slowly the people stopped going missing and the vampire scene of the town was driven out.

In one night alone, we cleared out a seedy bar which later became what it is upstairs today.

Campers and hikers stopped disappearing as Rebecca and I dressed up and posed like them, dealing with the vampires as they came for us. We took to hiding out after dark and we could easily take out a whole bunch in one go. We adopted that particular routine every couple of weekends and soon enough the town was being cleansed.

Other people joined in our efforts and for some time we had our own slaying crew. New rumours began to spread about us and our work to clear out the Heath for good, but when you're flying high, there's always going to be something to drag you back down. The Slayer Sisters soon came face to face with their arch nemesis: Alexis.

In a desperate move, he ventured into the town and came to find us. His hunched over figure limped towards me as I stood outside the bar, ready to lock the place up. That same old brown curtain cloak could be recognised from a mile off.

'Show time,' I said, with a freshly sharpened and varnished stake ready in my jacket pocket.

I stepped out onto the street and towards what was going to be what I thought was a pretty one-sided fight.

'You have strayed away from your roots Caitlyn,' Alexis said, from beneath his shadowy cloak.

From behind I heard a cry, it was Rebecca.

'Caitlyn,' she cried out, emerging from the bar doors. Beside her a pair of tall shadowy figures held her firmly.

'Shit,' I swore.

Alexis slowly pulled his hood away and stood taller.

'This whole deformed and broken man lifestyle has gone on for too long,' he said, stepping closer towards me.

'What do you want?'

'You have had an excellent run at killing my demographic most recently . Now this must stop...'

'Never. You will follow the ashes of your so-called 'friends'.' I stepped his way with the stake primed.

'This is a battle you will not win,' Alexis clicked both fingers and from every direction several shadowy figures approached. Two of them forcefully took my arms and pulled them towards each other.

Rebecca was dragged to me and there we stood surrounded; Alexis addressed us,

'Your actions have indeed gained my attention, but you have only merely chipped away at the surface, if vampire eradication is what you have hoped to achieve. I have come here this evening to discuss terms; terms where we can all live alongside one another in peace. In other words, where the two of you and your little town here can co-exist alongside with us.'

'Terms? Like what?'

'I will ask my brethren here to come out of the town's shadows and recede back to the trees. Anyone who passes through the forest is free game for us to feed on. That would require for you to only patrol the streets and not our land. Do we have an agreement?'

I looked at Rebecca; there was a fear in her eyes I hadn't seen before. She nodded to me, this guy meant business. He knew one-on-one we could take him out.

'We have a deal. Anyone who crosses into our territory, will face the ashes,' I agreed.

I could see across the street another shadow emerge. It came from the new store that had just opened; the Workshop.

A deafening rifle shot echoed throughout the dark street. Alexis and many of his shadowy brethren turned to see a young man wielding a rifle.

'Is there a problem here, ladies? Are these men bothering you?' a young Angus enquired. He wore the similar sort of get up that he had always worn.

'I'm just getting my store up and ready for opening next week, and see you two ladies from across the street being mugged, or something. You Sir, look to be in charge, what's the deal?' he asked, walking towards Alexis. As he did, more shadows moved in towards him.

'No deal here, Sir. I was just discussing terms with these two old acquaintances here. We will keep the peace, I assure you.' Alexis looked directly at the armed young man, and smiled. He nodded his head for the shadows to disperse and they did without Angus ever knowing.

'Peace is all I ask for in my neighbourhood. If you ladies are fine, then I'll resume work in my store. My family will be moving in soon, so I hope to see nothing like this happening again on my door step,' Angus remarked, turning away.

'I recommend camping in the forest for your family Sir,' Alexis said, in his slimy charming manner. At that moment, a chill ran down my spine.

'Yep. I been dying to check out the land. I may just do that. Now be on your way, all of ya.'

I could just smell Alexis marking Angus's card. The bastard did something to his family out in that forest, but I never found out what. So we stuck to what we had agreed, just to patrol the streets and stay away from the trees. People still went missing, but not in their huge numbers.

Bringing us to our present day and the amps have begun to arrive in the Heath; sent by Alexis as blood mules to keep tabs on me, the sole remaining slayer. Our crew, well it's just me and Splint most of the time and the balance is rapidly slipping back into Alexis's hands. Rebecca's older now and doesn't really fight much these days. She spends her time at the hospital as a doctor, concentrating on creating more cures for vampirism."

"Does she have anyone?" Blake asked, sitting forward.

"No, she lives alone by the hospital; it's at the other end of Main Street. Right, seeing as you guys have heard my story, some invited, others not…" I looked pointedly at Pam.

I jumped down from the kitchen counter top and headed to the bookshelf to open it up. The two shelves moved outwards with a creak to display a now well-lit weapons and potions container. Glass shelving held various bottles of chemical liquids and weapons hung in the light. In the centre, inside its own refrigerated box were five syringes; five cures.

"I guess I have to ask you all. I need a new crew. I'm gonna take out that son of a bitch, Alexis, for good, but I can't do it alone. So the ultimatum out of all of this is - do you want in?"

Part Three : Identity Crisis

* 16 *

I didn't intend for Caitlyn's story to take over the proceedings, but as I said at the beginning, perspectives will change and that's how this thing should be told. I noticed throughout her account and to my worry there was never any mention of the 'Darke Crusader'.

Even now I find it weird that she has lived for so long. I suppose that's what being a vampire is. If that wasn't enough to give me the creeps, then the whole witchcraft thing was for sure.

Who the hell was I to criticise? You know just as much as I do about myself right now. Something is blocking all my previous memories; I just can't remember anything from before the bus journey here, and now Caitlyn wanted me, Pam and Splint as her crew.

We weren't exactly the Justice League, but I guess she didn't have much of a choice.

"Now you've shared your piece," I said, breaking the lengthy silence. "It's only courtesy that I do the same," I added.

"Shoot," Caitlyn smiled, leaning against the kitchen counter in that 'not giving a shit' style. Even though I feared her slightly, it was still hot in my eyes.

"I'm shooting at the wind here, but if I said the name 'Darke Crusader', would any of you know what I am talking about?" I asked, throwing it out there.

Nobody even flinched.

Splint mouthed 'Darke Crusader' as if it was completely foreign and Pam stared vacantly back my way. Perhaps she was hungover.

Caitlyn just shook her head no. "I can't say that I have heard that name before," she said.

"Well, I read up about this guy online who came to Darke Heath. He posted some stuff up on a forum using the name 'Darke Crusader'. He said there was stuff going on in this town, well he sure as hell wasn't wrong, but the worrying thing is that he's missing. I can only presume the worst for him." I explained to the dead pan reaction all around.

"You read something on a computer. Sounds like you probably fell for that millennium crap too," Splint jibed.

"Look, it's all here in my diary," I added to Caitlyn and held up the leather-bound notepad.

"I didn't get around to reading that. What was this guy's name?" Caitlyn asked again.

"I've spent some time online, Mr Malone, and I have never heard of such a person who has come to the Heath," Pam said.

"That's strange; Angus employed him at the Workshop before me. That's what he said anyway," I replied, as Pam frowned at me.

"Another nerd. Great crew we got," Splint added, as Pam averted her gaze to him.

"There wasn't anybody else working for the Workshop before you. Angus is bending the truth yet again," Pam observed.

Strange.

"Okay, so this Angus cat has got some stuff to answer for. Noted. We can add that to the list of stuff we gotta do like burn out the rest of these vampires and Alexis. No sweat," Splint said, nodding.

"Angus knows something. Maybe he's the key to all of this," Caitlyn considered.

I had this feeling that everything we needed was there, we just needed to link it all together.

"But none of you answered my question. Are we all in?" Caitlyn asked.

"If we can discount all the computer talk, I'm in," Splint said.

"Yeah. Sounds cool," Pam answered, groggily.

"What about you, Blake?" Caitlyn asked.

"I may have only been in Darke Heath two nights and only just now realised that vampires exist. If that means getting to the bottom of all of this then what the hell, I'm in," I stood proud, and nodded to my team.

"I have to ask," I said, moving towards Caitlyn

"Oh come on man, more nerd talk? Mortals like me need some shut eye," Splint complained.

"You'll sleep soon enough, Splint. Our first job is to find out all we know about Angus and what he was doing out in the house tonight," Caitlyn said, as she closed the bookshelves together.

"The new crew has their first quest." Pam sprang to her feet.

"Do you think he will know something about that woman back at the house? She told me I would be back?" I questioned.

Her voice and shadowy image haunted my memory.

"The Mistress?" Splint asked, as he stood up.

"Yeah, she made a brief appearance tonight. Whilst you were out getting, let's say, more fighting experience," Caitlyn winked.

"Maybe she's a link," I said.

"She could be anyone; those amps have been talking about her before in the bar. Guess the rumours were true," Caitlyn muttered to herself.

"All I got on Angus is that his family split recently," I added, and then came the images of a dream flashing back to me; it was of the darkness and endless trees.

A name, Donnie, from a dream I'd had the night before I embarked on this journey to get to Darke Heath. That might have meant something.

"Hey, are you okay?" Caitlyn asked, as I must have visibly reacted to the memory.

'Swallow it down Malone. Don't let it haunt you.'
Donnie...

"Yeah. I'm just tired, that's all," I said.

Pam and Splint had already headed out of the door as I came to.

"Caitlyn, I don't really want to share this with the others, but there's something wrong. And I'm not quite sure what it is. Something is blocking all my memories from before I came to Darke Heath," I said.

"What about your diary? After all it's got why you came here inside it right?" she asked, as I began to slowly nod. "And if it's any consolation, thanks for coming out to get me." Caitlyn leaned in and placed her hand on my chest for a moment only, her dark eyes staring into mine.

"We'll find out who you are, Blake Malone. Now let's go and see what Angus's deal is," she added, and at that moment Splint poked his head back through the front door.

"That's a good plan and all, but I have a business to run each night so I'm gonna catch some winks. I'll holla if I see anything," he said, and tried to turn.

"What about the whole sticking together thing?" Pam asked, intercepting him.

"I'm good thanks," he replied and sidestepped around her. In a moment, he was gone.

"And four become three," Pam said shrugging, and as she did Caitlyn stormed towards her.

"What are you?" she asked, and roughly took Pam by the scruff of her band t-shirt, exposing Pam's necklace of flowers just under the neck line

"I can sense a charm from a mile off. Start talking." Caitlyn demanded, as her grip loomed around the much smaller Pam.

"It's just for protection... that's all," she whimpered, clearly shaken by the vampire face staring down at her.

"Protection from what? Vampires? well it's not that effective."

"No, it's just a generic protection charm. I was heading out to a bar tonight. We all know what this town is like," Pam explained.

"All the time Caitlyn was speaking about witchcraft and you didn't care to mention you're a wi..." I said, then being interrupted by Pam;

"I'm not a witch, trust me. This thing doesn't even work; look I read a lot of books and play a lot of role play fantasy games. I just kinda know a lot about stuff. That stuff in theory, I guess. I got a cheap spells and incantation book from the used book store."

She seemed to be telling the truth, well I thought so, anyway. Caitlyn let go of her and dropped her defence.

"My parents, they are a little weird. They moved here because of the rumours, of you know vampire and witch stuff, I guess it rubbed off on me. I know this isn't stuff to be messing around with. Hey, it probably didn't even work," Pam explained, looking up at Caitlyn through her thick glasses.

"Save the amateur witch stuff for another time. Now come on, it's nearly sunrise." Caitlyn grabbed her purple coat and led the way out.

Pam and I looked at each other for a moment.

"You may get an apology one day, Pam."

"It's okay, Mr Malone. Maybe I should have mentioned it before."

It had started to get light as I came the up the steps and towards Caitlyn. I couldn't help but grunt as the dull pain in my back just checked in to say hello.

"Still painful?" Caitlyn asked.

"Better. I guess," I said, noticing she was visibly pissed at something.

"Everything okay ?" I asked, knowing it wasn't, but that's what you say anyway.

"I just... don't know, Blake, if I can trust people." We slowly walked forward.

"What, Pam? She's just a little Korean girl who means no harm. She's just into that dungeons and dragons stuff," I comforted, but she continued to brood, or whatever it is miserable vampires do.

She looked at me with an intrigued face.

"I guess you're right, Blake."

"And me. Well, who knows who I am, so that's trustworthy right?" I joked, as we headed towards the Workshop.

From the front, it looked like nobody was home, so slowly we walked around the back. During this time it appeared to get lighter; sunrise was imminent.

"Do you have decent black outs?" Caitlyn asked, as we could see the rear Workshop roller shutter.

"Something can be arranged," I said.

The loud revving of a vehicle closed in from behind and I spun to see Angus's truck come bounding our way along the narrow back alley. It smashed a collection of trash cans out of the way as the bright headlights continued onwards. The truck snaked left and right, narrowly avoiding larger trash cans and a brick wall.

"He's not, uh... stopping." Pam froze along with me, as the truck loudly screamed towards us.

"Out the way," Caitlyn yelled, as she grabbed both of us. With ease, we were thrown into the roller shutter and out of harm's way.

The truck closed in and Caitlyn had no time, she just stood there with her back to the approaching threat. In a flash move her face morphed and she jumped up as the truck came forward.

I looked on with my mouth open to see Caitlyn jump and smash into the large windscreen. The glass shattered as she went through it and most probably into Angus. Tyres screeched as the vehicle swung past us. It violently shunted into a large trash compactor and that's where it remained. Two bright red lights staring at us as a plume of steam rose from the front.

"You okay, Pam?" I asked, as she grabbed her glasses from the floor.

"Fine, Mr Malone. I'm not so sure about Caitlyn or Mr Greene though."

She had a point, and so I dragged my ass up off the ground and as I came around to the side of the truck I heard a groaning coming from the front.

"Ah, that's gonna hurt in the evening." Caitlyn seemed okay. Apart from a trickle of blood that wept down her face, she was wedged in shattered glass where I could only see one arm.

"Could ya lend a hand?" she asked, and reached out to me.

I grasped her hand and pulled and after a loud groan and the sound of crunching glass, she broke free. Her purple coat had been torn to in a few places, but even worse that she'd sat on her arm somehow and now it was limp.

"Damn! Broke my arm again," Caitlyn said, sounding more inconvenienced than pained.

She shakily hopped off the truck and lowered herself down to assess the wounds.

"Anybody wanna check on the host?" she asked.

Pam stretched up to look through the driver's window.

"Mr Greene? Can you hear me, are you okay?" she asked, and reached to open the door.

"No don't open…" Too late. The door creaked open and Angus shot out.

"The Darke Crusader should have kept you all away!" he shouted in a strained voice.

"The bastards must have amped him," Caitlyn said, from her crouched position. We watched in horror as Angus clasped both his hands around the much smaller Pam.

He totally dominated her. His behaviour seemed wild and erratic, much like an amp as Caitlyn had described, with his mouth foaming and teeth out, Angus leaned in to take a chunk out of Pam. I stepped in to intercept and took hold of his flannel shirt. Damn, he was strong and heavy, but I managed to drag him back a small distance.

"A little assistance, please?" Caitlyn called, trying to reach into her coat pocket with the limp arm

I let go of Angus as he continued to terrorise Pam.

"Quick! Grab my stun gun," Caitlin demanded, as she tried to hold open her inside pocket. I reached in and took it.

"One buzz to the neck will do it. Make sure you or Pam are not connected," she added.

"No sweat," I said, and looked up.

'I can do this, no problem.'

Angus shoved Pam into the roller shutter and she struck it with a wrapping thud; the guy could have broken her in half with the strength he had.

"The Crusader compels you all to stay away from here..."

"Hey, over here!" I shouted, getting his attention. After another shout, he dozily turned and squinted my way.

"What do you know about the Darke Crusader?" I called, as his eyes locked onto me. In a sudden movement, he rushed my way.

'Oh, Shit. Here comes this mountain of man, amped up and looking to bite someone.'

I felt light on my feet as I tried desperately to dance around him; this guy was a heavyweight compared to me. His big hands reached out in an aggressive clasp, and I lowered finding myself now cornered by two large flannel covered arms. The hands took hold of me and I was hoisted up.

Somehow with my elbows angled down, I drove them into him and broke away for a moment.

"Do it, Blake. Now!" Caitlyn shouted.

My finger hovered over the discharge button.

'Now or never, Malone, before the saliva covered teeth come down on you.'

I thrust the business end of the stun gun upwards, my eyes firmly closed. To this day I don't know where I got him, only that I did.

The flash could be seen even through closed eyes as Angus let out a loud squealed grunt. My next image was of Pam clutching at both of her knees looking at her boss face down in the dirt. He didn't move.

* 17 *

At least a minute or two had passed before any of us did anything. Angus remained with his face down on the ground and Pam continued to look on, from my right came a gasp as Caitlyn eventually stood.

"Caitlyn. Are you okay?" I asked, rushing to her.

She waved her broken arm out at me. The bone seemed jelly-like as she flopped it.

"Minor fracture. Should heal in a few hours at most," she said, totally impartial to the obviously painful break of her wrist.

"Who is Blake Malone?" Pam asked, as she read something on the floor.

Shit my diary. It must have fallen out in the struggle and now it lay open for anyone like Pam to read.

"Who is Blake Malone?" she asked again, this time taking hold of the leather-bound book. Before I could snatch it back from her she'd flipped through several pages.

"This doesn't make sense. What is this? It just says the same thing over and over again." Pam looked at me and then to Caitlyn who had stepped away from me.

"This is your diary right, Blake?" she asked.

I nodded, but this didn't make any sense. That was my guide book to the Crusader and his forum. All my leads and stuff was in that book.

"Uh, yeah, that is mine," I said vacantly. In my head things tried hard to explain themselves.

"Would you like to share with the rest of the class?" Caitlyn asked, as I frantically searched for an answer.

'Who is Blake Malone? That's me isn't it?'

"I don't know what's happening. That is my diary, right?" I asked, and grabbed the familiar worn leather outer jacket.

"Somebody has to have switched it," I said out loud, eagerly scanning the pages. A chill ran down my spine as I realised this was my handwriting.

'Who am I?'

For a moment I tuned out of the world. The last two days, none of it made sense to me anymore. Was I just insane, and this was all some kind of sick nightmare I had found myself in? Desperately I tried to cast my mind back, before I came to the Heath.

Nothing, apart from the bus I'd arrived on and that blonde girl, the one I had exchanged glances with. Maybe her perspective meant she knew me in some capacity, or maybe those glances were looks of concern on her face for me. Everything was so damn sceptical right now, too many maybes. The bottom line question was this; who is Blake Malone? Because every time I ask myself that question, I feel less and less attached to the name.

A firm grip wrapped around my shoulder and shook me. My focus then returned to the alley behind the Workshop.

"Maybe you can have a think about who you are and tell us after we've got this guy inside?" Caitlyn said.

I looked at Pam helping Angus to stand.

"It's okay, Pam. I got this. Just got a little headache is all," Angus said, in his familiar tone.

He looked over to the see his truck with a large trash dumpster wedged into the front of it.

"Jesus, what a damn mess," he said, exhaling deeply.

"You better get indoors. Seein' as it's gonna be sunrise imminently, that don't fare too well for folk like you," he added to Caitlyn.

"Would be nice to find some shade," she said.

"We'll get a sling for that paw of yours, as well. Come on in," Angus shuffled sheepishly to the door, but Pam beat him and opened it all for us.

"Thanks Pam. I'm thinking we keep the Workshop closed for today. Maybe put up a notice saying we checkin' stock or something," he said.

"Yes, Mr Greene, maybe you should take a seat for a little while," Pam suggested.

"Maybe for a long while. I feel like death."

As Angus disappeared into the back of the Workshop, Caitlyn stopped us.

"This whole 'who is Blake Malone' is just a slight bit concerning for us all, especially you, Blake. Maybe we keep this to ourselves for now, until we find out what he knows. As Splint would say, get my drift?" she asked. I nodded as I tried to scan my mind for answers.

We walked into the back of the Workshop to see Angus leaning up on a workbench.

"Oh, I have been a damn fool," he said, rubbing his neck. There were two visible burn marks either side of his jaw line. The bastards must have buzzed him.

"They amped me after you two split. That Alexis is gonna rain holy hell on this town."

"It's okay, Mr Greene. Take it easy for a little while. Maybe sit in a more comfortable chair?" Pam asked, as Angus pulled out his office keys.

"Get my office chair and maybe some Bourbon from the top drawer," Angus instructed, as Pam headed to his office.

We stood around kind of awkwardly with this man who appeared to be broken. He had been through a lot in one night, same here for that matter, so talking wasn't something I really felt like doing, especially after the whole diary thing; right now I wasn't sure who I was.

"For a kid who just got to the Heath, you've sure been through a lot." Angus gently angled his head towards me as I stood up.

"Yeah, You could say that," I said softly.

Pam then returned with a large leather office chair and Angus slowly rose and lowered himself into it.

"That's better. Thanks Pam. No Bourbon?"

"It's morning, Mr Greene. Maybe some tea, I have some homemade stuff that will help with the headache perhaps?" Pam said.

"Pass, but thanks. Could you put up that notice now, then fetch something for this lady's arm? A sling, maybe?" Angus instructed. I got this vibe he was trying to send Pam away.

"Yes, Mr Greene." She moved away and headed to the front of the store.

"Please, call me Caitlyn, we have been neighbours for over twenty years. It would appear that we've got some stuff to talk about. Maybe you should go first; how much do you know about the Heath?" Caitlyn asked.

"Well, where do I start? Firstly, Blake; it seems neither of us has been honest with the other from the outset. That's okay, I think if we both come clean now there will be no hard feelings kid. I'm not sure about keeping Pam informed about things though…"

"She knows my story. No harm in knowing yours, I guess," Caitlyn said, before I could speak.

"I suppose. She's a useful girl an' all, but I don't really want to be scaring her away…"

"I don't think that will happen. Pam is actually quite well informed about the 'inhabitants' of the Heath," Caitlyn added.

"Is she now? Well then, I guess she better hear my story too." Just as he finished speaking Pam came back our way. She carried a green first aid box.

"This whole Darke Crusader thing has got a little out of hand. Unfortunate thing really, and before you ask? Yes, it was all me," Angus said with a slow bow of the head.

"Initially I thought of the idea to scare people from coming here. Most of these young kids today end up dead in a ditch drained of their blood. Some of them go trotting off into those woods to never come back or worse, they end up involved with that house out in the woods."

He slowly stood and took hold of the first aid box.

"So you are behind the Darke Crusader?" Pam asked, as Angus took out a large square of cloth.

"Yes, I did it all myself." Angus spoke like he was admitting defeat, then he signalled for Caitlyn to come closer.

"You're probably gonna have to take that jacket off, darling'," he said.

"Look, there was no other place I could turn," he added. After folding the fabric, he gently set it around Caitlyn's limp arm and put it into a sling.

"There ya go, Caitlyn. Not sure about healing times for folks like you, but I'm sure it ain't long," he said, and lowered himself into his chair again.

"So What happened, Mr Greene?" Pam asked.

"They took my family; those bastard blood suckers. All of them led by Alexis, he's the biggest bastard of them all." I could see Angus was beginning to get angry.

"Ever since that night he brought his hood gang into town, he's had it in for me. I should have dropped him there and then with my rifle. It took some years later for us to head into that forest and I tell ya back then I was naïve, and so was this damn town. There were no internet forums warning you of places like this. Hell, there weren't even many decent rumours."

He paused for a moment and looked at us all.

"Guess you better hear my piece."

* 18 *

"Marcy was draped over me as I woke up. There it was again; another twig snapping outside. Something was lurking out there nearby our tent and campsite. It had been doing this for the past few days now. You know when you can sense something, like human sonar or some other crap like that? Dogs pick up on stuff, and so do we I guess.

Geez, it never crossed my mind to bring the damn rifle, this was a family trip after all; the two kids were asleep just inches from Marcy and me.

Whatever happens now, or however close this thing gets, it's gotta to be afraid of us as well. Just don't react. Yesterday it went away, maybe that will happen again today.

Then another twig broke. This one sounded as close to the campfire we'd had that night. A louder than hell gasp came from Marcy's mouth as she awoke abruptly.

'Shhhh honey,' I said, as she rolled off me and sat up.

A cold sweat ran down my forehead and she softly whispered,

'Something's out there.'

I reached out to her and croakily whispered back,

'It's fine. Just stay quiet and it will pass. Probably a possum...'

Crunching sounds came from mere yards behind the thin canvas on the kid's side of the tent. That set them both off and now all four of us were awake in the dark. I lay there feeling the situation slip away from my control.

'Daddy?' my youngest Susie said.

'It's okay, baby doll,' I said, as I felt her arms reach out across to me.

Marcy took hold of her as I slowly sat up. I then awkwardly half stood in the tent.

'Let me take a look, okay? It's probably a whole load of nothing,' I added, and clambered over the sleeping bag.

That was when the screech came, only it was a soft screech followed by the sound of what seemed like sniffing. Air puffed against the tent wall as this thing began to smell what was inside.

'What is it Dad?' Donnie asked, curiously.

'Just be quiet,' I said, as the outside fell silent.

'You got that torch kid?' I asked, as Donnie offered it my way.

'Honey. No.' Marcy protested, as I headed towards the dividing zip between us and whatever lurked out there.

'Screw this,' I said loudly, trying to scare away anything nearby.

My hand grasped the zip and I pulled down. Still-cold air hit me as I fumbled out and my bare feet touched the woodland ground.

'Come on. Damn torch,' I said, smacking the damn thing as it lit up.

A beam of hazy light flowed over the tent and only the shadows of my family could be seen inside. My torch scanned the area around with the light powering on and off. The strobe effect played with my imagination as shadows bounced off other shimmering shadows. Was that a tall tree or a dark figure?

'What is it Dad? A bear?' Donnie asked, as he came outside.

'Go back inside...'

It crept up on me without any of my senses alerting or reacting. Wheezy short breaths caught my ear as I turned to see a cloaked figure standing only yards from me.

'Shit,' I said, stepping back and stumbling. The very sight of this figure weakened me in fear and I lost my footing, and the torch as I did; I began to breathe deeply, my heart beating painfully against my chest.

'Run!' I yelled.

Marcy and Susie both stumbled out of the tent, as Donnie picked up the torch and shone it towards the prowler.

He whimpered in fear and sprinted away; he went in the damn opposite direction as me. He knew that wasn't the way out of these damn woods. Only then Marcy and the girl followed him.

'Over here!' I shouted, and turned back. It was no use; they were headed off and away. Hopefully from whatever danger this psycho posed.

Twigs behind me snapped as I ran. My feet pounding on the soft forest ground and heart clanging in my chest, my lungs were heavy and aching, but I made it out into the clear and up the bank. It felt good to stand bare footed on the main Forest Road again. All I had to do now was flag somebody down; just anyone with a damn car to get me some help.

Small towns are renowned for their community and willingness to help each other. Everyone knew one another, and any real serious crime never happened. Yeah, some kids would set light to a trash can in the park sometimes or steal candy, but no real crimes were ever noticeably reported.

Looking back, I can see I was naïve then. To think the sheriff's office would even listen to what I had to say. They thought of an excuse for every damn thing

I said. It was the middle of the frickin' night and I had no shoes. Something had to of happened out there in the woods, but they straight up refused to believe me.

Bastards.

That was when I began to believe this town was more than just a few ghost stories, and tales of things going on in the forest at night. And no, I didn't just give up there, it had hooked me in. After being dropped home, I fetched my damn rifle and headed back into that forest. Every day for a month I searched in the daytime. Hell, I never even found the damn tent, or any sign that we had stayed there.

Such things can send a man insane you know, and I firmly believe this town will - if you let it. Eventually if you spend enough time between those trees you will find the house, and so I did, and as I walked out from the tress and into the long grass of a cemetery, there came this feeling; an almost magnetism, a fearful dread that draws you in.

Clutching my rifle and lugging my pack, I continued along until my foot stepped on something; a torch, Donnie's torch. It had been buried by the lengthy grass, but either way this belonged to my missing son and I wasn't gonna give up now.

On I trudged until I came to the mostly collapsed walls that surrounds the gardens of this house. Even in the daytime this place looked ominous. A crack of sunlight shone over a moss covered wooden door and coming closer to the building, I could tell the whole place smelled of ancient rotting decay. The windows above and below were blackened on the inside, but I could sense eyes were watching me, gazing at me. I could feel them burning into me.

Standing in full view of those windows I held up that torch and spoke loudly,

'This belongs to my son. He's been missing along with his sister and mother for some time now. I would like to know where they are.'

'This is not a question. It is a request,' I said, stepping up onto the rotten wooden decking.

I held up an angry fist and wrapped on the door several times. My presence was known, but not acknowledged that day.

It's a frustrating feeling knowing there is no help. The town authorities left me to it and anyone else who I mentioned it to just laughed me off.

Was I just going insane? Did Marcy and the kids leave me and this was some kind of a break down?

The answer finally came to me unexpectedly.

As I hung the rifle on the rack behind the seats of my truck, I got ready to head back into town after another full day of searching. Again I had visited the house with no result. As I was climbing into the truck, I was met by a figure. A dark hood stared at me from behind the passenger door.

I tried to reach back to my rifle, but another figure swiftly grabbed me. It was then I realised hooded figures stood in every direction. They put out my lights.

Sometime later, I eventually came around.

'Angus Greene of the Darke Heath Workshop,' a distinguished voice said.

As I lay slumped over my eyes gradually opened. 'Huh?' I asked.

I was in some dark room. The floor was wooden and candles surrounded me on every surface.

'What is this?' I asked, trying to reach out, but my hands were shackled.

Standing opposite was Alexis, in a lab coat. He glared at me.

'We can help each other,' he said, 'welcome to the Manor.'

I sat up and let him talk.

'You need me and I need you, yes?'

'Depends what for,' I remarked, cautiously.

'Marcy and the kids,' Alexis said, grabbing my immediate attention. I struggled in the chair and desperately tried to break free.

'Where are they, damn it? You tell me now!' I demanded, trying to kick out at him.

'Struggling will only dig you deeper into this mess,' he smiled, looking out into the surrounding darkness.

'You see, this wonderful but small community I have here, needs people like you. Good honest hard working folk, to do the work for me in a sense.'

'What do you want?' I asked, just wanting to see my family.

'I'm getting to that, Mr Greene...'

'How do you know my name?'

'The Heath is a small place and I have eyes and ears everywhere. My request to you, Sir, at least to begin with is really very simple. You are going to play fetch for me, my good Sir,' Alexis grinned.

'I ain't doing shit until I see my family.'

Alexis turned as footsteps came down into the cellar room we were in. There was struggling and commotion as two fellas dragged my wife down and towards us. She looked like shit.

'Marcy, what have they done to you?' I cried.

'Angus. I'm so sorry,' she sobbed out in tears; they rolled down her dirty face.

'It's not your fault,' I said, as Alexis ordered Marcy up and onto her feet.

'Here you can see your wife, relatively unharmed. Until now.' Alexis snatched at Marcy and forcefully pulled her to him. She flopped like a ragdoll. Jesus, he was strong with just one arm, he had full control, and then I saw it; his face changed and long sharp teeth protruded from his wide-open mouth. It closed around Marcy's neck.

'No! Goddamn it,' I shouted, as she breathed one last breath before blood trickled down her neck and she slumped to the floor.

'Now do I have your attention?' Alexis sneered at me. If I hadn't been chained in I would have been the ragdoll this time.

'You will do what I request, or the fate of your two children will rest the same way as her. My community is in desperate need of youth, but I will pardon them if you comply,' he said, and let go of me.

'Get her out of here. My bedroom will do,' Alexis said slimily towards me.

Bastard

'What is it? You name it,' I said admitting defeat.

'Just follow the instructions that you will receive.'

They clocked me again and this time I woke up in my truck. They had driven me back into town and parked me around the back of the Workshop. There I sat for some time in a daze, trying to gather what had happened.

Marcy's wide eyes burned into me as that son of a bitch sunk his teeth into her. I had never believed in vampires, that was until they took my family. The Heath is in denial about them and has been since they founded the damn place. I was trapped, and that's where I have been ever since; for fifteen years, I have been their errand boy.

This has mainly consisted of running weird medical equipment to them; electro shock therapy stuff, power supplies and components, wiring and generators. Basically all the stuff I could get my hands on through the Workshop. They used me as their supplier so they could run whatever weird experiments they were doing. Innocent people were snatched, some I recognised, some I didn't. They would hook them up and send volts across all parts of their bodies.

Eventually I got wise as to what they were doing, to what Alexis was doing. It wasn't some weird electro torture thing he had going, he was experimenting, looking for a cure. Along the way he discovered some kind of brain manipulation that had folks 'fetching' stuff for him, so he and the other vampires didn't have to go into town.

For a long time, I suspected that you, Caitlyn, was in on the gig they had running out there, that other woman also. Until last night that is, when they brought you in to do stuff to you. Then you, Blake Malone, come bounding in like a clumsy hero. You stirred up hell before busting out of there. They chained me down and did what they do to every other person they snatch.

Can't say I remember much between then and being jolted in the neck. Guess I have you three to thank for that.

I looked over to Blake and Pam, who were both in a level of shock. They also appeared to be working stuff out and putting things together in their minds Either that or they probably didn't believe an ounce of what I told them. Nobody ever has yet."

"What happened to your family, Mr Greene?" Pam asked, as Blake turned away, caught up with his thoughts.

"Haven't seen them in nearly fifteen years. He's still got them somewhere. Whether he has vamped them or shocked them to death by now, I don't know. Bastards, they took my damn family from me and left me dangling like this. I started the whole Darke Crusader thing to get this place some attention. A few evenings a week I'd spend in the bar opposite, just sat at the table in the corner listening out to hear what was going on in the forest. Believe me those kids were loud about stuff in there; so loud I began to write about it and post it on the internet. Soon enough word spread, for the better or worse, who knows? But it did something to the town' s rep.

Maybe I'd thought it could do something more to help me out and stop others from falling victim to them in the future."

"Your kids. They won't be kids, anymore right?" Caitlyn asked.

"My youngest Susie would be eighteen just last month. Donnie is older. I suspect they are both vampires much like their mother now, but I've never seen them," I said and saw that Caitlyn had that look meaning she was working things out.

"We can help," Caitlyn said, "your wife?" she asked.

"Marcy," I told her.

"She's the Mistress," Caitlyn added, as Blake and Pam nodded.

"And your daughter. I'm sure I heard her speaking when I was there in that creepy room," Blake continued.

"My girl. You saw her?" I asked, with the first glimmer of hope that this situation might turn good.

"It could have been her," Caitlyn said.

"So what do we do next?" Pam asked.

Caitlyn then stepped forward, "We hold back for now. I say we meet at the bar tonight. Get Splint in on the loop and take it from there. Mr Greene, you have given me the greatest reason of all to take out that son of a bitch Alexis. He will burn along with that damn house. As for your family, if they are vampires. They won't be forever."

* 19 *

The story Angus had told didn't do much to distract me from my current identity dilemma. There was a weird familiarity about his account and the whole running away in the forest thing, hadn't I seen it before? As much as I wanted to think about it, I had my own problems, mind you we all had problems right now. I felt sorry for the guy, but there was just the small case of who the hell I was.

"What do you mean they won't be forever?" Angus asked, with an air of desperation in his tone.

The now sling-wearing Caitlyn explained,

"There's a cure, an end game for vampirism. There are five solutions of them to be precise, I had envisioned one for myself in the long-term," she said.

"That does give me hope."

Angus looked up to me and for the first time that morning his eyes didn't seem quite so pained.

"All is not lost, but we must be tactical here. The whole town is rife with their errand boys and girls," he pointed out, then got up with a groan.

"Amps are easy to take down. Any high voltage will snap them out of it," Caitlyn said.

"Well that is something we got lots of here; components, batteries and the like. Real pokey stuff that can be found in an old TV nobody will miss much like your personal cattle prod. Maybe I can hash together a few homemade surprises," Angus said.

"I don't sleep much these days, so it would be useful if I did something. You kids get some rest and we'll reconvene tonight. It's probably best if I also unwrap the dumpster from my truck."

With Pam on her way home and Angus working in the Workshop, I found myself back in bed. My room was much darker than before because of Caitlin's jacket sprawled across the window blind; she just sat quietly facing the blacked-out window and hadn't talked in a while

Things were racing around in my mind, but I knew I had to sleep. As I began to slip into a dream Caitlyn did her thing,

"So, if you're not Blake Malone, then who are you?" she asked, and turned my way.

"Good question. There is something blocking my memory from before I came here," I said.

"I know what it's like to feel lost." A hand stretched out towards me and I took it.

"What are we?" I asked, interlocking my fingers with hers. "I mean what have we got here?"

"I'm too tired to answer that one, Blake. If that is even your real name."

"Guess we'll find out sooner rather than later," I replied before silence ruled over the dark room.

Again, my dreams were plagued with surrealism. There I was, sitting in a near dark square room with walls that were grimy and peeling. A sound came from behind, just a crackling to begin with and then music, it was the same music they'd played in the Manor. Then I realised, I was in that very room, you could even call it a cell.

I was in a rickety wooden chair looking up at a soft glow of light and as it came into focus I found it was a computer screen. For some reason my vision couldn't quite make up what was on the display, but it looked like a lot of red writing over a black screen.

Darke Crusader.

The music began to play but louder now, and in the background I swear I could hear screams of pain.

'You must take her heart.'

From the other side of the room the window abruptly rose up and opened. A breeze hit me and all around candles flickered. There came the sound of voices, just like the ones that had passed me by when I was out there. A girl spoke,

"I only remember this life. Everything before is blank, but there is one memory that I cling to, and that is of being a child and the person I came here with."

Darkness surrounded me as an echo of the girl's voice came from all around.

"Where are you?" I cried out, realising I now stood in the misty forest. Dark shadows stood all around, but they were just tall thick tree trunks.

"I've been here the whole time," the girl said.

"We all have, Blake, you are so close to us." she added.

My feet began to march forward. Was I walking towards the voice? I turned around in frustration.

"You can make it." The voice seemed closer and I began to run.

The mist grew thicker and thicker as the tree shadows thinned out. I came to a clearing and there she stood; a girl in all dark clothes, she wore a leather jacket and had smoky blonde hair. For a moment, I could have sworn it was the girl who I had seen before somewhere.

'Come on, Malone, you only have two days of memory. Work brain, damn it.

I gripped the girl's shoulder and she turned. Her concerned faced stared at me and I sensed a comforting familiarity. Her voice, the same as the girl who'd walked past the window back at the Manor. She had something to do with all of this.

"She will not approve," the girl said, and slowly held out an arm. Her hand pointed behind me, and so I turned.

It was dark now and the mist had gone.

The Manor faced me with brightly lit windows and I could see a silhouette standing there. It spoke in that comforting yet hypnotic voice of the Mistress.

"You have no power over us," she said, the voice sounding like it was in my head. In a flash her shadow had glided my way. A screech of white noise came crashing over me and that was when I woke. The last image was of a rotting woman's face, bugs and creepy crawlies staring at me along with those two dark eyes.

A cold sweat dripped down my face as I sat up. The room was now nearly in full darkness, even with Caitlyn's jacket removed and the thin blind just remaining. That meant early evening, so I must have had a long sleep; just what I needed as the pain in my back now seemed to be a mere ache when I stood up. My head was still full of identity thoughts, but at least painless; the not knowing was painful enough.

The sound of voices carried up to my door as I opened it. Heading down the stairs, I could see Caitlyn lugging a large TV under the direction of Angus.

"If you set her down with the back facing, I can get to the gubbins inside," he said.

"Ah, Mr Malone, you have risen," Pam noted, coming my way. She wore another dragon type t-shirt and handed me a fresh mug of coffee.

"Yeah. Sort of," I said, and was astonished to see the Workshop completely transformed. It was tidy.

"I got bored, and Angus was looking for a capacitator or something, so I thought could lend a hand," Caitlyn said, as the large TV was set down on a tidy bench.

"It's a capacitor. You'll learn. Someone has to," Angus grunted, as he took hold of a long screw driver.

"Your wrist. It's fine?" I asked, as Caitlyn moved her previously broken wrist in all directions.

"Perks of the disease," she said.

"Now, what I'm looking for is something not too heavy. Pocket sized, but enough to give someone an ungodly zap," Angus said as he unscrewed the back of the large TV.

I took a sip of the black coffee and I could feel it quickly begin to take hold and fully wake me up.

"I've managed to get my hands on an air gap capacitor; here." Angus said, taking hold of something no bigger than a soda can and presenting it to me.

"Don't look like much, but you shove that in someone's neck and they'll know about it," he explained.

I felt the heavy weight of the capacitor. "How quickly does it recharge?" I asked.

"Every so often, problem is it's too heavy to be lugging around. Not exactly user friendly, but I'll find something in one of these old things," Angus said, and put on a set of magnified glasses. He clicked on a small light attached to the glasses and got closer to the insides of the old TV.

"I guess it's dark enough outside for us to move. What do you say we go and disturb Splint? Put some kind of plan in place?" Caitlyn asked, already she'd started to put her coat on.

"You kids go on without me. You seem to have this together and I'll only slow you down. Pam, you be careful out there, make sure these two look after you."

"I'll be fine, Mr Greene," Pam said, defensively.

"The Heath is a rough place after dark and things tend to lurk in the shadows," Angus added, as he reached into the old TV.

"Yeah, things like me. Let's move out." Caitlyn led us to the door and out into the cold air.

As we came to the front door of the bar, it was apparent Splint had made 'arrangements' to let the townsfolk know how he felt about the current situation. An array of garlic hung above the door and on the handle. A scrawled sign had been wonkily taped to the blacked-out window. It read, 'Strictly no night folk'.

"Subtle," I said.

As Caitlyn went for the door it opened outwards and Splint appeared holding a baseball bat. He wore a range of small band aids scattered across the various scratches and cuts on his head. One of his arms was completely bandaged.

"After last night, I'm taking no chances," he grumbled, trying to shuffle us in.

"Is this your attempt at keeping them away?" Caitlyn asked, and reached up to the garlic. She ripped it off without a flinch.

"Actual garlic to ward off vampires is a very old wives' tale, Splint," she said, and dropped it to the floor. "However, garlic gas would be better."

I followed her and Pam into the empty bar. Splint closed the door and turned the lock.

"Well, I thought there would be no harm in trying to defend the place. Can I get anyone a drink?" he asked, heading around to the bar.

"There are more important things to discuss other than drinking right now, Splint."

"You're telling me. I gotta business to run." Splint reached down and set a bunch of bottles onto the bar.

"A business that is a front to lure amps and vampires in for me to slay," Caitlyn pointed out.

"I'll take one," Pam said. She climbed up onto a bar stool as Splint twisted off the bottle cap and handed one to her.

"Thanks, Pam," he said.

"You're welcome," she said, and sat there openly admiring him. "How are you feeling today?" she asked.

"Better," and then turning towards us, "so, did you speak to the old guy?" Splint asked us, quickly changing the subject.

"Yeah, he came back and was amped up. Totalled his truck out the back too. We snapped him out of it." Caitlyn replied.

"They've got his family," I said, and leant against the bar. "Have done for years apparently. Alexis is blackmailing the guy long-term," I added.

"Is he up for helping us take them blood sucking bastards down? I mean no offence to you," Splint grinned at Caitlyn.

"None taken," she nodded, 'he's reluctant to help or be seen helping. That's what he told me earlier," Caitlyn explained.

"They do have his family," Pam said, and she continued, "and it's apparent he would do anything for them." She tried to look Splint in the eye, but he didn't budge.

"Are his family vamped up?" Splint asked.

"He doesn't know..."

From behind came a gentle rattle; it was the door.

"Oh, hell no. You ain't getting in today," Splint said, and hopped over the bar. He rushed to the door with his baseball bat in tow.

"Now hold the damn phone, Splint," Caitlyn warned, as Splint tried to look through the blacked out glass.

"Can't see anyone," he muttered. "We're closed!" Splint shouted, and turned back to us. At that moment, a bottle from behind him hit the floor and smashed, just as Pam dropped to the ground from her stool whilst holding her head.

"Ah... It hurts," she whimpered, firmly gripping her head.

"Pam, what's happening?" I asked, lowering myself down to her. She began to convulse.

"What's up with her?" Splint asked.

As he approached the whole bar was rocked by a thunderous shockwave.

I lost my footing and cowered over Pam as a deafening smashing came from all around.

Every glass window including the doors shattered. The sound fractured our hearing as shards dropped to the floor. Then the realisation hit us; we were no longer safely locked in the Darke Bar. The street was now closer than ever, and so was whatever had just done this.

* 20 *

I kept down low and near to Pam as she continued to convulse. Her eyes rolled back and turned pure white. It wasn't clear what had taken out every pane of glass between us and the street, but we'd find out soon enough. Splint, of course, became angry and his band aid covered face screwed up.

"Oh hell no you don't. Someone's going to be paying for that!" he yelled, and wielded his baseball bat around. He skated dangerously over shards of glass as they broke under his weight.

There came another thud and an invisible force struck Splint in the gut. He grunted in shock as the power hit him, and the bat was smashed away and snapped against the barred window frame. He stood exposed and without a weapon; he had rushed in, the fool.

Before any of us could react, Splint was thrown backwards and into the bar; he landed on a table and tumbled through it and that was where he remained for most of what followed.

"Who is it?" I asked Caitlyn.

"It's her," she replied, and pointed out into the dark street. There, draped in a hooded red cloak stood a figure with the night breeze blowing over her. It ominously floated there like a ghost.

The Mistress.

She haunted us and waited for someone else to advance. I didn't make any effort to offer myself.

"What does she want?" I asked looking at the others, and then came the hypnotic voice,

"Caitlyn," she whispered in all our heads. A hand appeared and stretched towards us. One solitary finger pointed out to Caitlyn.

Without hesitation, she surged forward. "Let's dance then, bitch."

As her boots crunched on broken glass the Mistress clenched her hand out and an unparalleled force dragged Caitlyn forwards. The magnetic-like power made her look like a helpless ragdoll.

"Jesus, she's powerful," I said, as Pam began to groan.

In a flash movement Caitlyn was hoisted up and separated from her purple coat. It floated in the air and danced on the breeze as it came down. Caitlyn however crashed to the floor.

"No vampire can stop me," the Mistress whispered, but again everyone could hear. She caught the floating coat and took out the stun gun.

"Famous... last words!" Caitlyn shouted, as she shot up.

With her fingers wrapped around a wooden stake she rushed towards the cloaked Mistress.

They collided and both went down with Caitlyn on top. Before she could get anywhere near driving the stake down she was smashed back with a massive force.

"Silly little human vampire," the Mistress sneered, as she floated to her feet.

"I take that personally," Caitlyn shouted back and charged again. This time the Mistress grasped out and plucked the stake from her desperate but strong hands.

"You think this can defeat me?" The Mistress asked, and used her other free hand to reach out.

Her fingers wrapped around Caitlyn's neck and she pulled her in. With the stake primed, the situation was now borderline dangerous for the girl who'd kissed me the first night we met.

I had to intervene. Pam continued to convulse but there was nothing I could do, her eyes continued to roll back and forth, and so I laid her on one side and stood up. The Mistress continued to hold Caitlyn in the air as I looked around for a weapon of some kind.

There was no time, that stake would go down at any moment. If we lost Caitlyn, then this whole thing would go to shit. It was up to me now and before I knew what to do, my feet were stumbling towards them. The raspy cloak came at me and I threw myself at it while doing my best to barge into her.

"Leave… her… alone… dammit!" I cried out and collided with mostly thin air. It was enough however for Caitlyn to break free and she fell back to the ground; her lungs gasping for air.

The Mistress turned towards me and underneath the hooded cloak I could see two dark eyes staring right through me.

"Alexis was wrong to think you could do it. You are a failure to everyone," she barked.

"What?" I yelped in that high-pitched pussy-like tone that suggested I knew my death was probably imminent.

I looked at the stake in her grip, it wasn't too far from my reach and as she moved in to swipe at me, I evaded her and made to snatch it out of her hand.

The stake came free as I pulled, and now the weapon was in my hands. A piercing cackle came my way as the Mistress revealed two sharp fangs.

"Pathetic," she growled, and this time the cloaked sleeve hit me. I was thrown back with a powerful force as my feet temporarily left the ground. My back slapped against the floor and reignited the pain from my first night here. Lying there with the stake still in my grip, I found I had no motivation to move.

"Is there anyone worthy of challenging me?" the Mistress called out. I guessed there wasn't, but intrigue urged me to sit up and watch.

The Mistress moved closer to Caitlyn holding out both of her hands and clenching her fingers. Caitlyn was dragged to her feet as a bony witch-like hand wrapped itself around her neck again. There was nothing I could do, I was a mortal; Caitlyn wasn't and she still faced defeat. Slowly I lay back down on to the piercing cold ground.

"Take this one's soul for all eternity," the Mistress screeched, as she shook Caitlyn. A wave of exhaustion seemed to have come over her as the swipes she made became more and more feeble.

The potential girl of my dreams was being ragdolled; her life about to be taken away, just as I lay there looking up at the dark sky.

A pair of boots then stepped across my vision along with a dark red coat, much like Caitlyn's.

"Step away, witch!" A strong woman's voice ordered.

Again, I sat up and this time I saw a thin looking woman standing opposite the Mistress.

"Sister," Caitlyn said weakly, as she was let go and dropped to the floor. Worryingly she didn't move.

The Mistress turned and took down her hood. Her face seemed familiar to me, but I couldn't quite put my finger on where she came from. She was an elegant older woman, her steely eyes staring down towards this new arrival.

"Rebecca," I whispered to myself in realisation of who the red-coated woman was.

She resembled an older version of Caitlyn, her hair the same, apart from a solitary grey streak.

The two women circled each other in what would most probably be a face-off to the death.

Rebecca stood defensively and held out both hands. Her opponent did the same with neither of them averting their gaze.

"I've been wanting to meet you for some time," the Mistress said coldly.

"Fortunately, I no longer work with rank amateur tricksters," Rebecca seethed, as her fingers clenched and sent a blowing force effortlessly towards the Mistress.

Quickly the Mistress made reply with the same, but neither of them did anything more than blow stronger forces at each other.

"Maybe you would prefer it if I took the safety off?" Rebecca asked, as she lowered herself. Her arm swung around and reached towards the soft glowing streetlight.

After a bright flash the streetlight power seemed to fade. Rebecca stood there actively draining it of its energy; with a visible trail of light streaming up and illuminating her arm. In a sudden move, Rebecca spun on her feet and threw a bolt of lightning towards the Mistress. She side-stepped and caught the ball of sparks. In two hands, she caressed this energy which had lit up the street.

"You're powerful, for an Earth witch." the Mistress said, before totally consuming the energy.

"You have no idea," Rebecca muttered, standing firm.

"Oh, I do. Death will consume you all," the Mistress barked, as she rushed forward.

Her cloak hovered in the wind as she charged towards Rebecca with two outstretched hands. Her voice screeching, it was deafening.

Just as they were about to collide, Rebecca forced both of her hands up and blew the Mistress up and over; her hands swiping in all directions towards Rebecca, but to no avail. Before landing the Mistress sent a rain of fireballs her way, and again, the street lit up.

'Get out of there man.'

It was no longer safe to be in the street, that's what I thought anyway, and so I dragged myself up and headed for Caitlyn. She was in a daze as I approached.

The two witches collided, this time contact was made and Rebecca threw her attacker off. Just as she flew up she came back and Rebecca used her hands to force the Mistress to crash down onto the hard ground.

"Come on, let's get back." I helped Caitlyn away as the Mistress crashed down. She hit it with such force the concrete around her cracked.

Rebecca closed in and dragged her up with the power of her craft.

"You belong in the forest. This town is ours," she shouted, and took her by the neck with a veiny hand.

"I refuse to repent!" The Mistress screamed, and tried to break away kicking her arms and legs about. Rebecca reeled backwards with no choice but to loosen her grip. Recovering quickly, she was too far from the Mistress to regain her grasp, and so instead used her telekinetic force and raised both hands; the cloak that surrounded the Mistress flew up with her in the air and flipped her forward. For the second time that night she struck the ground hard.

I noticed the Mistress reach out to something as she lay face down.

"As I said... amateur," Rebecca stated claiming victory, only prematurely. She reached down to grab the Mistress.

Nobody could predict the scorpion that hid in the sand or in this case, the stun gun that had fallen from Caitlyn's jacket pocket. The Mistress had managed to get her hands on the device and as her foe leaned in, she let loose the high voltage stinger

There was a flash as the stun gun made contact, right in the neck. The shockwave hit her with such power it locked her legs. In a state of intense shock Rebecca stood. In a spiteful lunge the Mistress drove the stun gun again, but this time into her chest. Another bright spark flashed throwing Rebecca away from the jolt. She was already out cold before her deadweight crashed to the floor and didn't move.

"Shit," I said, out loud.

It was an underhand tactic, but it had worked as the Mistress now had the complete advantage.

"No! Stop!" Caitlyn shouted. She struggled to stand when finally she got up and moved away from me.

The Mistress closed in and swiped her away. I did my best to dive and wrap my arms around her waist as she fell; down we went together, again with my back bearing the brunt of our fall.

"This town is ours and will always be!" The Mistress pulled Rebecca to her feet and prepared to make the final fatal blow. Her free hand turned into burning flames.

"Death will rule you all."

"No."

I could feel Caitlyn move around in my arms as she stood up once again. This time her face morphed and from behind her strong white fangs came an angry growl. She careened towards the cloaked Mistress and tackled her head on; Jesus, this girl was tough.

Rebecca broke away only to fall again. Her body still limp from the shock, she looked worryingly half-dead.

Caitlyn threw out several punches; every one of them made contact and every one of them made no impact. The Mistress stalked forwards and threw out a firm palm wrapping it around the wild vampire neck of Caitlyn.

"I summon your soul to remain restricted..." the Mistress commanded, as Caitlyn desperately protested,

"No, you bitch. Stop!" she croaked and gasped for air.

As I watched, it seemed as if the Mistress used her free hand to drag something from Caitlyn; a misty type of aura began seep out and past the set of fangs.

"I banish your soul," the Mistress demanded, as the mist continued to flow from Caitlyn's mouth. In moments her head had flopped forward.

"Pathetic pretend vampire. You are no more," the Mistress said with disgust, as she pushed Caitlyn away.

She flew backwards, unfortunately out of my catching range.

It hadn't taken long, but now both Slayer Sisters were down and out. With one possibly dead.

"You underestimate my power," the Mistress triumphantly cried, and drifted like a breeze towards the collapsed Rebecca.

Suddenly with a flaming raised hand that she'd made ready to throw down on her. She said,

"You know what they say about witches? Burn... burn the witches until they're dead." Her voice rang with a witch-like cackle, her voice echoing throughout the street. As her flaming hand came down onto the helpless Rebecca, a burst of purple flew past me. It lit up the dark street and struck the witch. Abruptly she stumbled back and the flame from her hand extinguished

I sat there wide-eyed and wondering where the hell that could have come from, when my question was answered.

Light feet crunched over the smashed glass as Pam came out of the bar. Her eyes were no longer rolled back, but pure black. An aura of purple light surrounded her hands as she came forward. That's when I realised Pam had probably been bending the truth a little about being an amateur witch.

She tensed both hands around a powerfully bright ball of purple light and threw it like a dodgeball. This one made sure to strike the Mistress and knock her from her feet. She went down on her back: Check, and Mate, bitch.

Pam breezed by me with her night-black eyes and continued towards the now recovering Mistress.

"Levitate," Pam ordered and raised her right arm. The Mistress unwillingly stood, dragged by the cloak she wore.

"I am one with the earth and one with the sky. Let this witch's' powers temporarily die," Pam chanted as she threw out both arms wide. She opened both hands as her purple aura grew brighter.

Swiftly the Mistress broke away from Pam's force and tried to throw her own. Desperately she attempted to send anything out in retaliation, but nothing happened.

"What have you done?" she screeched.

"Stopped you from causing any more harm. Now stop." Pam said, as if she were talking to a child. Her glow diminished as she turned around and her eyes returned to normal.

What was to happen next? We still had this madwoman who was clearly some level of a threat. Caitlyn and her sister were both still down and I was sitting on my ass as our underdog saviour entered the game and saved the day.

From the very beginning of this journey, I had developed a rule when it comes to vampires and the Heath in general: Rule number one; never under any circumstances should you ever turn your back on a vampire.

I looked up at Pam's somewhat innocent face as she adjusted her thick glasses. A clever girl like her must have grasped this witchcraft stuff through book smarts alone. However, she wasn't so strong on the street smarts that she had no idea a batshit crazy ass vampire witch would charge her way. Teeth first, I might add.

"Pam watch out!" I shouted just as the Mistress pounced.

Her two fangs protruded as they sunk into Pam's shoulder. She screamed in terror as both of her knees buckled.

"No!" I yelled. Rebecca and Caitlyn were too far gone to stop the Mistress.

With the varnished stake still on my person, I charged and failed to raise my hand as we collided. I managed to separate Pam from the sharp now bloodied fangs, just before the deafening sound of rifle fire went off in the street.

I stood in between the now pain-ridden Korean witch girl and a blood thirsty Death witch with the fruits of her attack dripping from her chin.

"That's enough. I'm the one with the real weapon here," Angus shouted, as he made his way onto the street.

The Mistress wiped her chin and raised her hood.

"Are they hurt?" Angus asked, as he came closer.

"I don't know," I said, focusing more on Pam who continued to writhe in pain.

"And who we got here?" Angus asked, as he looked directly at the hood that covered the Mistress. She took a step back.

"Maybe you would like to have the decency to reveal who you are," Angus ordered. He began to raise the rifle.

"I can guarantee neither of you will like that," the Mistress said, with her stained chin and mouth moving in the low street light.

"Well, that's gonna have to be the consequence, I suppose. I seen some strange things around these parts for many years now. Now take down that damn hood, or I'll have no second thoughts about blowing it off."

Angus cocked the rifle.

"As you wish," the Mistress said, and slowly pulled back the hood. An unamused face, if I had to describe its expression stared back at Angus. Then it got real interesting.

"M... Marcy?" he asked, in a breathless weak tone.

* 21 *

I could see Angus weaken as he stood with the rifle aimed towards the Mistress. No more than six feet stood between them.

"I... I don't understand, how could this be? Marcy it's you, it's really you." He lowered the rifle and closed in.

"I'm not that person anymore. It's been a long time since I was the woman you speak of," the Mistress coldly stated.

Angus began to plead,

"You have been missing for so long, my family..." He became delirious with words. You couldn't blame the guy, he'd been carrying this shit around for a long time.

"My children, where are they?" he asked, and lowered himself down to his knees.

The Mistress stepped in and grabbed his rifle. In one movement, she had snatched it away and struck him full across the face. He went down hard to the floor.

From behind the scene came a pair of feet striding loudly. As they rapidly got closer, a sadistic laugh accompanied them,

"Very, very good. Wasn't she just good?" Alexis emerged, and stood with his one hand directed towards me.

"Now one could say this is the penultimate scene of such a tragic play, yes?"

He moved into centre stage and lowered himself down to Pam. She continued to hold her bleeding shoulder as her eyes looked up to him with anger.

"It's okay, I mean no harm. Even I have to admit those were impressive skills you demonstrated out there," Alexis observed, and wiped his finger across Pam's blood stained hand. She protested with a loud whimper.

He proceeded to lick the blood off his finger and then looked up at me. I stood with a stake primed.

"You son of a bitch! You tore Angus's family apart," I shouted, with my face screwing up. "You've kicked a man further down than he could already get." I said, and sharply turned to the Mistress.

I stood between them both with each foot wanting to charge in two separate ways. I still had more to say,

"Not only did you tear his family apart, but what about Caitlyn and Rebecca's?"

"Ah yes. The Turner family. You've been informed I take it?" Alexis questioned, and then not waiting for an answer continued,

"Shame about their Uncle. Edward, I was the one who pushed him into the path of a caved in tunnel. It was wise for me to get rid of any moral compass the ladies had, that worked out ever so well for me, but what about you? Nobody has thought of good old Blake Malone. Just who is Blake Malone?" he asked, never once averting his gaze from me.

"What do you know about me? Nothing," I said through gritted teeth, as Alexis spoke again.

"Oh, but I do. Rolling into town a mere few days ago on a rickety old bus? Then there's the diary Blake, a way of venting feelings and frustrations. But come now, it's time to admit who you are and what this is all about."

"I have nothing to admit. The only thing I don't know is who Blake Malone is. But it doesn't feel like me," I said, tightening my grip around the stake.

"For some strange reason I got a feeling you are at the centre of all of this," I added.

"Excellent, yes. Well done. So, you see that is your way back. A life you were set free from, but there were conditions, objectives even..."

The Mistress stepped between us,

"Enough toying with him; I may be a creature of the night, but my heart isn't fully black," she said, and placed a hand on my shoulder. She came closer and ran her bony fingers through my hair. This woman had a familiarity. Her gaze towards me seemed endearing.

"Does the name Donnie Greene mean anything to you?" Alexis asked, and my mind began to flash back. Bolts of lightning began to course through my mind and with it came the most horrific pain to my right shoulder, a stabbing and then burning sensation.

"There is some response, of course there would be," Alexis said.

"That's the name of Angus's son," I said, trying to shake it off. "The kid who went missing in the forest all those years ago," I recalled, as my head began to feel fuzzy, the shoulder continued to bother me. For a moment, I closed my eyes and Alexis' voice came to me.

"No. Donnie Greene is your name."

"No," I shouted in a pure anger filled rage. With my hand still holding the stake I pushed the Mistress away and barged into Alexis.

My body tackled his and we went down together. Erratically I lifted the stake up and took aim.

'The heart, end him now.'

My arm tensed as I threw the stake down straight into the centre of Alexis's chest. It hit with such force and yet the thing just sort of bounced off. I struck the wood down hard again for a second time, only for it to bounce away out of reach.

"Foolish child," Alexis said, and began to laugh. He revealed underneath his cloak and shirt a grey coloured and somewhat distorted chest. A leathery mass of skin covered his upper torso and right side, the side of his deformed arm. It had acted as damned armour.

"Deformities have to be embraced," he said, as my neck was grabbed and I found myself thrown off Alexis by the Mistress. She forcefully held me down.

"Blake," Pam shouted, and tried to make a rescue only for Alexis to push her back.

"This was all an ambitious and elaborate psychological experiment for the Darke Forest Asylum. You, Donnie my pet project, was an attempt to get Caitlyn back for me. You were my bait and I built a totally new identity for you. Years of work and preparation, just for you to fail at the final hurdle and show us who you really are. You were never worthy to be a vampire and so we used your blood for years," Alexis explained.

"No," I said groaning in defeat, but he continued.

"Freedom is what you wanted and so here you have it, at a price though, I'm afraid. You'll never see your mother again and your tear-away sister. She will probably embrace the same fate as Caitlyn once I have finished with her."

"Caitlyn won't be a problem any longer. Her soul has been... let's say, restricted?" the Mistress said.

"Good." Alexis said, and lowered himself to me. He signalled for the Mistress to stop restraining me and she pulled away as he spoke,

"I've only ever told this story once before. So many years ago I knew a man, a vile, loud and violent beast. He was incapable of nothing more than pure evil. I would eventually escape this terrible malevolent being and find the Heath, others weren't so lucky. I know what it's like to live in fear, and what it is like to be a slave. I watched my own family beaten, whipped and trodden on. All for the gain of another man, a much more privileged man. Like everyone, I once had a mother; the strongest woman I have ever known. Every day she was beaten and whipped in the same place, thrown down with wounds that never healed, but she rose up every time. Her resilience was indeed inspiring and defined her spirit. Eventually the body gives in, and as strong as she was, that final whip came and this time she stayed down."

"And why are you telling me this?" I asked, as Alexis leant closer to me.

"Because I have detached myself from the brutality of humanity..." he glared.

"You're just the same as that man you talk about," I interrupted, as Alexis fully pushed down on me.

"Do you want to know who this man was? Do you want to know his name? He was an Irish man made from pure execrable evil. He took a boy's mother away with a whip..."

"What does this have to do with me?" I asked, as he pushed harder on me. Breathing air began to feel like a privilege, and my hands flailed wildly around. I managed to grip the nearby discarded stake. Then I looked up to see his face as it morphed.

"I'll tell you what this has to do with you, because... this man, his name was Blake Malone." Alexis pushed off me and stood. "And instead of a whip, I have these two sharp teeth."

He and the Mistress turned away from me as I lay there, trying to comprehend it all and take everything in.

I could hear a commotion as Pam struggled with them. Something had me glued to the floor, as I kept my head turned away from it all. The sound of struggling began to recede further away as did Alexis and the Mistress, they had taken Pam. In all the time she screamed for help, nobody once answered her call. My realisation of the real truth had hit home.

Eventually silence ruled as the night time breeze blew across the street. I was cold now and so were my thoughts. How had I ever get to this point? To a reality where I wasn't Blake Malone, but Donnie Greene, missing for years, presumed dead or just forgotten. My own Mother had chosen the life of a vampire over me, and a sister I apparently had. Years of torment slowly flooded back into me, my shoulder ached and I reached in under my shirt to feel bare skin.

On the surface it seemed scarred from a burn, but deeper down the teeth mark scars stretched from the neck line all the way down to my upper arm. Pin pricks from the various sets of fangs that had fed off me over the years. They had almost bled me to death, but that would have been an easy way out. Each time my life had been drained, only for it to slowly grow back. I was whipped down and then dragged to my feet, only to be taken away again by another set of teeth.

The room, with the music playing; it had felt familiar because it was mine. For years, I had stayed there under the watchful eye of them. Plucked from my sleep and taken below, sat in that chair and told what to do.

'Take her heart.'

And told who I was.

'You are Blake Malone.'

They set me up with this elaborate backstory, gave me a trunk full of possessions and planted me on that bus. This whole damn life was a lie.

I could sense movement behind and so my trail of thought drained away. Slowly I twisted my body and got up.

"Son?" a pained voice broke the silence and called out to me.

My vision scanned around until it met Angus. He stood like a defeated man, holding his head and looking at me.

"Son? Is that really you?" he asked, coming towards me.

"Have I been so blind as to not recognise my own son?"

Although it felt forced and not exactly right, I spoke back,

"Dad." I exhaled loudly, and met him. Our arms wrapped around each other. He then pulled away,

"We are quite the pair, such an awful mess this all is."

I nodded to him and looked at the ground. It felt like there was nothing else I wanted to do right now, other than just find my bed and lie there, for all of time. Talk about defeated by the truth. All that 'truth will set you free' talk is just bullshit, man.

"What happened?" Rebecca asked, as she somehow came to. She looked all around and then at us.

I shrugged and looked over to a motionless Caitlyn.

"Sister," Rebecca cried, and hurriedly moved next to the fallen Caitlyn.

"What has she done to you?"

"She said something about banishing her soul?" I said, instinctively.

"No! Caitlyn can you hear me? She's in a state of shock," Rebecca said, and hurriedly took her pulse.

"Heartbeat is regular, she's just not there." Rebecca clicked her fingers in front of Caitlyn's open eyes, watching her intently as she lay there looking up at the black sky.

"The Mistress has done this. The only known way to break a Soul Restriction Spell is to kill the caster," Rebecca said, looking up at Angus.

"My wife. You can't…"

"We may not have a choice, Mr Greene." She shot up and came closer to us.

"What about this cure? If you cure Marcy of being a vampire, will that be enough?" Angus pleaded

"Not sure. This soul stuff is beyond me. I have only ever brought back my soul and one other, and both times the building almost fell down," Rebecca explained.

"That girl they took? She was powerful, maybe she can help, but for now I need to get Caitlyn inside. Splint?" Rebecca said as he appeared.

"What happened, man?" he asked.

"You were down and out throughout yet another spectacular fight. Come on, help me get Caitlyn downstairs," Rebecca instructed. She and Splint lowered down to pick up Caitlyn.

They shared the weight of her and lifted. I didn't even watch as they carried her away. Angus gradually followed, as I continued to stare at the floor.

"Are you coming, Blake?" Splint asked, as he and Rebecca stopped.

"I'm gonna sit this one out," I said, and turned away. My feet began to walk me away from the scene. I had to escape from it all.

"There we have the typical demographic Caitlyn goes for. Just going to walk away," Rebecca said in disgust, as they went in the opposite direction.

"Son?" Angus stood between the two departing groups; between them and me.

"We need you. I need you," he said, as I faced him.

"Your little sister is out there somewhere and Pam. She's been taken."

None of that seemed to matter right now. I was in defence mode and just needed to be away. I placed a hand on his pained shoulder. My face gave him the best look of defiance I could muster.

He nodded. Sometimes you don't need to say anything to say everything. His face looked back at me and he understood.

Either that, or he thought I had given up.

"I'll go and make sure she's alright. I know you like Caitlyn." He slowly walked backwards and spun away.

"God, I hope Pam is okay," he said, as he walked towards the bar.

"So do I," I said, and went the opposite way.

The final play seemed imminent, and yet there I was walking back to the dugout and bench. My hand was still clenched around the wooden stake as I headed up to the apartment, my only safe haven. To the place where only a few nights ago I'd spent with a girl who'd brought me so much wonder and mystery. Thinking of that time was a comfort, as I knew when I closed my eyes, all hell was coming my way.

The nightmares and flashbacks were coming thick and fast, now that everything had been made apparent, and I was in fact Donnie Greene. My consciousness wanted sleep, just to get all the information out in the open and have a good clear out. Then I could move forward, maybe even think about saving the day.

My body seemed to fall back in slow motion as it landed on the soft bed. The strong grip around the stake released and it hit the carpeted floor. My body slept, but my mind woke up. Vividly the sleep became deep and almost inescapable.

Memories unlocked of that night, the first night that I had led my sister towards the rotting wooden door of Darke Forest Manor.

The magnetic force drew me there from such a distance. A feeling of nothing but enticing comfort possessed me to go through that doorway. My sister couldn't feel it, she wasn't old enough then. I looked down at her, and for one last time I tried to put a name to her. The memory felt blocked, and so I passed it and into the Manor.

"Help me, Blake!" The loudest of voices shouted out to me, the volume rocked the world I stood in. This can't be, surely? I was standing in a memory, how could something new enter into it?

"You will stay here with your mother," Alexis said, as he appeared behind me. He stood in that ancient brown cloak cradling my mother with one arm.

"Don't listen, Blake. Just run," the voice cried out again, pleading with me to leave.

"Where are you?" I called back, looking all around.

Alexis instructed a nearby shadowy figure to lead me away. A veiny hand reached out, but I stood firm. The hand pulled and suddenly I gasped for air as I watched an image of my younger self walk out of me; he just took the hand and walked away. As I stood and watched, the realisation hit me, I wasn't living this memory I was just viewing it, a ghost amongst the shadows.

Time must have moved on an inch or two, because soon enough my sister came through the door led by our mother as she followed Alexis up the stairs.

"Come. You shall both stay with me," he said.

"What will become of her?" my mother asked.

"Whence she becomes of age, we will sire her also. For now, you are to protect her," Alexis said, as his voice trailed off up the stairway.

So that was it, the moment we went our separate ways; my mother and sister were to be vampires. I on the other hand had been taken to the cells of this asylum.

"Blake, just run from here. You don't need to relive any of this. Time is running out," the voice interrupted again.

'Caitlyn.'

"But where are you?" I called back, searching all around. I was standing in the candlelight of the Manor hallway.

"Outside. Come outside. Get away from there."

I turned and headed out of the old wooden door, and this time I passed straight through it. A bright flash knocked me forward, my feet stumbled but I managed to stay upright. Abruptly I heard from inside the house sounds of distressed struggling.

Once again I entered the house, but this time two vampires dragged someone forward. Looking closer, it was me; I was a few years older.

The cellar door was open as they tried to take me back down, but quickly I broke free and tried to make a dash to the door. Realising it wasn't possible I threw a hard punch out to the nearest vampire. Man, I used to be feisty.

Alexis appeared and literally walked through my ghostly body and to my younger self. He grabbed my neck and with one hand and lifted me.

"Disobedience will get you nowhere," he said, through gritted teeth. His hand released me and I was thrown backwards.

"Although we can influence certain traits out of your personality, Blake."

"My name is Donnie," my younger self said with that adolescent know it all tone.

"Would you both take 'Blake' downstairs? It's nearly treatment time," he commanded as the two vampires pulled me away.

"No!" I screamed, and watched as my eyes grew wide with fear. My escorts were too over powering.

"My sister, where is she?" I begged, as they dragged me down the stairs.

Alexis followed. "You have no sister, Blake. This is a hospital and we are here to take care of you."

I shuddered as the cellar door closed.

My shoulder started to ache as I realised what they had done to me down there. A combination of vampire torture and brain washing to ensure that I believed I was someone else.

"Blake, please..." she shouted out to me again.

I had seen enough of these memories. It wasn't hard to put it all together after that. The whole 'Darke Crusader' thing had simply been added to my persona to make things more real. Angus had made that up to stop people coming to the Heath, and Alexis had simply used it against him.

"I'm coming, Caitlyn. Where are you?" I asked, as I headed out of the house again. This time I wasn't going back in. Then, all the control I'd had in that one moment was lost and the very ground I stood on gave way.

In a flash I had fallen, only to find myself standing down inside that cellar again, shackled to the chair with my shirt off and a collection of scars all along my shoulder. Watching it all unfold. made me realise how much older I was now.

"Who are you?" Alexis asked, as he stepped out of the shadows. He wore that dirty lab coat.

"I... I... I am Blake Malone."

"Yes, very good. The patient now knows his own name. Excellent progress," Alexis said, looking towards the direction in which I found myself watching. There were others there as well, but I couldn't make out who they were.

"Now, Blake. What will you do?" Alexis asked.

"Steal her heart," I said, in a trance-like state.

"Very good. Then you will bring her to me," Alexis added. He looked towards where I stood again.

"He's nearly ready." Someone stated, and stepped forward. The soft female voice spoke,

"What about his scars?" she asked. A dark patch seemed to block the sight of her head out. I stepped forward to see her better, but no matter what angle I stood at this mystery girl had no identity.

"Who are you?" I asked, and waved at her. It was no use, I was a ghost after all.

"I will find a suitable way of covering up his... blemishes. Now please, leave us," Alexis instructed, as this girl turned and headed away.

What was it about her that stuck out at me? And her voice, I'd heard it before when I'd crouched down by that window of my room. She had come past. It was definitely her, the same woman. My only conclusion was that she had to be my sister. There was no real way of knowing though.

"Now this may sting a little."

I watched as Alexis dropped a flaming torch onto my shoulder. The scream I let out echoed throughout the cellar as my own shoulder burned in shared memory.

The bastard had covered up the years of teeth marks by burning my skin.

"As soon as he has healed, we shall unleash him to the world..."

"Blake, please!" Caitlyn shouted from high above. I wasn't going to stick around to witness any more of this torture, and so I ran. This time the surface appeared, and then the forest.

Now it was dawn. The sun was about to rise and all around it was still.

"You have to run to me." Caitlyn shouted, but I was already sprinting.

My feet seemed to cover miles in a matter of seconds. Trees flew past and Caitlyn continued to call out. The forest sloped upwards and then I came to a road. On the opposite side and down another slope stood a shadow, again she held something bright to her chest; much like that dream from before.

"My soul has been restricted, Blake. You have to help me," the shadow that was Caitlyn begged.

"How do I help? I'm no witch," I told her.

"You can work it out. Please help me," the light she held began to fade. Her heart was dying; she was becoming a pure vampire again. That was all we needed right now.

I turned to my right and there stood Caitlyn again but bathed in a brilliant light. She wore a dress from all those hundreds of years ago and smiled at me.

"Caitlyn." I said.

"Here we are. Both of us having been through so much," she murmured.

"How do I help you?" I asked her desperately.

Caitlyn continued as if it wasn't an issue.

"Maybe it's each other that we have in common the most," she reached out to take my hands.

Then it came to me. Her heart, maybe it didn't mean a physical heart, but her figurative heart.

Perhaps in all of her long life she had never found anyone to hold her heart. Maybe, just maybe love was the key that could set her soul free.

Before I could come to anymore conclusions everything faded to black.

The dream was coming to an end, and I was about to awaken.

Part Four : The Vampire Apocalypse of Darke Heath

* 22 *

My aching shoulder led me out of the deep sleep and into that comforting feeling between dreaming and wakefulness. I knew that I was lying there, even as the images continued to flow in front of me, the forest surrounding the unfolding scene. Alexis stood opposite me; my arch nemesis. If anything was going to happen, even if it meant I was going down, then he would be too.

My eyes opened and my consciousness became one with reality again. A cold sweat covered my forehead and the clothes I slept in were drenched. The question remained, how long had I been out? Slowly my rested body rolled off the bed and reached towards the world dividing blinds.

Sundown. My final figure of hours sleep sat very much above twelve. Maybe the best sleep I've had for a very long time. As I looked out at the orange sky, my vision focused down on to the bar.

Wooden boards covered all surfaces that were once glass. Jesus, the place looked shut down and derelict. As I was about to turn away and plan my next move, bright flashing lights approached and quickly shot past the apartment. For a brief moment

299

Darke Heath looked like a completely different town; an alternate version where the vampires had won and by sundown Hell had become a reality. Unknowing to me then, that was the theme to come.

I will briefly mention the hot steamy shower and burnt pop tarts before some clothes got thrown on, then I headed down. Again I had opted for the leather jacket over hooded top combo, with the stake now firmly rooted in my jeans back pocket. It was time to face what the world had made Darke Heath into since last night.

The sound of loud voices came from Angus's office, or should I call him my father? Either way it didn't feel right. As I approached he saw me and got up.

"Hey, Sport. Good to see you're finally up. How goes things?" he asked, seeming reasonably chipper.

"Better now after some sleep, I guess."

He then stopped listening to me and tuned into the radio playing. We caught the news reader talking,

"...Heath General Hospital, where they say their Emergency Department has had an influx of new admissions throughout the day. The town has never seen it this crazy before. Many of the patients coming in are all suffering from the same type of injury, that being of abrasions or cuts to the neck and shoulder area. Police are advising…"

"The whole town has gone to shit," Angus said, as he turned the radio down.

"Neck or shoulder area; bites," I said, as Angus nodded and sat back into his large office chair.

"This is bad. Caitlyn isn't showing any signs of improvement and now the town is rife with those blood sucking folk. Might be time to get the rifle and shoot our way out of this. Martial law style," he said.

"Where is everyone?" I asked.

"Rebecca is at the hospital, snowed under by all the admissions. She's a Doctor before anything else; taking down vampires is just her sister's calling apparently. She did spend most of this morning looking through old books mind; couldn't find anything to help her sister though. Splint, he's watching Caitlyn and there's still no sign of Pam. If her parents call, I don't know what I'm supposed to say."

"I'm gonna head over there. See what I can do," I said, and looked down at Angus. "Maybe there's something I can do," I added.

"You be careful out there. I know it's a short walk but it'll be dark soon," Angus lectured.

"I should be okay." Plus, I had the stake if anyone came too close.

Out I went into the crisp evening air. The fading orange sky above would soon be black, and who knows what would come out then. The smell of pine gave me some feeling of familiarity from my initial arrival here. Then I remembered that it was all a lie.

Was there anything that I could really do to help Caitlyn? My mind decided to throw me this curveball just as I was about to cross the street and head around to the back of the bar. This wasn't some fairy tale crap, and true love wasn't gonna move shit into our advantage. What could I actually do to help?

Instead I forgot the question and began to walk along Main Street whilst contemplating my thoughts. There was still a lot to think about, and so I did, with both hands in my pockets I just walked.

Soon enough my legs brought me to Darke Heath Town Hall, it was an old building held up by large stone pillars. The place originally designed by old man Turner and apparently before the days the vampires were unleashed upon this place.

I parked myself on the stone steps as more flashing lights and blaring sirens zoomed past. Another police car came and went and the whole mood of the Heath just felt aggressive and toxic. It appeared my fear for my life was only exceeded by my fear of losing Caitlyn; a love which had become painfully evident by my desperate need just to see her again.

'She looked like a damn angel in that dream.'

My story was beginning to intertwine with love. From what had begun as just a kiss with a stranger had grown into so much more; maybe I had a purpose now after all: Caitlyn.

Damn, it got dark around here quickly.

What was I doing just mulling it over? Go to her man, and tell her how you feel. This whole thing started with me being sent to steal her heart, truth is from the moment she kissed me on night one, she'd had mine.

As I stood with a purpose and place to go, a forceful push planted me back down.

"No. Stay," a demonic vampire face stared down at me. His blond hair and razor sharp features resembling much of these night creature types. Two hollow hungry eyes stalking its prey; me.

Instinctively I rolled forward and out of his path. I then realised another face stared at me with that same hungry passion. This one was a red-headed woman, and just as sharp featured as her counterpart. From near enough nowhere this couple had appeared, both dressed in leather jackets and tight denim. Piercing fangs were waiting for their next pound of flesh. I swore,

"Not mine, and not tonight."

"He's a fast one," the guy said, and stamped at me as if he were charging. I didn't flinch as the woman did the same.

"He shows no fear," she remarked disbelievingly.

"Stupid mortal. Shouldn't be out after dark in this town. Especially now as there's no Slayer Sisters to protect you," the guy added.

"Are you gonna talk me to death, or are you actually gonna do something?" I menaced, as my grip tightened on the stake in my back pocket.

Neither of them liked my wit and within an instant of talking he charged. Instead of pulling out the stake I took a page out of my younger self's book and threw out a punch. Screw him and these vampire pricks; I'm getting me some action.

My feet stepped into the hit as I struck the well-formed cheek. Anger channelled itself through and powered a punch I was proud of. Unfortunately for me, this seemed like a mere pat on the face for such a strong and dominant creature. He simply tilted his head in interest and seemed to wait for more.

As I pulled out the stake I was pushed to one side and the red-head charged with a primeval voraciousness, her urge to suck my blood was undeniable as she came at me teeth first, like a wild blood thirsty beast. No hands, just all gnashing teeth.

Even to my novice skills of slaying vampires, these two had seemed rather amateur right up until now. Not once had I felt threatened. Using her momentum, I just held out the wooden stake and let her do all the work. The force in which she approached was enough to impale her as the sharp wood broke into her ribcage. She exhaled loudly with a piercing screech as the stake pierced her heart, and the warm bright glow quickly spread as the burning began.

Two worried eyes stared back at me as they disintegrated into dust. The guy's face was alive with fear as he watched his probable love became nothing more than gritty carbon in the breeze. Right at that moment I should have said something, along the lines of a pun or there being a new slayer in town, but I didn't. Sometimes silence is louder than any shout.

"No! You bastard!" Of course, he charged and down we went. Now he was angry and looking for more than just blood.

Up I went as he took me by the scruff. Again, I could have just struck him at any moment, but chose not to. He semi threw me onto the hard-stone steps of Darke Heath Town Hall. Never once did I feel any fear; I mean I did put up my arms in defence but this guy was pissed and strong. Something gave me the strength to think,

'There really are more problems in my life than some Billy Idol look-alike blood sucking leech.'

A bright light closed in on us, followed by the loud revving of a motorbike engine. Before I knew it, the headlight and motor was killed and a shadow closed in; all the time with me still holding this angry vampire at bay, and him struggling to decide what to do with me. That same exhale and sharp piercing scream came as a stake went in through his back and faced me on the other side. It smouldered as his slaying became unquestionable.

A soft glow followed and his body became lighter than air. I pushed him off as he crumbled into a burning assembly of ashes.

I sat gathering my breath as the newly arrived eyes fell on me. Whoever did this had probably saved my life.

"Thanks," I said, and got myself up.

What faced me was a figure all in black; leathers again, a vampire I guessed, and a lady shaped one at that. A motorcycle helmet stared back at me until the figure slowly pulled it upwards. A mass of blonde hair flopped down as the girl revealed herself.

A pair of eyes looked at mine, and her vampirical glare disappeared. Now her face seemed conflicted and sad.

"Brother. It is you. They have been hiding you all this time," she said in a tearful whisper, and moved ever so close to me. Her arms embraced me.

After all these years and everything I had been through, I'd still never forgotten her eyes. That's what directed me to her on that bus. She'd been there for some reason.

My arms wrapped themselves around her. This was an emotional realisation.

"Sister," I whispered into her ear.

"I had no idea who you were. The truth has been hidden from me for so long. I can only remember from the night they sired me..."

"You don't have to explain. Memory problems run in the family," I said. My voice immediately calmed her erratic speaking.

"Do you remember me?"

"My past is kinda patchy at best," I told her.

"Call me Susie. From what I have heard this past night, you are my brother."

"Blake, I guess. The whole Donnie thing isn't sitting right with me."

She gently withdrew and looked up at me.

"Nice bike," I said, breaking the silence.

Susie began to smile and softly wiped her eyes.

"Dammit my eye liner is gonna run."

"We've all got our problems," I added, and cracked a partial smile.

"Like the rumours. Are they true about the Slayer Sisters, are they gone?"

"I wouldn't say gone, maybe incapacitated. Caitlyn is anyway," I explained.

"Caitlyn, the one Alexis obsesses over."

I nodded in agreement.

"This town. It's becoming overrun with vampires. Alexis is getting his way, he has to be stopped," she said, looking out at the night sky. More sirens could be heard in the near distance.

"How about our mother. She's pretty close to him..."

"The Mistress? She can burn like the rest of them," she interrupted. Her face shifted at the mention of our mother.

"My conscience has only just come to terms with all of this. I didn't know you were my brother. I am truly sorry, Donnie. Blake," she added.

"I didn't know until last night either. How did you find out about me?" I asked.

"Last night when they came back to the house, they had some girl with them," Susie said.

"Pam."

She nodded and continued,

"They took her down to the cellar and are doing who knows what to her. This must stop. After hearing about you Blake, I had to get away from there. You break a vampire's heart and they regain their conscience, that's how I see it anyway. Well, the guy I loved and who sired me is gone now. Some people came out to the house a few nights back, he didn't make it." Susie clenched a fist in anger and then looked up at the black sky again.

'Greg I presume, yeah, uh... sorry about that.'

"They sent me out with you to make sure you arrived here on that bus. That's why I probably looked like I was giving you some kind of weird eye. No more though. A vampire's life is no life," Susie added.

"You know, there is cure for what you have. I'm sure the sisters could spare one for you, and maybe even our mother. She is family after all," I said.

"Family, huh? And what about our dad?" Susie asked.

"Angus? he owns the Workshop. Alexis blackmailed him into being an errand boy for years." I lowered to take a seat on the steps, and she followed.

"The man with the green truck... that's him? There's so much I don't know," she muttered.

"Same."

"I've been running around town trying to clear up this mess. The Sheriff's department is overrun; people are being sired left, right and centre," she added, and at that point I stood up.

"That's real noble of you to help out, Susie. Caitlyn told me that most vampires have no conscience, I guess you found yours. No asshole gene for my sis. That's what she called it, and that's why we need to do something about it," I said, feeling a reminiscent fondness for Caitlyn.

"Even in vampirism blood runs thicker than water, Blake, but if we don't do something soon the whole town is going to be engulfed by vamps."

"Come on. Time to meet your old man," I added

"Then what?"

"We try and snap Caitlyn out of whatever spell our mother has cast on her; something about a soul restriction."

"Witch stuff? Great," Susie said drily, as we headed towards her bike.

"There has to be some kind of spell to counter the Mistress," she added.

"Either that or something else," I said.

"Get on." She got on the bike as I perched behind her.

The engine echoed loudly through Main Street as we took the short journey back. From a distance, we could both see something was happening at the bar.

"What is it?" I yelled into Susie's ear as she lifted her visor. She slowed the bike and spoke back.

"Looks like vamps and amps," she said, and then we saw fire.

As we cautiously approached, we could see the bar had been taken over by a mass of people and that some of them had dragged away the large boards covering the smashed-out windows. They threw them onto a fire in the middle of the street.

"The Darke Bar is open!" a shirtless man shouted as everyone roared in unison. Some had clearly got to the booze already and begun to drink leaving their faces marred with a glare that was hungry for blood. A few even had blood stained mouths.

"This is getting out of hand. Splint is gonna be pissed. Head around the back, and we can handle this later," I said, and pointed for Susie to bank right.

The bike veered across the street and we turned away from the riot conditions that had taken over the bar.

"Through here," I instructed, as the bright headlights filled the alley behind the bar.

She killed the engine and we coasted forwards. I stepped off as she parked the bike.

"What about meeting Dad?" she asked.

"We'll have to put that on hold for now. Right now Susie, I have some business to take care of. Come on. It's this way." I headed towards the steps leading down to the apartment.

"You love her, don't you?" Susie added, as she took off her helmet.

I stopped in my tracks and turned to her.

She placed the helmet on her bike and stepped my way.

"I can smell it on you." She placed a hand on my shoulder and smiled.

"Sucker," she added, in that playful childish tone.

"She has become something that I need," I said, and turned in a way that could only be described as heroic.

"She might even have some eyeliner for you to borrow," I joked, whilst going down steps.

"Hey, is it that bad? I'm paranoid about it now," Susie laughed almost piling into me.

We stopped dead in our tracks, staring in horror at Caitlyn's apartment door standing wide open.

"No!" I shouted, and began to run forward.

* 23 *

With the gathered demographic having taken over the bar upstairs, I feared the worst for Caitlyn, and whoever happened to be in the apartment at the time.

I walked in to see the place a mess. My eyes moved erratically in all directions urgently scanning the kitchen surfaces with their books sprawled out all over, some still left half open. The fridge stood slightly ajar, and then there was the shelving where most of these books had lived, many now thrown to the floor; all the tell-tale signs of a panic and struggle.

Maybe I had been selfish to walk away from all of this, or perhaps I was just too damn late and this story had moved on without me. Self-reflection was something that I had needed along with sleep, and in doing so I had let this happen. Crap.

Susie followed me into the apartment and quickly pointed to the sofa.

"Splint?" I called out to him. He lay there face down unmoving, his one visible and bandaged hand stretched out to a book that was standing up.

"Shit." I said, and made my way to him. I looked over to the bedroom area where the archway was covered by a dark curtain. Behind was where Caitlyn must have been hopefully.

As I opened my mouth to speak, Splint stirred and turned over. He was just sleeping. The book he held fell over and clapped shut.

"I think he's asleep," Susie said, whilst keeping back. She looked at Splint in a way that would best be described as passive aggressive.

"Yep, he's out," I agreed.

"What happened in here?" she asked, and took hold of a book.

"I'm not quite sure."

Splint seemed to be fine, so I made my way towards the curtain. From above came a loud thump.

We both looked up.

"The bar is literally above our heads," I said.

"I'll stick around out here. Maybe wake this dude up," Susie said, as I disappeared behind the dark curtain.

Suddenly finding myself plunged into flickering candlelight, I could see the outline of Caitlyn under the dark covers of her circular bed. She lay still and with her eyes closed, her two pale arms resting on top of the silk sheets. To me in the low light she looked elegant and peaceful.

'Her deathbed.'

Caitlyn always seemed to have a stern glare about her whenever she was awake, but now that was gone. An entire peace had taken her over, almost coma-like.

"Caitlyn," I whispered, and sat on the edge of her circular bed.

"I'm here now." My hand took hold of hers, but it was cold to the touch and stiff like she had slipped away. For a moment I feared the worst.

"Caitlyn, can you hear me?" I said, with a rising panic and moved in to gently shake her body.

Although her chest didn't move up and down, I still wasn't quite sure on the whole vampire thing. Did they need to breathe? Was a heartbeat needed for them to live? My fingers pressed onto her inner wrist; I waited for a pulse. It came ever so faintly and in no orderly fashion.

The heart they had started years ago had begun to fade. Nothing more than a less than frequent beat existed there now.

God where was Rebecca? Why wasn't she here trying to help her sister?

I leaned in close and whispered,

"Caitlyn, I am here. Can you hear me?" I asked.

No reply.

"What about now?" My lips softly pressed onto hers, warm touching cold. The dreamer in me wanted her to wake just there and then, but she didn't.

I held her hand again and gently squeezed it. The pale skin that covered her seemed transparent, her life was draining away minute by minute.

"So what do I do now?" I asked the empty room. Defeated, I moved away with my head in my hands. "You know, there isn't much I remember ever wanting in my life."

I spoke as if she could hear.

"It's funny because my memory has been messed with more than I actually know. But there's one thing I can remember wanting above all of this; someone like you." I turned in hope that she could hear me.

Her body remained motionless whist I stood rooted to that position. Absolute fear came over me as I accepted this girl had met her fate, and was slowly slipping away.

"If I knew how to save you I would. You know that? Because ever since that night you kissed me, you've had my heart. Hell, you can have the damn blood in my veins as well," I said, and leaned forwards staring at the floor.

For some moments, I'm not sure how long; I just sat there and trailed away lost in my thoughts. Maybe I should have gone back out to check on Susie and Splint, leaving them alone for so long could have dire consequences. Instead I stayed anchored to the spot, and then after a couple of deep sighs it suddenly clicked; my brain was struck by the lightning of thought.

'Blood. She's a damn vampire, what do you give a vampire? Blood.'

As I burst through the curtain Splint shouted,

"It's you from the forest! You and that chump tried to take my wheels. What do you want?"

Susie stood in the kitchen area as Splint glared her way. He rose shakily and began to approach her with that heavy-footed chest out threatening lurch.

Susie's face rapidly morphed as she braced for a brawl.

"Whoa! Splint, she's with me, man," I shouted, as he came within swiping distance of my sister.

He looked over to me and then did a double take. A confused frown flashed mine and then Susie's way.

"She's on our side," I added.

"Okay," Splint said slowly, and then scanned the apartment.

"We're just letting every damn biter in off the street now?" he asked.

"Well, maybe if you thought of closing the door before you decided to take a nap, we wouldn't have this problem." I said, as Splint backed away from Susie; her face slowly morphed back to normal.

"Some of us have been up all night trying to save Cait," he snapped back, and dropped back down to the couch.

"This your girlfriend?"

"Actually, I'm his sister," Susie said.

"You know anything about soul restriction spells? There's just nothing in any of these stupid books to tell us what to do. I mean what do you give a vampire on her deathbed?" he asked, and threw the book back down in disgust.

"Blood," I said, and my feet stepped towards the shelves. I grabbed the two books which handily concealed the handles.

The shelves pulled forward and revealed the well-lit cupboard behind. A range of weaponry, crucifixes and all kinds of stuff hung on a white glass backdrop.

"What are you doing man?" Splint asked.

"I'm gonna give Caitlyn what she's been lacking for quite some time," I said, and grabbed a curved dagger.

Susie and Splint followed, they looked warily at each other as they walked side by side. Before I headed back into the bedroom I watched as Splint spoke out,

"Maybe we should put that encounter we had back in the forest behind us. No hard feelings about that vamp we slayed. He was your fella, right?"

"If I hadn't lost him, then my eyes wouldn't have been opened to this situation. You did me a favour," Susie said, and nodded to him in solidarity.

"I'm glad you could both have this moment, but it was me that took him out, so I'm claiming credit for the slay. My first to be precise," I stated, and began to push through the curtains.

"It may have been a favour, but I didn't say I was happy about it," Susie said.

"Well I'm your older brother and I know better."

They both followed me into Caitlyn's bedroom.

"Do you wanna explain what you're gonna do with that blade?" Splint asked, as he watched me perch next to Caitlyn.

"Just watch," I said, and pulled up my jacket sleeve. Hesitantly I offered the blade to my own flesh.

Just above the crease of my elbow, I knew it wouldn't take much. Looking away I was about to swipe when Splint shouted,

"Don't do it, man."

Suddenly the curtains burst open and Rebecca appeared, she stormed my way.

"What is going on? Who are you?" she glared at Susie.

"And what are *you* doing?" she then demanded from me.

"I'm gonna give Caitlyn what she needs," I said, and stood with the blade against my under arm. In one slow swipe, I sliced myself. The electric shock of pain seared through me.

"Oh man." Splint turned away. "That's hard-core man."

"This is all a tad extreme, don't you think?" Rebecca asked, as she tried to come close.

"Let me take care of that," she added, and grabbed a small medical kit that sat on the dresser.

Susie just stared and remained fixated on my blood.

"Don't get any ideas," I warned her, and held out the knife for her to take.

"You probably shouldn't give that to me," she said, and Rebecca took it away.

"All your sister has ever wanted is to have someone she could give her heart to. Well she can have my heart, and blood if she needs it," I said powerfully, and turned to Caitlyn.

I extended my arm out and offered it to her. The blood trickled out and down my elbow. Slowly it began to drip onto her lips.

"She hasn't had blood in over thirty years..." Rebecca said, trying to interfere and then it happened.

Caitlyn's nostrils flared and she took a deep breath. Her eyes opened. From a peaceful sleeping face she transformed to full on vampire frown. Then the pain really set in as she opened her mouth and two long fangs clamped down onto me.

"She's awake," Splint said, as everyone looked on in shock.

I could feel my own blood being sucked; it gave me a kind of woozy feeling, like my own life force was being taken from me. It took some effort to pull her away, but I did after Rebecca helped. She wrapped my arm in gauze and as she began to dress the wound there came a growl from Caitlyn.

Her eyes stared into my soul. She looked at her sister and tilted her head.

"We'll give you guys a moment or two. Don't give her any more blood," Rebecca instructed, as she took steps back and away from the bed.

Splint and Susie followed her through the curtain and then we were alone. Perhaps not the ideal situation to be in as a vampire stared me down, my arm oozing fresh blood under the gauze.

Her hands reached up and took hold of me. In one sweep, I was flipped over and pinned down onto the bed. She looked down at me through her primeval eyes.

"Caitlyn," I said. "It's me."

She took hold of my arm and easily plucked the gauze away. Her hands began to shake as she tried to resist the bloodlust.

"I am alive," she said, and clenched her fist. The muscles in her arm tensed, veins bulged as she began to come back. She reached down to my hand and pulled it to her chest. It was warm to the touch and I could feel a pulse.

"You feel that?" she said in a typical Caitlyn tone.

"You're back," I said, as the room began to shake. Candles fell to the floor along with anything else that sat on a surface. Caitlyn held out both arms wide as a bright light appeared around her. A white mist appeared and as she opened her mouth, it entered into her.

"Her soul! It is returning. Stand back!" Rebecca shouted, as she stood with Splint and Susie in the archway. However, I was left pinned to the bed as the transformation began to happen.

The mist diminished as it entered through her mouth; it hit her with such a force she was thrown off the bed. A flash of light filled the room for a moment, and then came the silence.

I lay there still as anything, not sure what to do.

"I heard everything you said, Blake," Caitlyn whispered from the floor. She immediately stood as I did and we met at the foot of her bed.

Her face resumed back to normal. There she was in a nightgown opposite me.

"All I have ever wanted is someone like you, as well." She said, and held out her hands. I took them and our grips entwined.

"We are both victims of this. We are together in this."

That was the epic moment we sealed our love with a long impassioned kiss. My arms moving themselves around her.

"I have never tasted blood like yours," she said withdrawing. "It's hypnotic."

"Thank you." Again, her lips locked with mine.

"You're welcome," I said, as she pulled back and smiled.

From behind the curtain came a loud throat clearing cough. That was when the three appeared.

"Sister," Rebecca said.

"It's me. That Mistress is powerful, but she's going to meet her match tonight," Caitlyn said, and then glanced over at Susie.

"The legendary Slayer Sisters? I have heard stories of you both? I'm on your side," Susie said.

"Good to hear, because tonight this all ends. What is that noise?" Caitlyn asked as she looked up.

"The bar is kinda open," Splint explained.

"Well, not by my choice, but Susie here says they just helped themselves." he added.

"Guess they are first then. Let's gear up." Caitlyn strode out of the bedroom. She approached the open cupboard and went straight to a concealed compartment. After revealing a key pad, she entered a code; a loud unlocking click followed.

After a clunking hiss the two shelves opened wider and slowly revealed an opening. The shelving had actually concealed an entire room. It resembled a command centre with gym equipment and a racking shelf system. There were workbenches and countertops, all of it decorated with the same white glass and elaborate lighting.

"This is going to be a battle. So, we are gonna need everything we've got," Caitlyn said, and headed into this futuristic looking space.

I stood with Susie as she stared up at the small fridge. It contained five syringes of half red and half white liquid.

The cure.

"Is that it?" she asked.

I nodded.

Rebecca opened the fridge door and a plume of dry ice came out.

"We take these with us tonight. Cure who we can. Blake and Susie, priority is your mother. Come this

324

way," Rebecca ordered, and we followed her into the room.

"For what she has done, I say let her burn," Susie said, causing Rebecca to turn. "She's behind most of this," Susie added.

We came to a central table most of it taken up by a large grid type map of the Darke Heath. Much of it had been annotated with writing and directions.

"You guys get the same decorator as batman?" Splint asked, as he took hold of a large sharpened crucifix.

"Back when we had a crew, we put these quarters together." Caitlyn stood admiring a display case.

It contained an outfit similar to the gear she would normally wear, but this version was lined with a type of armour and padding. A fresh purple coat hung complete with elbow pads and strengthened body. Next to it were dark red jeans, also padded and accompanied by a long sleeved top. A pair of metal lined heavy duty boots sat at the bottom.

"I haven't used this outfit in a while," she said, and opened the glass case.

I noticed a much smaller box mounted on the wall nearby.

Inside this container, and divided by glass, was a severed claw-type hand. The flesh had begun to dry and peel as it fell off the long bones. A range of long rusty nails kept it pinned to the wooden board.

"We'll save that for another story," Caitlyn said, as she noticed me looking up at it.

"Let's just say there are more than just shadows lurking in the darkness of those trees," she added.

"What happens when you take the cure?" Susie asked, as Rebecca placed the syringes in a strap. She moved onto the racking and took hold of a long rifle.

"The patient is fully cured of vampirism and the soul returns there and then. It is best to administer it in the neck, the same place where vampirism begins in a host." Rebecca placed the rifle down on the table.

"Using this dart gun means we don't even have to be close," she added.

"What about Alexis?" Susie asked.

"Alexis..."

Caitlyn interrupted her sister,

"Alexis can burn. I say we all take a cure and that leaves one for your pee shooter there."

"If I take them all then there is no chance they could get lost or end up in the wrong hands," Rebecca argued.

"Yeah, I don't do so well with needles," Splint said. He took hold of a dark football style helmet and put it on.

"This fits just right," he added.

"Maybe she's right," I said, not warming to the idea of holding a cure. I wasn't the most responsible of people.

"Look. I say we give out cures to who wants them. Me for one." Caitlyn took the strap containing syringes and unclipped one. She handed it to me.

"Blake. Use it on whoever you think would benefit. All you gotta do is pull the cap off and stab. The syringe will do the rest. I take one and Rebecca keeps the rest for her rifle. Now it's time to stop the vampire apocalypse of Darke Heath," Caitlyn said, and grabbed her purple jacket.

24

"We've prepped for both amps and vamps upstairs," Caitlyn explained, as she put on her final layer of armouring. She stuffed her trusty stun gun into a pocket and spun a varnished stake in her hand.

"Something gives me the feeling that the whole amp barrier has fallen down. We're gonna be facing vamps mostly," Rebecca said, as she appeared from behind the shelving. She stood in a similar jacket with armouring as her sister, but in the colour of dark red. She held a large crate in her hands which she set down on the table.

Splint instantly closed in and took out a varnished stake.

"Everyone take a wood and a sparker," Caitlyn said. She handed out stun guns to both Susie and me.

"Splint, can you be trusted with such a device?" she asked, as Splint snatched it away.

Rebecca then pulled out a strap filled with green glass tubes.

"Garlic gas, good for crowd dispersal and disorientation of vamps, not so good with amps. Blake and I will take a supply," she said, and threw the strap my way.

"What about crucifixes?" I asked. Susie helped me with the strap and clipped the buckles together.

"Crucifixes are only effective if they contact a vamp. We tend not to take them out with us as they are bulky and generally a pain in the ass to carry. Vamps can't touch them either," Rebecca said, as she took the one Splint had found.

"I don't mind bulky," he said, and pulled it back.

I concealed the stun gun in my jacket pocket and kept hold of the stake. Something told me I would be needing it more. In my back pocket was the other stake; a spare and probably needed at that. Alongside it sat the syringe, the cure, and my only target was Alexis. Take away his vampire life and then his human life.

We were ready to do battle. Both Caitlyn and Rebecca were our leaders, the Slayer Sisters; then there was Splint, the clumsy mad man fighter, his look was completed by the wild looking helmet he wore; then came Susie, the leather clad blonde vampire and my sister.

I stood feeling like the weak link of the crew.

"What's the play?" Susie asked.

"It's closing time at the Darke bar, time for the locals to settle up and get out. Everyone thought the world was going to end when the millennium came last year, but now it's gonna end for them. It's all just fragile lives and shattered dreams," Splint said, as he cradled the large crucifix.

"Exactly. We'll head out to the front and take down whatever is up there. Then we move on to the trees. Any questions?" Caitlyn asked, but she had already begun to move out.

"Do you think maybe I could get a little more armour than a strap of garlic gas?" I asked, but nobody answered.

We came out into relative darkness and followed the walkway forward, loud voices and the rowdy nature of the bar could be heard from around the back, so up the steps we went and to the back area of the bar.

"This your wheels?" Splint asked, admiring the bike that belonged to Susie.

"Oh yes," she said.

"Nice. A vampire with taste. That's new."

Caitlyn turned back and glared at Splint momentarily.

"What about vehicles?" I asked, knowing the Mustang was behind the nearby garage door.

"We come back for them afterwards. I don't want to announce our arrival," Caitlyn ordered, and we followed her out towards the street.

My stomach began to knot at the site of facing so many vampires. Although I was in good hands, this still didn't bode well. A hand gripped my shoulder,

"Stick with me. We'll get through this," Susie said, and we hung back behind the others.

The Slayer Sisters marched forward with determination, while Splint followed behind; he held his crucifix to the ready. They turned into Main Street and we followed just as flashing blue and red lights shot past. Blaring sirens filled our ears as two police cars screeched to a halt. They had arrived at the scene.

Four uniforms got out wearing armour and carrying shotguns, and yet none of them advanced anywhere near the bar. By now the fire in the road had become an inferno. Surrounding it and heading into the bar were scores of shadows; some with their primeval glare turned towards the arriving officers.

Over a bullhorn came the shouting orders,

"Police: Disperse immediately."

"Let's see how this pans out," Caitlyn said, as we dropped back into the gloom.

A few straggling vamps began to approach the police cars, just as the officers stood behind their open doors ready to fire.

"Stay back and disperse. Hands where I can see them, I won't ask again..."

And like that the four officers were mobbed. A shotgun fired up into the air, as teeth sunk into an exposed police officer's neck. Blood flowed as the mob of vamps tore these men apart.

"Damn savages," Splint said, and spat on the floor.

The mob had taken over the situation and pulled the officers away. They were heading for the large fire.

"We can't let them do this," Susie cried out, and we began to advance forward. I had no choice but to follow.

Splint decided to make a dash for the police cars; he made it and ducked down. Then he did something none of us appreciated or could have predicted. He jumped up onto the car bonnet and then onto its roof, in his hand was the bullhorn.

"Hey, is this thing on," he echoed towards the vampires.

Some of them dropped what they were doing and looked up at Splint. He was cradling the large crucifix in one arm and the bullhorn in the other. Static screeched in reply as he offered the microphone to the grating of his helmet.

"I'm curious to know who I am dealing with here..."

"What is he doing?" Rebecca asked, as she shook her head in disapproval. We all hung back and watched the vampires turn their attention to this madman standing on a police car. In the flickering light of the flames eyes stared up at him; lips licking at the sight of another fresh body filled with blood.

"Who here is with Alexis? You know, creepy guy lives out in the forest. If you could just raise your hands?" Splint asked, as the nearest vampire jumped up onto the police car bonnet.

The stalking vampire slowly raised his hand and then came a demonic smile. From all around came laughter as the creature eyed Splint in front of his audience; one step and he would be on the car roof.

Splint chose to remain and laughed visibly,

"I get it. Class clown. There's always one," he said, as the vampire stepped up onto the car roof.

In flash move Splint charged forward with a head-butt. His solid helmet sticking out as it struck the vampires head. He pushed the crucifix forward. The cross pressed against the dazed creature and smoke began to rise as it connected with vampire flesh.

His spectators reacted in anger as the burning vampire screeched and dropped to his knees.

"Anyone else here with Alexis?" he asked, but continued speaking before anyone could answer.

"Last orders at the bar was yesterday. So if you blood sucking assholes don't mind, would you be so kind as to get your ugly asses out of my goddamn bar? Get my drift?" and he drove a foot into the downed vampire.

"Nice to see you have taught him well, Sister. Tactical as always," Rebecca grinned.

"He's more of a self-taught type of guy," Caitlyn smiled back.

Vamps began to charge towards Splint who showed no signs of fear, and as another stepped up onto the bonnet, he swung the bullhorn and clocked the vamp over the head.

"Plenty more where that came from," he shouted and swung out again.

"Guess we should probably help him," Caitlyn suggested, and we ran forward into battle.

The attacking vamps mobbed the car as we charged. Caitlyn and Susie lurched forward; their warrior-like ability to fight didn't go unnoticed, while I just kind of held back with Rebecca.

"I'm way too old for bar fights," she said, with her stake primed.

Soon enough the car had become overrun and surrounded. Splint held his rooftop haven and kicked out at anyone who got near him. Susie made a successful job of pulling some vamps away as she pushed them into an open space where Caitlyn stood ready; both of them in unison plunging stakes into vamp chests.

The brightness glowed as the burning began, their victims turning to dust.

It would take an eternity to drag every vampire away from the car, and with no way to get to Splint, I had to do something.

'The garlic gas: used to disperse large numbers of vamps. Perfect.'

I pulled the glass tube from my sash and took aim.

"Fire in the hole," I shouted, and threw the glass tube forward. My gut instinct was to get Caitlyn and Susie away, so I gripped them both and pulled. They followed as a large cloud engulfed the car including Splint.

We watched as Rebecca charged forward and into the thick green cloud. Many of the vamps became entangled in the gas as she made easy pickings of her prey. Her stake came down in quick succession on to many of her targets, lighting them up as bright sparks before bursting into clouds of crumbling dust. In an instant, she had made her way through to the car.

"Maybe give me a hand, Splint?" she asked, as Splint dropped to one knee.

He offered a hand out and Rebecca grasped it. With a pull she scaled the car just as the green gas began to clear.

"Come on. We'll work the bar," Susie said, as she led Caitlyn away.

They dashed around the police cars with stakes at the ready. The numerous mobbing vamps didn't see them slip past, as they covertly slayed their way into the bar. Then came my moment; as the mob dispersed one particular vamp came my way.

She shook off the garlic daze and discovered me standing there.

Her teeth were primed as she pounced. My grip tightened around the varnished wood. This was it. Time to enter the battle.

I screamed at the top of my lungs as the stake surged into her. There came a flash, and then a cloud of ash softly fell over me.

"Take that," I shouted, as a rush of adrenaline engulfed me. Easy.

'Come on, Blake, you can do this.'

I moved forward towards the crowd, my arm arched, ready to strike. Another came my way and quickly the stake turned him into dust.

Rebecca and Splint worked together making short work of dragging their victims up to be either bashed with the large crucifix or staked, or both.

"We're kinda cornered here if you get my drift?" Splint shouted, as I looked on. The mob separating us had left me helpless towards their situation.

"I'll say," Rebecca replied, and then she reached a hand out towards the large fire; with a dragging motion the flames flickered brighter.

"I'm no Fire witch, but I'm not afraid of playing with matches!" she shouted, and a faint trail of burning embers began to move. The orange glow formulated out of the main burning fire and grew stronger. As its strength grew, it headed snake-like towards the vampires, surrounding them at floor level. Flickering heat crawled closer until it reached the first vampire.

Like fast growing vines, this veined finger of burning fire wrapped itself around the legs of a now screaming demon. The flames cut her and others down swiftly as it burned stronger and brighter. Smoke filled the air and an unpleasant musk of burning flesh hit me.

"Like the flowers of the wild; make these flames rise," Rebecca commanded, as she waved her arms around powerfully. The trail of burning did a series of laps around the car leaving anyone who'd been standing nearby to be abruptly taken by the flames. Some of them were immediately fully engulfed, whilst others just had their legs taken from them.

I could feel the heat as this endless trail of flames grew higher and higher. The dancing embers licked at the police car, and then it became clear that

337

Rebecca had lost control. She threw her arms down, an effort without any reward.

"Look out," I shouted, as Splint took hold of Rebecca. They would have been next on the burning list if it wasn't for him. They jumped off the car just as flames engulfed it.

For a moment, I thought the worst.

Keeping my distance, I ran around the other police car, as flames caught another vehicle. All the while my feet darted over the various half burnt bodies of slain vampires.

Relief spread through me as I saw Splint and Rebecca slowly stand up and appear unharmed.

"Fire is the most difficult to work with," Rebecca said apologetically, as she looked towards me in terror.

It was then I fell forward. I struck the ground with such force everything jolted to black momentarily.

An erratic and blood thirsty vamp flipped me over, its rabid teeth loomed as a face of pure malevolence stared down at me.

"Oh shit," I said, trying to move the arm that held a stake, but it was pinned down by a strong grip. A demonic smile came my way as the vamp began to lean down and seal my destiny.

My saviour came from the unknown. Not in the form of anyone presently there, but from the crack of a rifle. The bullet struck the vampire clean in the face. He smashed backwards, leaving me with the realisation that I was saved.

"Huh?" I said in a panic, and got up. My instinct was to drive the stake deep into this writhing demon and so I did. I looked up to see a shadow emerge from the Workshop.

Angus stood with his rifle aimed forward. A jagged length of wood was lashed to its smoking barrel.

"You seemed to be in some trouble, son. Thought I could lend a hand," he said casually, and then aimed the rifle past me. Again, he fired at another straggling vampire. "Time to clean this place of vermin," he said, and this time Splint made the final slay.

"Dad," I said with meaning for first time in a long time, my breath still short.

"It's okay, son. Stay by me and we'll get through this shit," Angus said.

He walked onwards with that older man type of roll and stoop, his rifle firmly aimed forwards . Then another charging vamp came and this time Angus stepped in to meet his attacker using the jagged length of stake to drive it straight into the heart.

"That's a sure bad ass looking rifle," Splint said, as he and Rebecca joined me in following Angus.

"Stay close, son," Angus said to Splint as he held out the crucifix.

From behind came the wild battle cry of an approaching amp. He quickly stalked Angus and closed in.

"I got equipment for your types as well," Angus said, and spun on his heel. He flipped the rifle to reveal the butt had something attached to it.

The amp had no time to react as Angus stepped in driving the butt of the rifle forward. A bright spark flashed into the face of an amp and he fell back.

"Shit, that's badass man," Splint admired, as Angus faced the scene again.

The vampires noticed the flash and so he aimed upwards. The crack of fire echoed through the street.

"You'll be clearin' out of here right abouts now, if you know what's good for ya," Angus shouted.

The remaining vampires began to disperse at the sight of this man who had taken everything from their blood sucking ways. Rebecca stood alongside him and threw out a garlic bomb.

We could see Susie and Caitlyn had made short work of the bar's inhabitants. They stood waiting for us as we cleared away the final vampires, most of which had fled into the night.

Angus remained on guard until both Caitlyn and Susie had changed from vampire back to human. That was when it hit him,

"Susie…" he said, and stumbled forward whilst becoming breathless.

"Dad?" They looked across at each other. Angus visibly weakened at the sight of his now adult daughter.

Without introduction both of them knew who they were to each other.

She sprinted towards him as he let go of the rifle. and Rebecca stepped in to catch it.

"My baby girl, what have they done to you?" Angus asked, as he reached out to Susie. She embraced him like a child.

"Daddy, I'm fine. I'm here," she said, keeping him upright. Her hands softly placed themselves either side of his face.

"You're beautiful. Just like your mother," Angus said, as he did the same with his hands.

"I'm just a vampire, is all," she added.

"But there's a cure, Right? Doctor Turner?" Angus turned and looked to Rebecca.

She nodded.

"She's more useful as a vampire right now," Caitlyn casually observed as she wiped the blood off her stake, then realised it was pretty much broken from all the constant slaying.

"Useful? This is my daughter," Angus said, protectively.

"And he is your son. He's been through a lot, worse than me. Trust me, it's better I stay this way for now," Susie said, looking at me.

"She's right. We've got more chance in a fight with her like that..." From a distance came the large thud of an explosion which interrupted me. The ground shuddered ever so slightly as we looked around in all directions.

"This damn place has fallen to hell." Angus took back his rifle and kept his head bowed.

"So let's do something about it," Caitlyn said, as she threw her stake into the large fire. "Most of the vamps are headed back to Alexis now. How's about we mop them up on the way," she added, and looked straight at me.

"And so comes the final battle. Guess I'll go and get the Mustang," Splint muttered.

"No, you leave that here. We'll go in my truck; it's already beat up and right now if I get my way with Alexis, I don't much care what I come back in," Angus said.

"Are you sure about this? Are all of you sure? It could just be me and Caitlyn that go, it should be us," Susie said.

"I've waited my whole damn life to get that son of a bitch. If it be the last damn thing I do, I'm going with ya. They took Pam, an innocent kind hearted girl who harmed nobody. Now come on," Angus growled, as he headed back towards the Workshop.

* 25 *

The recurring theme of my backache continued as I found myself sitting in the back of Angus' truck; the metal rattling and vibrating under me whenever we passed over a pothole. Next to me Splint perched whilst cradling the blood covered crucifix. In the partial light, I could only see the outline of his helmet. Neither of us spoke as the streetlights zoomed past.

Rebecca pulled the elder sister rank and rode in the passenger seat while behind us I could see Caitlyn holding on to Susie as she rode her bike. That way, if there were any straggling vampires, they were together.

We were heading out to the trees. It would end right where it had begun for all of us; at that house. I insisted on a plan that saw me go ahead and try to get Pam out first, before any other attack was made. With Splint's supervision, I would make my way into the house. After all, we'd got in before, so there was no reason why we couldn't do it again. Splint would help me get inside and then head back to the others and if they didn't hear anything after five minutes, then the attack would begin.

Again, came that strange magnetic feeling of being drawn towards the trees, it was clear that something in this forest was off.

Now that I knew some of the story, anything left to the imagination was just pure terror; stories of those twisted creatures, screeching through the night and being able to turn people into their own kind, followed by the blood sucking tirade that came afterwards. This whole story was a complicated mess intertwined with the past; a past I longed to forget.

The girl was mine if I survived, that was always the way in the old-fashioned stories of redemption, it came part of the deal. My thoughts became distracted as the truck slowed down and I could see we were heading towards the town limits and the hill. There suddenly came a brightness followed by an intense heat.

We watched in horror as an apartment block stood in flames, with not one sign of the fire department or any other help on the way.

"Jesus this town really has gone to hell," I said.

"There's only one way out and that's gonna be up," Splint muttered, as the truck slowly climbed the hill and away from the heavy glow of flames.

Susie revved her bike loudly, an indication for the beaten truck to go faster and so it did, with me and Splint jolting forwards and backwards as gravity insisted on being present.

"You got that cure ready?" Splint asked me.

I dipped my hand into my back pocket.

"Still intact," I said, with Splint's helmet nodding.

"Who's name you got written on it?" he asked.

"Straight up, I don't know. I wouldn't mind giving Alexis a piece, just so I can take him out as human," I said.

"I get ya drift. I think everyone wants a piece of that guy." Splint slowly moved out of his perch and leaned against the green metal.

"Nice night for it either way," he observed, and looked up at the clear sky. Moonlight shone down on us as we came closer to our tree filled destination.

Angus sped the rattling dented truck past the trees swerving erratically, causing Splint to jolt across to me. I grimly held on to the dark green frame of the truck as it weaved around a straggling group of shadows.

"Vamps," Splint warned, as he looked out into the road.

The headlight from Susie's bike turned as she and Caitlyn prepared to take down the stragglers. We left them behind, much to Splint's complaint.

Angus slid open his back-cab window,

"They'll take 'em out and loop back to us. No need for the whole group to go riskin' life and limb for a few stragglers," he said.

"That'll give you two time to find a way in and get this Pam out," Rebecca agreed.

"I'm not warming to the feeling of leaving anyone behind," Splint said, as the headlight dipped out of the horizon's view.

I didn't like the concept of leaving both my sister and Caitlyn behind either, but they were both vamps so I reckoned they could handle it.

Soon enough we had made it through to the Forest Road turn off point.

The brakes squeaked as Angus brought us to a slow stop; he banked right and off the road we went. We went from being under a canopy of moonlit stars to a canopy of shadowy branches; the silhouettes of a thousand bony hands spreading out above us. The moonlight trying its best to break through, but instead of creating light it only cast unforgiving shadows that could be either creature or tree.

Tyres crunched over the fallen twigs and stones as we ventured further along the beaten path laid out ahead. Here the trees were thicker and concealed every speck of light from the outside world.

As I've said before, you've never known true darkness, not until you have faced the Darke Forest, armed not only with weapons and cures, but the darkness of your past. An urge to carry on through that blackness and know that the light will be there somewhere on the other side. Well that was my hope anyway.

Gradually the truck went down and then over a small hill, a sign that we were nearly there. Splint thumped on the truck for Angus to kill the headlights and slow down. He did. Then the truck pulled over to one side and edged down an inclining bank.

"We're off the path here, and you gotta be lookin' hard to see us. I say we park it here and you kids do what you gotta do," Angus told us, as he killed the engine.

"Let's move out," Splint said, and a faint figure of his shadow hopped out of the truck.

As I came past Angus's door he powered on the cab light. He held out a hand to me and softly gripped my jacket sleeve.

"Be careful out there, son."

"I will," I said, and headed out towards Splint's moving shadow.

As I caught up with him, he stopped. Both of us glanced up towards the old Manor, candlelight was flickering inside the front windows.

"We've been here before," I said quietly.

"Follow me. We take the same route as we did last time and hope that the window is open," Splint said, as he set off again.

"I got a feeling it will be. It always is. That's Alexis's way. You can climb out anytime you like, but you can't leave," I said.

"Ah right, Hotel California. Cool reference," Splint added smiling.

We came closer to the house. This time we had no care if anybody saw us. In fact, I wanted confrontation now that I'd had a few slays in me, it gave a certain rush. I held the stake firmly in my hand; Splint cradled his crucifix.

The long grass surrounding the old Manor was freshly moistened as we trailed through it, and again we turned the corner to see nobody around. The window stood in plain view, and open. I stopped and looked out into the black, before me would have been where the Darke Forest Village had stood before it collapsed and caved in.

"Come on man," Splint said, as his arm gripped my shoulder. I jumped slightly as I'd been lost in my train of thought.

"It's open. Ready to check in?" he asked, and crouched down to give me a leg up.

I slipped the stake into my back pocket and obliged. My hands wrapped themselves around the peeling wood as I hoisted myself inside. From climbing in I could easily see that the room wasn't occupied.

"Any sign of Pam?" Splint asked, in a loud urgent whisper.

I leaned out of the window and shook my head.

"You should head back. I'll find her and get her out. Go," I said, and turned back to the cell-like room.

"Okay man, I'll tell them you're in. The clock is ticking son," Splint said as his voice trailed off.

I stood strong and forced my brain not to flash back; the bed in which I'd spent so much of my time recovering from the severe blood loss and torture. The computer given to me with the intention of being reeled in by the 'Darke Crusader'.

'Shake it off Blake and go find Pam.'

From above me I could hear creaking. Upstairs, somewhere I had never been. Trying to be as light as possible on my feet, they took me to the slightly open cell door. With a stake held in my tense hand, I opened it to discover an empty hallway. Through the shadows I went, past the various cell doors, some of them now open, unlike before.

Perhaps Alexis had unleashed his worst upon the Heath. Hopefully Caitlyn and Susie were mopping them up as I as I made my way through the Manor, every now and then stepping on a creaky floor board.

The old wooden panelling of hallway faced me, only this time I recognised some of the paintings and portraits. One particular man stood out; his look was astute and upstanding, a Lord of the Manor perhaps? Or even Edward Turner, the man who had perished not so far from where I stood; in the cave-like tunnels beneath the ground.

I began my ascent up the old creaky stairs, its thinning carpet softening my footsteps until I reached the summit. Flickering candlelight cast shadows along a dark hallway and lit up the nearest door facing me. Without so much as a single step towards this entrance, it began to creak open.

Shit! Was someone coming my way? I froze in an idiotic looking stance, only to realise that a light breeze must have opened the door ever so slightly as I felt it blow back towards me. Wood gently knocked on wood as the gap into the unknown thinned.

Phew, but still this was tense. I stood in unfamiliar enemy territory and at any given moment a carnivorous beast of a person could emerge teeth first. That's why I had the stake held firmly in one hand as I placed the other flat on the door.

My hand pushed it open and the bedroom revealed itself to me.

A four-poster bed took residence within the middle of this square room, with the various odd half melted candles placed on to various surfaces. An overpowering smell of old, damp and rotting decay assaulted my nostrils. Still I moved forward towards the occupied bed. A head of dark hair lay resting as I approached.

'Pam.'

Her head faced away from me and into the thick shadows. A prominent double puncture wound dominated her neck. They had already got to her, and now she slept until morbid immortality came.

"Pam?" I whispered, and placed my free hand on her arm. She was ice cold to the touch.

Any moment that head could turn towards me and a set of demonic eyes would look upon me and alert the others to my presence. I tried to distract my thoughts to something else, but I was drawn to the vampire-like glare of Pam, even though she didn't face me.

Something looked at me, and I had an overwhelming realisation; even with the candlelight there were shadows in every corner of the room, and I wasn't alone.

The human psyche does interestingly weird things upon being discovered. I stood there feeling their eyes upon me from the shadows, and yet I simply continued as if I hadn't been discovered.

"Pam, are you awake?" I said, my voice sounded different to me, as if I were acting.

My eyes stealthily searched the room without moving any other part of me. Where are you, you sneaky bastard?

The faintest creak came from behind, and with my fingers wrapped around the stake I swivelled with all my might. Only the darkness faced me, until a voice came from a darkened corner.

"Your efforts can only be commended," Alexis said, as he came forward and I faced him.

A hand then gripped my shoulder and I turned to face the Mistress.

"He managed to hold his temper for around ten seconds," she said.

I tried to lash out and fight, but something kept me from moving. My arms hung rigidly beside me; as a last resort I tried to speak, but even my spoken words failed me. This overwhelming force paralysed me as I stood there, unable to control even my own physical being.

"It's nearly feeding time for this one," Alexis said from behind me, and in the corner of my eye I could see his white lab coat on the bed.

Off all the words I wanted to say, nothing came out. The desperation must have been etched into my face.

"You always were cute when you were angry," the Mistress laughed, and as she walked away my paralysis lifted. My arms were mine again and so were my words. Just as my lips opened and my feet prepared to charge, a blunt force struck the top of my head.

All I remember from that moment is going down on to the floor and my shoulder preventing my head from impacting on the carpet. Then it went dark.

* 26 *

As my eyes opened, they ached from the powerful glare of the tripod lamps shining down onto me. My wrists were shackled and my shirt was ripped across my scarred shoulder. They had kept the jacket on me and I could still feel the pocket with the stun gun inside. The dry musky smell I knew all too well and had now become synonymous with the pain which faced me; feeding time.

Behind me, I could hear the humming of electricity from their various 'medical' devices they used to amp people, then I realised that Pam was standing with her back facing me. Voices came from beyond her, I could just make out it was Alexis and the Mistress. There seemed to be some level of uneasiness in their tone and then they all turned to face me.

"Ah our host is awake," Alexis observed, as he approached me.

"You remember the drill, don't you? Now you must bear in mind that our project to let you off into the real world has failed miserably; your job was to bring Caitlyn to me…"

"Bullshit," I said, and spat on his white coat. I had nothing to lose anymore. He paused for a moment and then turned away.

"Denial only puts us back to square one." I watched as he came back. The bright lights glinted off something he held.

"I remember everything Doctor, and I have been told some other stuff too. Right now I just choose not to think about it," I sneered, as his concerned face stared back at me.

"Denial is not something we do not encourage our patients to immerse themselves in Blake," he said, and stepped closer.

"And again, bullshit," I said, only this time reserving my spit.

"You kept me here a prisoner and as part of some kind of weird project to feed your sick fixation of Caitlyn," I added, just as he began to lean into me. Then he stopped, and I spoke again.

"You named me to avenge someone you never could; a name that belonged to someone else, not me. Using the name Blake now is because the time I spent as Donnie was wasted being your prisoner. My family were torn apart because of you. Caitlyn's family, the same…"

"Enough!"

Then the searing pain came as Alexis slowly dragged a scalpel blade across my scarred shoulder. I screamed in agony and my arms tensed. The shackles seemed loose for a moment as pure pain took over. A slow emergence of dark red liquid oozed from the slice. My own blood lay open to a trio of vampires.

"There is much to do tonight," Alexis said. He moved to the equipment rack and unhooked something. "For we are not only going to use your blood, but we will also be testing the extremity of my equipment." I tried to move away as he stuck two cold probes beneath my jaw line. He then placed a firm grip on my exposed shoulder. I retched in pain as he turned to Pam.

"You must feed now, then your siring will be complete," he said.

As she noticed the blood trickle from me her face morphed. She twisted her head and spoke,

"Do not worry, Mr Malone, the pain won't last. You must remember my power needs feeding," she said, and held out her hand. A purple aura surrounded it for but for a moment.

Alexis moved away and inclined his head towards me. In the background the Mistress continued to watch without any trace of my mother inside of her.

Then came a noise; a loud shattering crack from above, both Alexis and the Mistress instantly turned and looked up.

"Guests?" he asked, and headed towards the stairs. The Mistress followed him and up they went, their footsteps trailing to the stairs and away.

As soon as they had gone, I tried my best to reason with the looming Pam.

"Pam, look it's me, Blake. You don't want to do this," I pleaded, as she moved seductively towards me. Two long white fangs revealed themselves as she came closer.

A gentle purring came from her mouth as I insistently pleaded,

"No. Stop..."

A piercing agony rocked through me. A combination of adrenaline and pain flowed from my shoulder as I almost jumped out of the chair. Then the shackle on my left wrist snapped.

I was free, and with that realisation my hand gripped Pam's hair. With all my strength I pried her from my flesh and pushed her back. She stumbled back as I frantically freed my other hand.

"Playing hard to get won't work with me," Pam licked her blood-soaked lips.

I threw up a foot and kicked out hard as she came forward. This time she fell back on to the wooden floor.

"Mr Malone, this will only end badly for you."

I reached into my back pocket and tried to get out the stake, but however hard I pulled on the wood it wouldn't budge, the damn thing had got caught in the denim.

'Dammit.'

Pam pushed me and I had no choice but to fall back into the chair. This time she climbed on top of me and held one hand down against my chest.

"Maybe I'll just have myself a snack right here, and the rest later," she drooled. A drop of my blood fell from her chin as she moved in. Her small hand rigid with strength, I was pinned.

Shakily I reached into my jacket as the searing pain of her teeth clamping onto me became inescapable. My own blood was being sucked as I took out the stun gun. There wasn't long to decide, it was either jolt her now and possibly myself, or have my life sucked from me.

My fingers gripped the stun gun as it slipped out into view. I took one look at it before saying,

"Pam, I'm sorry."

She pulled away and looked directly at the flash as I drove it into her neck. Somehow in a miraculous turn of events the shock never got to me, but it took her down.

Pam jumped back and crashed into a nearby tripod lamp. It went over and smashed to the wooden floor, with the glass bursting into a thousand pieces. I saw sparks spread out in all directions. All it would take is for one of these to contact some dry flammable wood and the place would burn.

My wishes were answered. Underneath the lamp a cloud of smoke began to form. I could see that Pam lay far enough away not to be harmed and so I stood up. Looking around one last time, I never wanted to see this place again, let it burn.

I pulled off the two cold probes that had been stuck to me and threw them towards the equipment they were connected to. The wiring looked like a damn death trap, and all it would take is for the right short circuit in the right place.

As I turned to look for something a fist struck me. It took me by complete surprise as Alexis stood with an angry vampire glare. I stumbled away and managed to pull out the stake.

"This is not how it's supposed to happen," he shouted, and looked over to see Pam discover a small fire had started by her feet.

"Whoever put you in control of my destiny is wrong. I'm taking it back," I shouted back and stepped in.

With the stake wrapped around my fingers I threw out a fist and connected with Alexis's face, the wooden point scratching against him. He groaned as the wood sliced along his cheek, his whole body lowered down in defence and that was when I dropped my weapons and grabbed his white lab coat.

Using the adrenaline fuelled 'live or die' strength inside me; I swung both my arms that gripped Alexis. He stumbled forward and the momentum sent him straight towards the racking. His destiny consisted of being the short circuit that would blow his equipment sky high, and so I released my grip.

From slow motion to fast forward, he went without any control straight into the racking and faced a mass of sparks. I turned away, but in the corner of my eye he continued onwards as the equipment tipped over and fell into the cave below. A blast of smoke and sparks rose up as he, and everything else, crashed down below.

The basement was then plunged into a powerless darkness, the only light came from the now spreading fire that had begun to fill the wooden floored area.

"Rest in peace. Son of a bitch," I said, and headed for the stairs.

Not once did I look back. Smoke began to rise up the stairs behind me as I climbed. My breath shortened as the door faced me, and then from below came an echoing plea,

"Mr Malone? Come back, I only want to talk, it won't be so bad. You can be like me," Pam entreated, her set of feet quickly climbing the stairs.

I burst through the door and back into the candlelit hallway. For a moment there was silence, then a deafening crack of rifle fire filled the hall. Instinctively I ducked and moved forward. The front door had split into several pieces as another loud rifle shot came from outside. Bright lights shone in, presumably from Angus's truck. This was it, the final attack.

Shadows emerged from behind the brilliant light outside, they came and stopped at the threshold. I watched as from the stairs came the ghost-like movement of the Mistress. She floated down the stairs at speed and with a piercing scream.

"Get away!" she shrieked, and stopped dead at the foot of the stairs. A burst of energy streaked out from her and towards the shadows that stood at the door.

"Get down," Splint shouted, as he pushed Angus out of the doorway. The burst of energy struck him and he smashed back away from the house.

"I banish you all from this Manor," the Mistress screamed, and threw another burst of energy out of the house.

"Honey? It's me," Angus said, and appeared in the doorway again. His silhouette held out the rifle.

"Please. This has to stop," he added, and came closer to the now silent Mistress.

She lunged forward and grabbed the rifle,

"No!" She cried, and pulled Angus into the house. She powerfully turned as he kept his grip on the rifle.

Angus was thrown to the floor when she let go, the rifle landed a distance away. He didn't move.

"No! Stop. Dad?" Susie shouted, from outside.

"Daughter? Where are you?" The Mistress called, as she stepped outside.

I crawled towards Angus; he started to come around as I helped him up. We slowly headed away and into the shadows.

"Why do you defy me, daughter? Why don't you fight me?" The Mistress demanded.

"Because your fight is with me." From behind us Rebecca appeared, she had got in through another entrance. In her hand, she held a ball of light.

The Mistress floated back into the house and screamed in anger at the sight of Rebecca. There they stood, at either ends of the hallway when the cellar door burst open. Pam appeared between them and immediately caught wind of what was happening. From both her hands came a brilliant purple light.

"This woman is an intruder in our house. She must be destroyed," The Mistress commanded in a powerful voice.

"This house will destroy you all," Rebecca replied, and looked at Pam. She threw the ball of light away and held out both her hands towards her.

The Mistress replied with her two bony hands held out, and the two witches wrestled with an invisible force between them. As they inched closer to one another the house began to shake; picture frames on the wall wobbled and eventually fell. The whole world seemed to vibrate as these two powerful forces headed towards one another.

Pam stepped in between them and raised both her hands. They tensed into fists as she screamed,

"Stop!"

Both Rebecca and the Mistress abruptly stepped away and their forces diminished.

Pam stood and glared at the two witches standing either side of her. Inside her anger grew and the house shook and rocked more than ever.

I watched as two more shadows came towards the front doorway. They moved with a steady quickness, one of them approaching the Mistress.

"Mum," The first shadow pleaded, it was Susie. "This has to stop," she added as her Mother turned.

Her bony hands clasped onto Susie as a red glow surrounded them.

"You have betrayed me daughter..."

An exhaling scream abruptly filled the air as the Mistress lost her glow and grip. She stumbled backwards as a bright light surrounded her.

I realised Caitlyn was standing with the dart gun aimed at her; the syringe still poking out of the Mistress's neck.

"Marcy," Angus shouted, as he limped to her. He caught her and stopped her from falling as a mist enveloped them both.

"We would have loved to see what was going to happen here, but business is business as they say," Caitlyn remarked, as she stepped closer to Pam.

"Pam, now it's your turn," she took out a syringe and loaded it into the dart gun.

"I am too powerful for your potions and cures," Pam intoned and dropped her head, suddenly she became swathed in a purple light which seemed to encase her.

"Sister, now!" Rebecca cried, as Caitlyn took aim. She fired the dart and a short burst of air hissed towards Pam. It bounced off the purple shielding and fell to the floor.

"You cannot defy me. All of you," Pam shouted in a demonic voice, as her arms spread out. A burst of energy cut through everything it touched. Luckily everyone ducked. Wood panelling became engulfed in smouldering embers and the ragged carpet was quickly scorched away as her burst of power swept along the floor.

Steadily she left the ground and floated there.

"My power cannot be tested," she said, and ceased the burning.

There was a call from the front door and standing in the white headlight beam was the outline of Splint, complete with his helmet.

"Pam." Without fear or hesitation he stepped towards the looming purple light that encased her.

"Who is this mortal who speaks to me?"

"Pam. It's me Splint."

"The man that I like?" Pam said, as her feet touched the floor. Slowly her glow faded.

"I came here with the others to rescue you," he added.

"Splint?" she said, as if those words had never been spoken. Her hands reached out to him and he grasped them.

"I am here for you," he said, as she pulled him down to her height.

I leaned over towards Caitlyn as she looked at me,

"This could either end really well or really badly," she whispered, as we all watched.

Pam looked into Splint's eyes through the helmet he wore.

"Will my noble Knight known as Splint reveal himself?" she asked, as Splint took off his only protection.

"Come on, Pam. Let's get out of here," he said, as she pulled him in closer.

They kissed, or she kissed him I guess.

As they began to withdraw Splint held up his clenched fist. He thumped it down into Pam's neck.

She screamed in fury before pushing Splint away. Then the same bright light flashed, that had had appeared over the Mistress.

"Yeah, man. It's happening," Splint shouted, as he stumbled back to his feet. As he stepped towards a now weakened Pam, her legs buckled. Instinctively he caught her and went down as well, he managed to retain some grace by taking the fall for her as she landed on top of him. The mist that surrounded her disappeared into her mouth as her soul returned.

I stepped out of the shadows with Caitlyn, my arm and shoulder felt thankfully numb and dead by this time. I held a stake in my hand, but then came the realisation; I no longer needed it. My grip released as it fell to the floor and rolled away. The stake just kept going back and disappeared into the shadows.

"Blake," Caitlyn said, as she looked at me.

I stood weak and ready for her embrace, but it didn't come. All around everything seemed to slant backwards. After a thunderous snapping sound my whole world was sent crashing and tumbling backwards.

* 27 *

The very foundations of Darke Heath Manor must have collapsed by the great heat that was generated from the cellar depths. From what started out as a small electrical fire, eventually burned the dry wooden support beams into weakened charred embers. This, combined with the hollow cave underneath, made the whole thing slip easily into the ground.

This happened as we all congregated after what appeared to be our great victory.

Much like the village collapsing way back when, the house was now heading the same way. I was too far down into the depths of the ruined house to make it out.

Splint however had by now carried Pam out with Rebecca hurriedly following. Angus had managed to drag out his reunited wife, and so that just left me looking up from a rather deep chasm that had opened up under the house. Susie and Caitlyn's whereabouts, I still didn't know.

Smoke bellowed upwards making my path to safety unclear and treacherous. The house ruins seemed so far up, I couldn't imagine a way to safety. My fate had been swallowed whole by a house that had tormented not only me, but several souls for generations.

I shakily stood on a slanted floor made of ripped carpet and snapped floorboards. My lungs were filling with smoke and so I had to get out of its cloudy path. Using my only good arm and shoulder I pulled myself up, and as I climbed a hand came down to meet me, at first it flopped, but then sprung to life.

The sleeve that was connected to it was shredded and charred, remnants of a white lab coat made me realise this wasn't someone I wanted to help me.

A demonic face stared down at me as Alexis's hand gripped mine. He hauled me up to his level and pinned me against the earthy root filled wall. Dirt crumbled away as he pushed me.

"Look at what you have done. All that I have created now destroyed. You are just a weak shell of a man," he snarled.

"Now you shall face the flames." He dragged me away from the safety of the dirt wall and towards a steep looming edge.

Below me most of the charred remains of his cellar lay. I could see shards of jagged metal and sharp wood projecting their deathly fangs towards me. From where I stood nothing could survive the drop, and so I was pushed towards the ledge.

My feet flailed on the loose gravel, it was all the difference that stood between me and solid ground.

This was really it, the last two days flashed before me just as Alexis's insistent pushing ceased; from arriving at the Heath on that old bus, to meeting Caitlyn in a bar; from stealing a kiss in the darkness to fending off some amps; I relived it all in seconds.

I suddenly came to the realisation I was about to shuffle off this mortal coil when something happened. Up from above a leg swung down and crashed into Alexis's head, and he fell to the side and away.

Caitlyn dropped down and faced me; she was covered in dirt, and like me looked like hell. She pulled me in close and away from the ledge. Alexis rose up, his clothes dirty and his face covered in ash. Again, he came my way.

"Caitlyn, my love. You have returned to me..."

"You... you will never represent anything like love. This man does," Caitlyn shouted back, as she held on to me. "You never deserved me and you never deserved to be a vampire. For that I take it away!" Caitlyn let go of me and charged. In her dirt encrusted hand was a syringe and with a firm grip she plunged it into Alexis' neck.

For a moment he didn't react, before his whole body unexpectedly jolted.

"What have you done to me? I am more creature than man..."

I stepped in and threw out a hefty punch. My fist connected into his face just below the eye and he snapped back into the dirt. Cloudy mist surrounded him just as the dirt gave way.

Caitlyn and I watched as everything near him fell into the cavernous depths.

"Quick we need to get out of here," Caitlyn said, and reached up. She took hold of a rope with one arm and wrapped it around herself. I ran to her and gripped it. She yanked on it twice and within a moment we were pulled up just as the ground gave way.

The whole house seemed to fully collapse as we emerged at ground level and finally saw the forest before us. With my last glimpse down, I was just able to make out Alexis falling away into what I felt was an appropriate grave.

Susie, Rebecca and Splint held the rope firmly which was anchored to Angus's truck. They pulled until we were clear of the now cavernous crater that stood where the old wooden Manor house had been.

My grip remained around Caitlyn as we lay on the soft ground. She looked at me and smiled,

"It's over, Blake."

As we both got ready to stand, Rebecca and Susie came over to help.

"Did you get him?" Rebecca asked to her sister.

"Well, I've got no more syringes left, so that's a yes," Caitlyn said.

I reached into my pocket and took out mine.

"Still got mine," I said.

"Keep it," Caitlyn added.

We walked away from the scene and towards Angus, who now stood with the fully restored Marcy. I looked at them both; two people who had been through hell. I almost collapsed at the very sight of seeing my parents again. Luckily Caitlyn was there to prop me up and I embraced both of them for the first time since I could remember.

"Our son, I am so sorry for this," Marcy said as she put her arms around me. She then realised Susie stood nearby and called for her,

"My daughter," she said tearfully.

I withdrew and went back to Caitlyn again.

"You get your family back, even after all of this. Good work for a guy who only just turned up in town," she said.

This would be a perfect place to stop telling my story and roll the credits. Everyone had endured their conflicts and there was even some resolution. Pam had got the man she liked and they sat attached to each other. My parents were reunited after so many years and the Slayer Sisters looked down into the smoky abyss where their home had once stood.

What an ending, but it wasn't. I have come to learn that you should embrace the unexpected, it rules over us all.

This wasn't over and from the giant hole that stood in the Darke Forest there came a piercing screech. The culprit emerged, looking less like Alexis and more like what was left of Alexis just before the moment he was sired.

More creature than man burst out into the night. Wearing rag-like clothes, Alexis stood hunched like the wild creature he now resembled. Both Caitlyn and Rebecca were stunned into immobility as this man with a claw-like hand swiped at them. A hand that had been dormant for years now seemed more animated than ever. He grasped the syringe that still protruded from his neck and discarded it.

I watched in fear with my feet rooted to the ground as this beast came our way. He closed in as Angus reached into his truck for the rifle.

It all happened too quickly to fathom. As Angus took hold of the rifle, Marcy stood between him and this creature. It looked back peacefully into her eyes for just a moment, then cocked its now weirdly formed head and tried to speak,

"If I can see you... They can see you!"

The creature lunged with his razor sharp clawed hand. The talons disappeared for a moment into Marcy and then protruded out the other side where Angus stood to catch her.

He screamed not only for her, but in pain as the claws had exited her and pierced him. They both fell to the floor. My life began to move in slow motion.

Splint had jumped up and run towards the creature with his crucifix.

"No! You bastard!" he shouted.

Everyone panicked as this bloodthirsty creature screeched at the top of its lungs, before disappearing into the trees. Its damage inflicted.

The Slayer Sisters ran to help as I stood by watching and not knowing what had even just happened.

My mother lay covered in blood, dead instantly. My father collapsed with several serious puncture wounds in his abdomen.

The last thing I remember about that scene was the huge searchlight which shone over us from the arriving helicopter above.

As dark as that forest could be, nothing seemed blacker than how this had all ended.

* 28 *

Some hours had passed and I found myself sitting on the back of my father's green truck in Darke Heath General Hospital's parking lot. Rebecca's experience as a doctor had pretty much saved him. We got him back with probably a matter of minutes to spare. Still, my insides stung when it came to thinking of my mother.

There came a point where there was nothing else I could do, other than let the medical professionals work. I slipped away from it all just to gather my thoughts about the past few days.

'What happens now?'

Then I heard a familiar comforting voice,

"Did you want any company?" Caitlyn asked, as she approached. It was near daylight and sunrise would be here at any moment.

I looked up at the sky.

"Should you be out here?"

"That's kind of what I wanted to talk about," she said, and sat next to me. She looked at me and held out a hand. I slowly took hold of it and she moved her hand away.

"Not that," she said. "I want to know what the sun feels like on my skin again." She held out her hand again and this time I reached into my pocket.

Caitlyn stood up in the back of the truck and I joined her. She took hold of the syringe and popped the cap off.

"Well, here goes."

My hands took hold of her waist as she came in close. Our lips met and she closed her eyes whilst pushing the syringe into her neck. A brilliant white light surrounded her and the mist appeared once more. I stepped back to watch her return to humanity . It seemed to drain her life momentarily, and then I caught her.

"Caitlyn?" I asked, as her head bowed. After a moment of silence she came to life.

"Blake."

"How does it feel?" I asked.

For the first time Caitlyn smiled at me as a mortal, her teeth were no longer fangs, they were just normal.

"You're gonna have to ask your sister what it's like to be the only good vampire in town," Caitlyn said, as she looked up to the sky.

"Caitlyn Turner, the vampire with a heartbeat. Now you're just Caitlyn Turner with a heartbeat," I said, as I took her hands.

"And together we can face anything; we are going to clean up this town," she said, as we watched the sun emerge. For the first time in almost forever the orange glow fell upon the pale face of the girl I loved. She looked better than ever.

And so you have to ask yourself what else is left to tell in this story? Shouldn't things just end now? Well my friend, every opportunity to end a story is the opportunity to tell another.

There were some characters who lived happily and others who just lived. Some resumed their transformation into hell-like beasts and disappeared into the woods.

A few weeks passed and I tried my best to gather a life I'd once had and put it back together. The mystery of when I first 'arrived' at the Heath will always be a fond memory. That was before I found out who I really was and what the actual story was. Never the less, I survived it and now I'm sitting in the bar with my friends.

Splint cashed in big on insurance and remodelled the Darke Bar. It's now called 'The Cure' more appropriate for an upmarket wine bar, but there's still a pool table. I was sitting in a booth with a near empty beer and writing a nearly finished story, when just as I was about to close the notepad a familiar song began to play; Splint shot me a look from behind the bar.

"A perfect way to give the new sound system a test drive," he said, bouncing his head to the lengthy introduction.

"Want another beer?" he asked.

On a dark desert highway, cool wind in my hair.

Of course I nod and head his way, past the numerous people all drinking there tonight. Then the door opens and I see a face that I haven't seen on his feet for a while. Angus, my father, slowly limps his way to the bar.

"Mr Greene. Good to see you back on your feet," Pam said, as she rushed from behind the bar to embrace him.

"Pam, nice to see you, honey. Splint, the place looks good," Angus said, as he looked towards me.

"Son."

"Dad," I said, and slowly embraced him.

"Hey there, stranger," Caitlyn said getting off a nearby bar stool to greet him.

"Caitlyn, good to see you. There she is," Angus added, as Susie appeared and folded her arms around him.

"Careful now, stitches are still healing."

"Sorry Dad," Susie said, as she withdrew and turned to the bar.

"Now what is the purpose of tonight's meeting?" Angus asked, as he faced Splint.

"I'm meeting the parents tonight," Splint said, as he set down a beer for both of us.

"My folks are coming in and I wanted to introduce them to you. Here they are now," Pam said, as a Korean couple entered the bar.

Introductions took place, and Angus led them over to a booth.

"Hey Susie-Q. Can you watch the bar a while?" Splint asked, loudly as he threw a towel at her.

"Sure, free drinks all round," she announced, and headed behind the bar.

"Now that is an offer I am willing to take up," the voice of a man said from the pool table. He looked to be drinking whisky and quickly finished the glass.

"I'll have another, but I'm happy to pay for good whisky," he said.

I noticed he looked rugged in appearance and wore a creased flannel shirt. His face was unshaven and covered in scars. He seemed to look around the place as if he was working it out.

Welcome to the hotel California.

I leant against the bar and nodded his way.

"How you doing?" I asked.

"Not bad. Nice bar you got here."

"Yeah, just re-opened," I said.

"We had a slight re-modelling," Caitlyn added, approaching and sensing my suspicious interest in this guy.

"I can see you kept the pool table. Good choice and the music too. Anyone wanna shoot?" he asked.

"Sure, I'll play a game." I said, and moved closer.

"You sure about this, Blake?" Caitlyn asked, remembering our first night.

"Hey, I'm networking," I laughed.

The man quickly set up the table and got ready to break.

"So, the yellow taxi outside? That's yours right? Looks old school," I said, and the man stopped his aim.

"Yeah, that old thing, it gets me about. Don't take much passengers these days," he said, and broke firmly. I took the cue from him.

"I never got your name," he said.

"It's Donnie. But my friends call me Blake. Blake Malone," I said, and offered a hand to shake. He obliged and looked me in the eye,

"Well, Blake Malone, the name's Randy. But people call me Twister."

And so I spent a little time getting to know a man called Twister. Perhaps we would become more than just two people making small talk in a bar. Maybe there's another story waiting just around the corner.

What I do know is that true darkness is out there and I may have temporarily shined a light through it. But I know it still lives on in those trees.

A place where many a wild vampire lurks and of course the creature we released once known as Alexis.

Where the Manor house once stood, there was now a plain of scrubbed ground. The soil had been churned and the many subterranean networks disturbed. Where there were once blockades now stood paths.

The Lord Edward Turner had spent an eternity pinned down by heavy stone, but he was still immortal after all. With the memory of his betrayal at the very forefront of his mind he never ever forgot what happened. As his own Manor house collapsed he became unleashed. His grave lifted, and the heavy stone released him from his apparent confinement. A bony blood deprived hand burst out of the soft earth and into the night air. There had been an awakening. He was free, and so his journey of retribution would begin, just as a piercing screech sounded.

You can check out anytime you like, but you can never leave.

The End

Authors Note

I began writing Darke Blood with the intention of creating a stand-alone story centred around vampires and witches. A genre that seems more popular than ever in both literature and television.

Although my journey when putting together this tale was indeed long and difficult, I dug deep into my imagination to answer the same question I face in every book I write. *How am I going to do this?* This time around, I just spent more time answering that question through narrative.

This process compares differently with my first novel Open Evening which reads more like a film, whereas Darke Blood reads more as a book, making them perhaps polar opposites. They are very much linked as the various references throughout culminate with the appearance of a well-known Open Evening character in the final chapter of this book.

Of course if you have read both books you should know by now they reference each other with an eventual plan to cross over both stories.

In creating both worlds and the universe they sit in hasn't been a solitary experience and I must give a great amount of credit and a thank you to my editor and publisher Nicky Fitzmaurice.

I would also like to extend my thank you to everyone who has joined me on this journey, whether that be sharing a selfie of my book on social media or simply clicking 'like' on one of my posts.

For the most up-to-date news and free content be sure to follow my website via email at leehallwriter.com

Thank you for reading and of course I wouldn't be an independent author if I didn't say; make sure you leave a review, that is 'if you get my drift'.

Printed in Poland
by Amazon Fulfillment
Poland Sp. z o.o., Wrocław